THE TRUSTWORTHY ONE

THE TRUSTWORTHY ONE

SHELLEY SHEPARD GRAY

THORNDIKE PRESS
A part of Gale, a Cengage Company

LIBRARY OF CONGRESS CIP DATA ON FILE.
CATALOGUING IN PUBLICATION FOR THIS BOOK
IS AVAILABLE FROM THE LIBRARY OF CONGRESS

ISBN-13: 978-1-4328-7852-8 (hardcover alk. paper)

Published in 2020 by arrangement with Gallery Books, an imprint of Simon & Schuster, Inc.

Printed in Mexico
Print Number: 01   Print Year: 2020

For Lynne, my first reader and friend.
Thank you for being you.

Dear Reader,

Thank you for reading *The Trustworthy One*!

The theme for this particular novel was trust, of course, which made me think back to when I was teaching elementary school and had a discussion with one of my classes about this topic. I remember being so touched when the children talked about who they thought was trustworthy. Some mentioned their parents, others mentioned best friends, a couple mentioned God. To my surprise, all of the kids agreed that trusting someone was a scary thing — especially if they'd been betrayed in the past. I can't help but think that those same feelings are true for everyone, no matter a person's age. Gifting someone with trust is a precious thing, indeed.

I hope you enjoy Kendra and Nate's story, as well as the whole Walnut Creek series. Though the series ends with the upcoming e-novella *Promises of Tomorrow,* this book is the fourth and final novel about the Eight. As always, I'm sorry to see this cast of characters go. I loved writing about a group of lifelong friends who have stood together through thick and thin.

But as I write this note, I've already begun a new series, the Berlin Bookmobile series!

The first book will be published at the beginning of 2021, and I'm so excited about this trilogy featuring a retired *Englischer* matchmaker who travels the back roads of Holmes County delivering books and hope to all sorts of library patrons — many of whom are Amish. I hope you'll look out for those books in the near future.

If *The Trustworthy One* is your first novel by me, thank you for giving one of my books a try. If, perhaps, it's your tenth or twentieth or even fortieth, thank you for giving me your trust. I promise, I never take my readers for granted. I appreciate you and am grateful for your support.

With my thanks and my blessings,
Shelley Shepard Gray

Trust in the Lord and do good.

— Psalm 37:3

Instead of pointing a finger,
why not hold a hand?

— Amish proverb

PROLOGUE

Right about the time she'd discovered that mercurial, insidious emotion called envy, Kendra Troyer had been envious of the Eight. Though it shamed her, she understood it.

Why, just about everyone who wasn't in the famous clique envied them something awful. They were good-looking, loyal to one another, and led great lives. Their close friendships had already lasted a decade, and they were only in their early teens.

Above all that, just being around their group made a person feel better about the world. They constantly seemed to be in good moods, loved teasing one another, and always had something new and exciting planned.

So, sure, Kendra got why the group was popular with most everyone. But it didn't make sense. After all, they shouldn't have fit in anywhere, given that they were a combi-

11

nation of all the different groups in Walnut Creek. Some were English, some Mennonite, and others were Old Order Amish. Why, one member was even New Order Amish like herself.

The Eight were on her mind as she walked through the middle school parking lot on Friday afternoon. Two girls who sat behind her in choir had been talking about *Englischer* Andy Warner and his Amish best friend, John Byler. Both boys were handsome as could be, and Mary Kate and Cassidy had seen them splitting a pizza together the night before. Instead of singing, they'd been whispering about the boys, wondering if they'd ever give a girl who wasn't part of their tight circle a second glance.

Kendra had wondered that a time or two herself.

She'd also wondered what it would be like to have a big group of close friends — or at least a group of friends who wanted to go have pizza with her on a Thursday night.

As she continued through the parking lot, each of her steps feeling like lead, Kendra half pretended that she was on her way to anyplace other than home.

She'd stayed late at school to help one of the teachers get ready for Saturday's science fair, not that she would be presenting

12

a project or anything. Even if she had been smart enough to design an experiment, she couldn't have done it anyway. Projects like the ones the other kids were showing cost money. That was something she didn't have. Something she'd never had.

She hadn't minded helping Mrs. Kline set up the table, though. She liked being helpful. More importantly, since this was her eighth grade, and therefore would be her last year in school, she wanted to do as much as she could. Next year she wouldn't be so lucky. Instead, she'd have to stay home to take care of her four younger siblings even more than she did now.

Realizing it was getting late, she sped up her pace. Their father was going to be home soon, and there was no way she would let her younger siblings be alone with him if she could help it.

Slinging her backpack over one shoulder, she pushed the crossing button at the inter-section.

"Hi, Kendra!" E.A. Schmidt called out. "Are you walking home, too?"

"Jah." She smiled at the red-haired girl with bright blue eyes. As far back as Kendra could remember, Elizabeth Anne had gone by E.A. It was rare to hear anyone ever call her by her given name, except maybe some

13

teachers on the first day of school.

Most people did whatever E.A. wanted. She was pretty, one of the Eight, and most importantly, she was probably the smartest girl in the whole school. It had always been that way, too. Every year E.A. seemed to get smarter and smarter. She was always receiving awards for earning the best scores on tests or getting straight A's or tutoring her classmates or little kids.

E.A. didn't push all her gifts into everyone else's faces, either. She just went about her business, never acting like she was better than anyone.

But everyone in Walnut Creek Middle School still knew she was brilliant.

"Want to walk together for a while?" E.A. asked.

"Sure." Kendra smiled at her. Maybe she had a chance to be part of the Eight after all.

When the light changed, they crossed. "So, how come you were here so late today?" E.A. asked.

"I was helping Mrs. Kline set up the science fair in the gym."

"Really?" Her blue eyes looked incredulous before she quickly masked her surprise. "Why, that's wonderful. What is your project? Mine's on Newton's Second Law of

Motion."

"I don't have a project. I was just helping out Mrs. Kline."

"Oh."

And . . . there it was again. The confusion that wasn't quite masked. It wasn't E.A.'s fault, though. "I, uh, saw your booth. It looks really good."

"Do you think so?" When Kendra nodded, she smiled. "Thanks so much! It's taken me forever. My mother kept trying to tell me that it was good enough, but I wanted it to be really special, you know?"

What could she say to that? "Good luck. I hope you do well."

"Thanks! I know it's prideful to want to win first place, but I can't help myself. I'd love for that to happen," E.A. said just before her smile widened. "Hey, look who's walking toward us."

"Who?"

But E.A. didn't hear her. She'd already turned all her attention to the approaching boys. "Hey, Andy! Hiya, Nate."

Andy Warner grinned. Next to him, Nate Miller raised a hand.

Andy Warner! Kendra smiled cautiously at the boys, thinking that things really were changing. First, E.A. wanted to walk with her, and now, here she was, stopping on the sidewalk to talk to the leader of the Eight! If Mary Kate and Cassidy saw her, they'd be so jealous.

As the boys got closer, E.A. turned back Kendra's way. "You know them, right?" she whispered.

"*Jah.*" It was the truth, too. Their community was a small one, and most everyone knew everyone else, at least slightly.

When the boys waited for them to catch up, Kendra pasted what she hoped was a pleasant smile on her face. She feared she just looked desperate, though.

"Hi," Andy said when they all were standing next to one another. "What are you doing getting home so late?"

"I was tutoring. Kendra, here, was helping set up the science fair," E.A. replied. "What about you two?"

"Andy had baseball practice, and I stayed late to finish a history test," Nate said with a groan. "I *canna* wait until I'm done with school."

Andy grinned. "You only have a couple more months until you're done for good. I still have four more years of high school to get through." He shifted his duffel bag to his other hand as he turned back to them. "So, I've got a game tonight. Are you coming?"

16

"Of course," E.A. said. "Marie and I are going to cheer you on every time you get up to bat. You better hit a home run."

Andy laughed. "I'll do my best. Hey, afterward, my parents said I could have people over. Want to come?"

"I'll try," E.A. replied. "I've got to ask my parents, but it shouldn't be a problem."

Kendra could hardly believe it. He'd asked her over. It was happening! She wasn't just going to talk to E.A. and Andy on the sidewalk, she was going to get to go to Andy's house and hang out with all their friends! She'd sneak out if she had to, even though she would get in so much trouble for leaving the house.

She noticed then that his expression was a little sheepish. Maybe a little embarrassed. "Hey, Kendra. Um, you're welcome to come over, too. I mean, if you don't have anything else to do."

Time practically stopped.

Andy hadn't meant to invite her. He'd been talking to E.A. alone, as if Kendra hadn't been standing right there, too.

She'd been invisible to him.

"Danke," she said. "But . . . I've already got plans."

Looking relieved, Andy grinned. "Yeah. Sure." He turned to Nate. "Miller, you know Kendra Troyer, right?"

Nate looked at her and nodded. "We know each other."

Kendra had gone to the food bank once with her mother, and Nate had been volunteering there. Her mother had been sporting a black eye, and Kendra had felt as if every person in the facility had been staring at them.

Though that had been years ago, Kendra felt shame slide deep into her chest. She half expected Nate to tell them about that day.

She needed to get out of there. Quickly, she pointed to their left. "I'm headed that way. I'll see you later."

"See ya, Kendra," E.A. said with a smile.

"Yeah. Bye," Andy said.

Nate just stared at her.

But when she was about halfway across the street, she heard Nate say, "That girl is all right, but she's got a real messed-up family. And they're really poor."

"She can't help that. There's nothing wrong with Kendra Troyer," E.A. said.

"There's nothing good, either. I've seen them go to the food bank. And there's all kinds of rumors going around about her father, too. Like, he drinks and is as mean as a snake," Nate added. "You got lucky

18

Kendra ain't coming over to your house, Warner. Your *mamm* would have to hide all her stuff."

"Ouch. That's harsh," Andy said.

She didn't hear what E.A. said, but it didn't matter. Kendra felt like she was choking.

As she hurried home, she had a change of heart. From that moment on, she decided she wasn't going to be envious of the Eight. Not at all. No, from now on, she was going to be real glad that she wasn't a part of their group.

And as for Nate Miller? She hated him now, and probably would for the rest of her life.

ONE

"So, it's been a little over a year since Andy died," Katie began to a large group of friends in the gathering room of her bed-and-breakfast. "I'm sorry I didn't plan something last month, but to be honest, I just couldn't do it."

"I don't ever want to gather on the day of Andy's funeral," Kendra said. "He would've hated that."

Ten Years Later
September
"What do you think, Miss Troyer? Will these improvements suit your needs, or would you like us to make some additional changes?"

Kendra walked farther into the recently painted and carpeted storefront and ran her hand along the countertop that had just been installed. It was refurbished wood and had been sanded and polished until it shone. It was the final component that she'd needed to complete her vision for Tried and True Furnishings. She intended to sell both vintage and new eclectic pieces of furniture, rugs, and accessories to make any house a home. Just looking at it all, she felt a burst of pride. This place was quite an accomplishment for a girl who'd grown up in a place that was barely two steps up from a shack.

"I don't think anything else will need to be done, Mr. Grayson," she replied as calmly as possible. She so wanted to sound like a lady. "It looks just as I had hoped. Thank you so much."

Mr. Grayson, who was fond of wearing overalls and flannel shirts no matter what time of the year, stuffed his hands in his back pockets. "So, should I tell Jan to send you the contract?"

"Yes. I'm ready to sign a lease."

He grinned. "That's real good news. I know you've been back for a while now, but this feels official. Welcome back to Walnut Creek, Miss Troyer."

"Thank you. I'm glad to be here." And it really was almost the truth.

After they shook hands, Clyde Grayson gathered up his backpack and strode out of the building.

Leaving Kendra to stand alone for the first time in her very own shop.

It was the culmination of what felt like a lifetime of hard work. After struggling through school for most of her life, things had finally clicked well enough for her to get her GED and eventually apply to a small design school outside of Columbus. Miss Wilson, the volunteer who'd helped her with her coursework, had been her angel. She'd boosted up Kendra's low self-esteem, encouraged her when everyone else hardly looked her way, and even found additional scholarships and grants for Kendra so she could have free room and board at school.

Remembering the day she'd left on the bus for college, Kendra shivered. She'd been so, scared to venture out to the big city. Almost as scared as she'd been relieved to leave Walnut Creek.

After boarding the bus, she'd stared out the window, not thinking about anything other than the fact that she was about to change her life.

And she had.

She'd gone to design school but had lasted only two semesters until she'd let the pressure and insecurities get the best of her. She'd started drinking, sometimes even trying pills. Anything to help alleviate the guilt she'd felt for leaving her siblings — and to help block out the memories of what she'd endured in that house.

Feeling the familiar weight of remorse press on her chest, Kendra shook it off. It did no good to dwell on the bad. Especially since she'd gotten sober, found a good job, and had started a new life for herself. She'd been determined to stay in Columbus, too, until Andy Warner had died and her little sister Naomi had called her one evening crying, saying that she missed her.

As always, Kendra's personal goals had been no match for her brothers' and sisters' needs. Soon after that phone call, she'd begun to make plans for her new life in Walnut Creek.

And it was a new life. She was now good friends with the remainder of the Eight, had a pretty little house she'd gotten for a song, and was about to open up her own business. She was just a few minutes away from her siblings, in case they needed her.

That was what was important.

She'd just begun a list for office supplies when the glass door opened and Nate Miller strode in. Just like it had been for the last decade, she felt a twinge of dismay at seeing him. And, maybe, a fierce rush to turn away and hide.

24

"Hey, it is really you," he said. "I saw Clyde walking down the sidewalk, and he shared that 'Pretty Miss Troyer' had just decided to lease this building."

His hazel eyes looked almost green in the morning light. They were just as sharp and perceptive, though. Every time he looked her way, she felt like he was searching for all her secrets.

She needed to keep a firm hold on her composure. To do anything less would let him see all the chinks and cracks in her armor. And if that happened? Well, he'd see that her insides were just as flawed as her outside was.

Turning her face away from him, she ran a finger along the countertop. "There's a lot of Troyers around. I'm surprised you thought of me."

He laughed. "*Jah*, there are a lot of Troyers, for sure. There's not a lot of pretty ones, though."

The comment was so irreverent and surprising, she looked back at him.

Meeting her gaze, his grin deepened.

What could she do? She smiled back in spite of her better judgment. "I suppose there's a compliment in there somewhere."

"Come now, Kendra. We both know it's not hidden. I put that out there as bold as

25

brass." He walked closer, reminding her just how good he looked in his dark pants, boots, and white shirt. Yes, he was wearing the same clothes most any Amish man in the county wore. But somehow, he managed to wear them better.

He was practically daring her to look anywhere but into his eyes, and realizing that it was getting harder and harder not to let her eyes stray, Kendra coughed, then looked back down at her list. She reckoned it was an almost believable stance. Well, it might have been, if there were more than two items on the list.

Nate shifted. "Kendra, Clyde also told me something else that I found interesting."

She picked up a pencil. "And what is that?"

"That you've been visiting this shopping center for a while now. Several weeks, in fact."

Her chin popped back up. "It's no secret that I moved back to Walnut Creek." She'd been all over the area with her friends.

"What I'm getting at is that my hardware store is just two doors down. And since Walnut Creek Hardware was started by my grandfather and we have a lot of the same friends, you had to have known that I was running it now. Didn't you?"

26

"I did." She looked at him curiously.

"I thought you would've stopped by."

"There was no reason for me to." She picked up a hammer from a counter. "I already have enough tools."

"Come on. You still could've come in to say hello. I mean, we're friends, right?"

Suddenly, all of his words just made her feel awkward. He was acting too sure of himself. Too slick. "Nate, though we've known each other for a long time now, we've never really been friends."

"Are you serious?"

As much as she wanted to act like nothing he ever said about her had bothered her, she couldn't do it. "I wouldn't lie about our past."

All the humor faded from his expression. "Maybe we should talk about that," he said slowly.

There he went again. Looking at her too intently. Seeing too much.

Feeling trapped, she stepped away from the countertop and stuffed her notebook back in her purse. "I don't think so. I mean, there's nothing to say that hasn't been said before. Now, I think I'd better get on my way home."

"Hold on a sec, wouldja?" Looking troubled, he spoke again. "Kendra, I'm sorry,

27

but I think there might be some things that need to be said." He stepped closer, bringing with him the scent of soap and peppermints. "For years, you've acted like you want nothing to do with me, even though we have all the same friends. Every time you've come back to town, you've hardly ever said a word to me — even when I've tried to ask about your job or how your family was."

"Nate, I'd rather not talk about you and me."

"I really wish you would, though." Looking at her directly in the eye, he said, "What did I ever do to ya?"

He'd embarrassed her. Made her feel like she was less than everyone else. And that had hurt so bad that she'd tried to avoid him at all costs. In short, Nate Miller was a constant reminder of how badly she'd wanted to fit in and how impossible that goal had seemed back when she was fourteen.

But to dwell on that made her feel churlish and petty. They'd all moved on. "I don't think there's any reason for us to start rehashing things that happened ten years ago."

His eyes lit up with triumph. "So, I did do something. When? Ten years ago?"

Ugh. The conversation was not only awkward, but she was also somehow making things even worse. "Don't worry about it. It's not important anymore."

He stepped closer. "Sure it is." He lowered his voice. "Kendra, what exactly did I do? I honestly can't recall when I hurt you so bad."

"Nate, you used to laugh about me to your friends. You put me down. You would point out how I wasn't smart and had to go to special classes." When he opened his mouth, she talked over him. She couldn't help herself. "You used to remind everyone that I didn't have any money. That my family was poor. That I had to go to the food bank while you did your volunteer service there." Though she knew she should simply shut up, she added in a choked voice, "Nate, I heard you make fun of . . . of my whole situation." That was as much as she could say about her abusive father and her in-denial mother.

All the color had washed out from his face. "I . . . I don't know what to say other than that I'm sorry."

She felt herself breathing hard. All of her hard-earned poise had just disintegrated in a flat thirty seconds. *Good job, Kendra.* Now she was just a couple more seconds away

29

from showing Nate that she was still awkward and unpolished. Just seconds away from losing everything she'd ever hoped to attain. "Look, I know it was a long time ago. I'm surely being too hard on you. Let's just forget about it."

"Kendra, I remember a lot of what you are talking about. I was a jerk and I really am sorry." He waved a hand. "But you can't seriously hold me to task for that now, can you? I mean, I was just a kid when I acted like that."

She didn't want to hold a grudge, but that explanation felt like a sharp jab into her side, because he was neglecting a very important point. He might have been just a kid when he'd done all of those things, but she'd been just a kid, too.

Just a fourteen-year-old abused girl with four younger siblings and not a lot of hope.

"I know, Nate," she said. "But see, you acted for the world like you were better than me. You volunteered. You *helped* the poor and needy. You acted like you were friends with just about everyone, but it was all for show. Inside, you weren't all that nice at all." Though it was hard, she continued to look at him in the eye. "I'm sorry, Nate. I know you were just a kid and everyone makes mistakes. But as much as I try to give

30

you excuses, there's a part of me that thinks you were old enough to know better."

A muscle worked in his jaw. "You're right. I really am sorry."

His easy agreement took her by surprise. "All right."

"So, do you forgive me?"

She nodded. "I forgive you."

"So, maybe we can be friends now?"

She hadn't expected that. Caught off guard by the confusion she was feeling, she gripped a fold of her dress. "Let's take things one step at a time, *jah*?"

"I hope you'll at least try. I mean, every moment counts, true? Especially after Andy died."

"This isn't about Andy."

"Of course it is. It's about friendships and hurting and not doing enough to make things right. It's about missing opportunities."

His voice sounded brittle. Hurt. She exhaled, hating how upset she was by his words. How confused they made her feel.

"Nate, I . . . I don't know what to say."

"How about you say that you'll try? Just say that you'll try to trust me again. I promise, I'm worth it."

While she gaped at him, he paused, looking like he was going to make a speech, but

31

he seemed to reconsider. Seconds later, the door closed behind him with a satisfying click, leaving her alone again.

Standing there in the silence, Kendra thought about his words, about his promise that he could be trustworthy again. However, she knew that wasn't going to be the problem.

The problem was that she'd never trusted Nate Miller. And how did one repair a relationship that hadn't actually been there in the first place? She wasn't sure if that was possible.

Of course, whenever she thought about her late teens in Columbus, she shivered. Kendra knew what it was like to be alone, and it was hard. There was also the memory of Andy. She'd always liked him and thought she'd have her whole life to one day renew their friendship.

But he was gone now, and she'd have to live with that. Regrets always tasted bitter, and she didn't want to have any more of them if she could help it.

As if the Lord was nudging her forward, Kendra knew she had to discard her hurt where Nate was concerned. Though they might never patch things up completely, she owed it to herself, Nate, and maybe even Andy's memory to try.

TWO

"I feel the same way, Kendra," Katie continued. "But I have to admit that I was relieved to know we were going to talk about Andy tonight. So often I hate to bring him up. I'm ashamed to admit it, but I feel if I mention Andy, I'll make everyone depressed."

"I've done the same thing," Will said. "My only saving grace is that I think Andy would have completely agreed."

"Well, yeah," John said. "Andy used to place a lot of importance on a good time."

Two Days Later
Saturday
"Are you ever going to stop glaring, Nate Miller?" his assistant, Benjamin, asked.

As Nate blinked, he realized that he'd been lost in thought, no doubt staring blankly at a display of batteries they'd just placed on sale. "I haven't been glaring."

"Sure you have. All day long, too." With a grunt, Benjamin started sorting a new shipment of electrical supplies. "And just for the record, yesterday wasn't any better."

"Did you know that I didn't hire you to comment on my disposition?"

"This here is a bonus. And believe me, you need all the help you can get. You're practically scaring young children."

Benjamin was fifty years old, knew more about hardware and building materials than most anyone in town, and was a little too free with sharing his opinions.

Nate picked up the assortment of cleaning supplies he was about to display and started to walk away. "Exaggerate much?"

Benjamin picked up two brooms and followed him to the showroom. "All I want to know is how I can help you. What's wrong? What's gotten you so irritated?"

He was going to keep his thoughts to himself but decided to share. Benjamin knew so much. Maybe he could help Nate figure out how to patch things up with Kendra. "Kendra Troyer is opening a shop two doors down."

Ben nodded. "*Jah.* It's a knickknack and decorating shop."

"I think she calls it a design studio."

"Hmm. All I know is that it's sure to be full of girly items. Which is a good thing, but not my cup of tea, *jah*? Is it not yours, either?"

"Not really, but that's not the problem."

Benjamin gazed at him seriously. "So what is?"

Nate put the box on the floor by his feet and straightened. "I offended her back when we were teenagers, and she hasn't forgiven me." Looking at Benjamin in the eye, he added, "See what I mean? It's been ten years. Don't you think that's a little long to hold a grudge?"

"I suppose. What did she say all those years ago when you apologized?"

That caught him off guard. "I never apologized back then."

Benjamin recoiled like Nate had announced he was going to close up the shop and move to New York City. "Say again?"

"Come on. You heard me." And yes, he was embarrassed about it.

"I heard that you know you were wrong, but you never had the guts to apologize for it."

He hadn't had the guts. That had a ring of truth to it that didn't sit especially well with him. "I always kind of thought it was

35

better to let sleeping dogs lie."

"Son, sometimes even sleeping dogs need to get up and stretch their legs every now and then. You need to apologize."

"I did yesterday."

"Ah."

Little by little, all his righteousness slowly evaporated. "I think I've always known that I shouldn't have made fun of Kendra," he said at last.

"I should hope so."

"I'm not proud of myself, Ben. It hasn't been easy to admit that I hurt her and never apologized."

"You don't have to answer this, but what did you say that was so terrible? I mean, in general?"

Nate figured that since he was in for a penny, he might as well go in for a pound. "I used to make fun of her for not being smart . . . and for being poor."

Benjamin, who Nate was fairly sure had mastered the art of the poker face around the age of eight, stared at him without a single bit of recrimination or surprise in his features. "Ah," he said again.

Nate hung his head. "I know. I knew better then, and I certainly know better now."

Benjamin pulled out a stack of gardening gloves and started arranging them in the

36

center of a table, fanning them out in such a way that it looked like they were standing in the middle of a fancy clothing store. "Nate, I've never been the man my father was. But if he was still with us on Earth, I know he'd encourage you to rectify this situation as soon as possible. I think that's what you should do."

"I will. I promise."

"Gut."

The ringer at the door sounded, bringing in a group of five people, three men and two women. Nate turned on his heel, took a deep breath, and approached them with a smile. "Hiya. Let me know if you need any help."

One of the women smiled up at him. She was pretty, with dark hair and light blue eyes. "Thank you so much! We heard a lot about this store, so we thought we'd look around."

"I'm glad you did. Take your time."

She smiled at him again, this time a little warmer and brighter. After her gaze lingered on him another long second more, she turned away. For a moment, Nate was about to follow her — she was the type of woman he would usually want to get to know better — but now he realized that despite her pleasing looks, he was hoping only that she'd buy something.

He realized that his priorities had changed. He'd finally grown up. He no longer put much emphasis on either a woman's outward appearance or her social standing in the community. Thanks to Kendra, all that mattered were the things that couldn't be seen. It was humbling to realize that he was finally doing what he should have been doing all along.

On Monday morning, Nate was still stewing about his need for that apology. So much so, he knew what had to be done. After telling Benjamin that he would be back shortly, he walked down the row of storefronts until he stood in front of Kendra's.

The door was locked. But there was a light on, and he could see Kendra sitting on a white ladder-back chair scooted up to a small side table with ornately carved legs that someone had stained light blue.

She was wearing a simple long dress in a rich shade of plum. The sleeves were short, displaying tan arms, and on her feet were a pair of leather Birkenstocks. Her long brown hair was neatly plaited under a white *kapp*.

She looked fresh and pretty.

He rapped on the door lightly, hoping and

praying that she'd consent to give him the time of day.

Immediately, her head popped up. Her eyes widened when she looked at him, and he could tell she was trying to force herself to walk over to him.

How had that happened?

No, Nate, his conscience corrected. *It should be how come it was still happening?* They were both carrying the load of what had happened a decade ago. It was up to him to try to rectify things.

He stood still as she unlocked the door. "Nate?"

"Hey. I know you don't want to talk to me, but will you give me ten minutes?"

She tensed. "Why? What do you need?"

"I don't need anything. But I do have something I need to talk to you about."

"Now's not really a good time."

"Please?"

She looked shocked that he'd said *please,* which embarrassed him all the more. After another few seconds, she stepped backward. "Come on, then."

"Thanks." He closed the door behind him.

She was now standing a few feet farther away, almost leaning against the wall, like she needed distance from him in order to feel safe. The sight made him feel even worse. Boy, what kind of person had he been?

He now realized that she wasn't going to say another word, wasn't going to offer to let him sit down or make small talk. He needed to speak his piece.

"Kendra, I came over here to apologize for the way I behaved back when we were teenagers."

She blinked. "You've already done so."

"I realize that, but I don't think I said enough to convey how ashamed I've felt about my behavior."

"Oh."

Oh? What did that even mean? Maybe she was waiting for him to say something better. Though it hurt to do it, he forced himself to be more specific. "To tell you the truth, I'm not even sure why I used to think you weren't very smart. And I know that I had no business saying things about your living situation."

"My living situation." Her voice sounded hoarse. Or maybe it was more hollow? "Um, yes. It was really bad of me. I still feel bad to this day for talking about you the way I did."

She studied him, seemed to weigh her words, then, to his surprise, she walked over to the door and opened it again. "Now that you've said your piece, you can go."

"Wait a minute. Don't you have anything to say to me?"

"Nate, the truth is that I wasn't very smart. I had a learning disability, and it was really hard for me to learn to read. Even now, I have to read things slowly and sometimes twice to make sure I understand something. So, you weren't wrong. I wasn't very smart."

He hadn't thought he could feel worse, but he did. "I was way out of line. I'm so sorry."

But it was like he hadn't said a word and everything she was saying pained her. Kendra continued, "As far as my living situation . . . you were right. We were poor, I can't deny that." Her voice lowered. "I was always hungry, and my father beat me. Often." She met his gaze. "So, it was a real bad living situation. You didn't lie."

Why had he thought a simple five-minute apology would make everything all better?

More guilt piled on. How could he have been so callous? How could he have thought all this time that it was okay to simply pretend he hadn't hurt her so badly? "Kendra, I . . . I don't know what else to say."

"I don't think there is anything else to say, Nate."

41

She was practically shooing him out the door. But if he left, Nate knew he wouldn't be able to get back in. He stepped to the side, out of the doorway. "*Nee,* Kendra. I came to clear the air."

"I'm sorry, but I think you came over here because you were suddenly feeling ashamed and wanted to feel better. I believe you need to hear me say that all is forgiven and forgotten so you can leave and not think about it again."

She was right. Yet again, he'd been concerned with himself and not her. Feeling like a worm, he swallowed, trying to come up with the perfect words to say to make everything better. But though it seemed he could charm just about anyone, he couldn't think of a thing to say.

Kendra's dark brown eyes studied him closely. "It's probably best you went ahead and left, Nate."

"What is it going to take for you to forgive me?"

"I do forgive you." When he still looked skeptical, she added, "I promise, I do."

"But?"

"But . . . well, I am sorry, but like we both just agreed, there isn't anything else to say. Ain't so?"

She didn't look near tears. Instead, she

looked resigned and maybe disappointed, too.

He'd somehow just made things worse. He hung his head and walked out, wondering if there was ever going to be a way to make things right between them.

THREE

Katie looked around. "I think over the year, most of us have shared a story about him. But I'd love to hear from someone new. Kendra? Nate? Would either of you like to talk?"

"You go, Kendra," Nate said. "Remember that story you told me the other night? Share that."

Feeling shy, but also feeling just as sure that she could share something about their friend that was worth remembering, Kendra stood up. "I'm not a great storyteller, but I'll do my best."

Tuesday

"Kendra, when were you going to reach out and ask me and the other girls to help you?" Katie asked as she walked into the shop.

She knew the answer to that — never. It

wasn't that she didn't appreciate her girlfriends or think that they could give her a
hand. It was more that she wasn't comfortable asking for help from anyone. Not when
she'd been berated at home when she made
mistakes and been made fun of at school
when she couldn't do things right.

But all of that sounded far too pitiful to
admit out loud. "I know you're busy. All of
you are busy now."

"Not too busy to help you," Katie murmured as she walked around the store, running a hand along the wooden shelves made
from reclaimed wood that Kendra had just
gotten installed. She'd elected not to get
the shelves sanded and repainted. She
preferred the way they looked now, with
chips of faded blue and red paint on the
grain.

When Katie stopped to pick up a spool of
soft yarn made from alpaca fur, Kendra
rushed over to help her. "Don't be bending
down like that, Katie. You're gonna hurt
yourself."

"I'm pregnant, not sick."

"You're seven months pregnant. You
should be sitting, not picking up things off
my shop floor." When Katie looked like she
was on the verge of protesting, Kendra
guided her to an overstuffed chair that she'd

just bought. "Sit down and put your feet up."

Katie wrinkled her nose but sat, placing her feet on the ottoman. Seconds later, she'd kicked off her tennis shoes. "Oh, this feels so much better. I hate wearing shoes now, my feet are so swollen."

A memory surfaced of when her mother was pregnant with one of Kendra's younger siblings. Once, when her mother was near her time in the middle of August, she'd sat down and rested on the front porch. Her father had been so angry.

She shook her head in an effort to block out the rest of the memories.

Worried about her friend, she murmured, "What does Harley say?"

Katie blinked. "That he feels bad for me, of course. Last night he made me a foot-bath. It felt like heaven."

"Oh." Of course that's what Harley did. He might have been quiet, but he was such a good man. He would never be upset with Katie for complaining about swollen feet.

"So, when is your store going to open?"

"In two more weeks, I think. I am waiting for some things I ordered to arrive. I'm also making a couple of items that I need to finish."

"Like what?"

46

"Just some table runners and place mats. A few bowls and vases, too. You know, things that people like to buy as gifts."

"Are you throwing pots again?"

"I haven't started, but I plan to in a couple of months. There's a lady over in Millersburg who lets me use her kiln for a *gut* price."

"You are so talented. It's amazing."

The compliment was as sweet as it was hard to hear. She tucked her head. *"Danke,"* she mumbled.

"You know, we're all really proud of you, Kendra."

"I haven't done anything yet."

"One day you're going to learn to accept a compliment."

Kendra chuckled. "It's not a crime to be modest."

"Moving on, how is it being so close to Nate Miller all the time?"

"Nate? Oh, I don't know."

"He's so very handsome," Katie continued in a singsong voice. "Marie and I were just talking about how he's single, too."

"Hmm." She doubted her girlfriends were "just talking" about Nate.

"Did he help you put up the shelves?"

"No. I, um, I hired someone from over at Kinsinger's Lumber in Charm."

47

"Why would you go all the way over there for help when Nate is just a couple of yards away?"

"You know me and Nate don't always get along too well." She felt vaguely awful about saying such a thing. After all, she'd promised Nate that she'd forgiven him.

"You know, I don't think I knew that." Katie sat up and slipped her shoes back on. "Well, I came over to offer help, but you seem to have everything well in hand."

"You can still stay here while I work. I'd be glad for your company."

"I would stay to chat, if I didn't fear that I was about to fall asleep. I think it's time for a nap. I've got some guests arriving around three or four this afternoon. They're first-time guests to our bed-and-breakfast, so I'm going to have to give them a tour."

Kendra walked over to help her up. "*Danke* for coming over. It was so kind of you."

Katie scoffed. "It wasn't just out of kindness. I like you, Kendra. I like you and I want to help you." She gave her a hug. "I'm not the only one, either. Don't forget that."

"I won't."

Katie smiled at her again before waddling out the door.

Kendra carefully closed the door behind

48

her and locked it. She was alone again. This was the way she preferred to be, but suddenly it seemed lonelier than ever.

Three hours later, just as she got back to her little house, Naomi knocked on the door.

Kendra hadn't seen her sixteen-year-old sister in weeks. They had a complicated relationship. Kendra had tried to shield Nanny — their nickname for Naomi — from their father as much as she could, but she hadn't been all that successful. Later, when she'd moved away, Nanny had been mighty upset with her. Kendra hadn't blamed her but had known that she wasn't going to survive if she'd stayed. She'd justified her choice by knowing that Mary, Jeremiah, and Chris had all still been there.

But Nanny had depended on her. And Kendra knew why. After all, she'd essentially raised her.

When Nanny had turned twelve, she'd left to go live with their mother's parents near Canton. Mommi and Dawdi had a soft spot for Nanny that they'd never seemed to have for the rest of Kendra's siblings — or maybe it was just Kendra.

"Naomi, what a lovely surprise!" Kendra exclaimed as she let her sister inside. "It's good to see you. Did Mommi and Dawdi bring you here today?"

She nodded. "I asked them if I could stay with you for a couple of days." She paused, reddening a bit. "I mean, if that's okay with you."

"You know you never have to ask about that. All you have to do is simply be here."

"Danke."

"Do you have everything?" Nanny had decided to live as a Mennonite like their grandparents, which meant she now traveled with a large suitcase filled with all sorts of things.

Privately, Kendra thought that her sister's tendency to carry half her belongings with her had more to do with her being Naomi than being Mennonite. The girl always claimed she needed a good number of personal items in order to feel settled.

"My suitcase is with Mommi and the English driver."

"What are they doing?"

"Mommi wanted to visit some shops, and Ramona, the driver, said she'd go with."

"Where is Dawdi?"

She frowned. "He went home. I mean, to see Mamm and Daed."

"Why?" Kendra wondered what had happened. Their grandparents had never been

50

shy about voicing their disapproval of the way their parents had treated Kendra and her siblings. It had all seemed like a bit of a game to her. They talked about how they didn't like the way their son-in-law treated their daughter and grandchildren, but they never actually did anything to intervene.

"Our father is sick," Nanny said. "Dawdi fears it's his liver." She lowered her voice. "No one seems to think he's going to ever get better."

"Oh." Maybe in the middle of the night when she couldn't sleep she might feel differently, but she couldn't say she felt anything other than empty inside.

Nanny, whose pale blue eyes were so different from Kendra's dark brown ones, gazed at her intently. "Do you think we should go visit them, too?"

She was never going to step foot in that house again. "You know I'm not going to do that."

"I don't think Jeremiah will, either. Or Mary."

Or Chris. Kendra didn't know if any of them would ever see their parents willingly if they could help it. "I'd be surprised if they did."

When Nanny's shoulders slumped, Kendra murmured, "Naomi, each of us has to

51

make our own way through life."

"Uh-oh. I know you're serious if you're using my real name."

"I am serious. What I'm trying to say is . . . if you . . . if you want to visit our parents, then I think you should." And boy, did that statement feel like vinegar on her tongue.

Now that the decision was solely in her hands, Nanny looked a whole lot less sure. "I'm not certain if I want to visit them or not."

"That's all right. You don't have to be sure."

"Truly? When do you think I'll know?"

"I can't tell you that," Kendra replied, feeling as old as she used to when they were growing up. She'd always had to be her siblings' substitute mother and had memories of being twelve years old, with Chris or Naomi on a hip, trying to make enough spaghetti for the five of them.

She'd also become skilled at giving vague answers to her siblings' questions. It was usually because she hadn't wanted to give them the real answers, which were always filled with bad news and pain.

And just like when she'd been a little girl, her sister looked frustrated.

"Kendra, that is no help."

It was time to redirect the conversation. "Since you're here, would you like to have something to eat? I made a lasagna yesterday that I was going to heat up for supper."

Nanny moaned. "Oh, yum. You have the best food, Kendra."

Watching her little sister, who was already making her way to the kitchen, her pretty pink dress perfectly fitted and her wavy brown hair fastened in a bun under the spotless white covering, Kendra felt herself relax. She knew she didn't have a lot. She was a broken mess and she wasn't even sure if she trusted anyone completely. Sometimes, even God. But she did have love inside her. Love for her siblings. Love for her friends. She even loved that she wasn't hungry and she wasn't hurting.

Over the years, she'd come to understand that was enough.

FOUR

Because it wasn't just the Eight there, but quite a few of their siblings, other family members, and friends, Kendra cleared her throat. "I should probably begin by reminding you all that I wasn't always so outgoing. I used to be really shy."

Tuesday Afternoon

The note that Benjamin had put on Nate's desk that morning was weighing on his mind. Every time there was a break in customers coming in, he found himself circling back to the handwritten letter on lined notebook paper and reading it again.

Dear Mr. Miller,

I'm sorry to bother you, but I'm in a tight spot. Someone told me that sometimes you work on people's homes, and I hope you will work on ours.

I know it's a lot, but will you think

54

about it? See, we have a leak in our bathroom floor. My mother seems to think it's a faulty pipe that is causing the problem, but we're not really sure. Anyway, it's making a real mess and hurting my bedroom, too, since the bathroom is right above my bedroom.

My mom tried to fix it, but she's no plumber. Then, there's the fact that she's real sick and can't work too much. And since she can't work, we can't pay anyone to come in to fix it. So now I'm really getting worried.

I know you don't know us from Adam, but if you know of someone who maybe wouldn't mind helping us patch it up, I'd really appreciate it. Things are getting pretty desperate around here.

Thank you for your consideration,
Allison Berry
1617 Palmer Dr. N.W.M

She was desperate. Well, that said it all, didn't it? Moreover, she'd been right. He did, in fact, do some pro bono work around town from time to time. Of course, the men in his church community helped one another out in times of trouble, too, but this girl didn't seem to be Amish, so she wouldn't have been a usual recipient.

It wasn't anything he advertised, though. He had a business to run, and he wasn't a construction worker by trade. He was simply handy and wanted to help others when he could. Usually it was a friend of a friend or someone he knew through church.

This was the first time he'd gotten a letter like this. It was so sweet, and it was from someone in need. He doubted she was much older than thirteen or fourteen. If she was old enough to get a job, he had a feeling she would have done that.

He knew where his mind was going, too. Back to the guilt he felt about Kendra. It seemed he was destined to do what he could to help others, since he'd done nothing to help Kendra and her siblings when she'd needed someone most.

Walking over to Ben, he held up the letter. "Do you know this girl?"

"The one who wrote you that letter? Not really."

"What do you know? How old is Allison Berry?"

Benjamin shrugged. "You know I'm no good at guessin' ages. Fourteen, I'd say. Maybe fifteen?"

So, just about what he'd thought. "She said they've got a leak, and it's messing up her bedroom ceiling."

"A real shame, that is."

Nate looked at him carefully. "Any particular reason why you passed this letter on to me instead of helping her out yourself? You're a lot better at construction than I am."

"Couple of reasons. One, I'm not as young as I used to be. And though I've got a good feel for construction, you're the better plumber. And two? She asked for you."

Nate almost rolled his eyes. "Ben, that's not much of an excuse."

"It's a good one, though. And the truth. You're the one who has the reputation for fixing things. Not me." His eyes lit up when the door opened. "Hiya, can I help ya?"

Seeing that Ben had the customers well in hand, Nate stared at the letter some more, then finally decided to go over to this little girl's house and see what was going on.

He drove his buggy down to Palmer Drive, feeling a sense of guilt he got now whenever now he passed the road. Kendra had lived on this street, which meant that he avoided it at all costs.

Time hadn't made it any better. If anything, the houses looked even more ramshackle and in danger of falling down in a real good storm.

When he pulled up to Allison's address,

57

sadness filled him. Unlike some of its neighbors, the lawn was neat, and no trash littered the yard. But that said, it was obvious the house and its inhabitants had fallen on hard times. Tape covered one of the front windows, the siding was peeling and in need of fresh paint, and there was a gap around the front door that no doubt let in mosquitoes in the summer and cold air in the winter.

Two lights burned in the hallway though, so he was hopeful that someone was home.

After patting his pocket to reassure himself that he had Allison's note with him, he knocked on the door twice. He'd already decided that if her mother or father opened, he'd show them the note and say that he'd be happy to help if they'd like the assistance.

But instead of an adult, a skinny teenage girl with tangled blond hair peered out at him through the front window just to the left of the door before opening it.

She was wearing jeans that were a little too short and a knit T-shirt that was a little too big. She also had brown eyes just like Kendra. They looked as sad as he remembered hers being, and he felt a lump form in his throat. After a few seconds of studying him, she said, "You're Nate Miller,

58

aren't you?"

"Yep." Taking care to keep his voice gentle, he added, "And I'm guessin' that you're Allison Berry."

"Yeah." She nodded. The door opened a few inches wider. Her expression was so hopeful yet wary that he had to take a minute to collect himself. She was obviously having a hard time, but here she was, trying to take care of her home.

He pulled out her letter. "So, I got this today. Does it look familiar?"

Her eyes widened. "Yes." She looked like she was hoping to ask him about it, but instead she bit her lip, obviously waiting for more information.

"Your letter was . . . well, it meant a lot to me. I'm glad you sent it."

"Really?"

There was that whisper of hope again. The lump in his throat was beginning to feel like a boulder. "Oh, *jah*. I've been thinking lately that if more people ask for help when they really need it, the world might be a better place."

"I know I'm not Amish like you, but I didn't know who else to write."

"*Gut*, because I reckon the Lord intended for me to read it. The moment I did, I came over here. I thought maybe I could come in and see your leaky floor."

"Really?"

Boy, did no one ever honor their promises to her? "Really." He held out his hands. "I mean, I'm here, aren't I?"

She nodded again, then stepped backward so he could enter.

Nate was immediately surrounded by the acrid smell of bleach and Pine-Sol. He looked around the small living room. It held a cheap card table, a worn-down couch, and two chairs, the kind one might find in a diner.

Everything was spotless.

"Is your mother here?"

Allison looked stricken for a moment, then shook her head. "No. She went to work. She cleans houses."

"Ah." Well, if she was working, she had to be feeling better. That was a blessing, he supposed. "How about you go ahead and show me where the problem is?"

"Yeah. I mean, thank you. It's over here." Her voice was as hopeful as if he'd mentioned he was going to take her on a shopping trip to the mall. She pointed to a narrow stairway that led to a loft of sorts. "It's up here."

"Lead the way." He smiled when she looked at him doubtfully before climbing the stairs.

The little loft looked as exhausted as the front room. In the corner were a made bed and a table with a variety of medicines on it. "I'm guessing this is your mother's room?"

"Yes. She likes being up here by the bathroom."

He followed her to the next doorway. When he peeked inside and saw the condition of the shower pan and the floor around it, he winced. Allison had not been wrong. There was a real good leak, and from the looks of it, it had been leaking for a while. Even at first glance it was obvious that the floor was rotten and that the shower was almost unusable. She'd been right to reach out to him. Someone needed to help her.

"Let's go see your bedroom."

"Okay." She looked relieved to be going back down the narrow stairs. The moment he got to the main floor, she turned down a hallway and into a small room that was about the size of his storage room at the store. Inside were a twin bed, a chest of drawers, and a metal table with a lamp on it. There wasn't much else.

Though it shouldn't have mattered all that much, the sparseness made him even sadder. It didn't look that different from a lot of Amish rooms. But even he knew the bare walls and lack of possessions was out of the ordinary for an English teen.

"See?" She pointed to a dark patch on the ceiling. It was black mold.

Unfortunately, that wasn't the worst of it. Stains marred the wall, and the linoleum on the floor was curled at the edges. He had a pretty good idea that there wasn't mold on just the ceiling. She was surrounded by it.

Allison was standing at the doorway, motionless and obviously afraid of what he was going to tell her.

Nate couldn't help but compare her reaction to some of the men and women he dealt with. Usually they were full of questions, sometimes full of excuses about why things were the way they were. This girl, on the other hand, had no words. Instead, she was simply staring at him. Waiting for his verdict.

It was humbling.

He realized then that the Lord was giving him this task as a blessing. It was his chance to help someone, to try to do some kind of penance for all of the cruel jokes and determined indifference he'd felt about Kendra and her family.

No, it wasn't going to change anything. Maybe it wasn't even going to make a difference to the Lord. All he could do was concentrate on the fact that he couldn't right the past, but he could improve this girl's future.

This isn't about you, anyway, a voice whispered in his head, and he knew this to be true.

Finally he walked to Allison. "I have *gut* news," he said. "This is just the thing I do all the time. I'll be happy to fix your leak and repair the damage it caused."

"Thank you so much!" Almost immediately, worry filled her eyes again. "I don't know how to pay you back, though."

"No need for that. It's my pleasure, Miss Berry."

When she smiled at last, he felt like crying. Instead, he said, "Now, let me go up to that loft and look at things again. I need to make some lists."

FIVE

"Some of you might know that my home life was pretty bad." Impatiently, she shook her head. Reminding herself she wasn't going to cover it up anymore. "*Nee,* what I meant to say is that when I was a little girl, I was abused."

Wednesday

Naomi Troyer had a secret. She hadn't come to see Kendra just because she wanted to visit her for a couple of days. She wanted to move in with her. She might be only sixteen, but she knew it wasn't going to be an easy feat to convince her big sister that it was a good idea.

She had nothing to lose, though.

Mommi and Dawdi were nice enough. But because they were their mother's parents, they didn't always want to admit to all the problems Rosanna Troyer had. Even now, though none of Rosanna's children had much of a relationship with her — and more than enough reasons to never see her again — their grandparents still had a ready supply of excuses for her. *She'd been overwhelmed because she'd had five* kinner. *She was spoiled because they'd done too much for her when she was a child. She'd married a bad man and had been a victim, too.* Or Naomi's personal favorite: *Rosanna put on such a brave face and kept so much to herself that no one was ever sure how to help her.*

The fact that their grandparents refused to place any blame for their abuse on their mother's shoulders was something Naomi knew she'd do her best to keep from her other siblings — especially Kendra. Their mother had spent the majority of their lives pretending everything in that house was just fine, but the truth was that they had had a scary childhood and spent much of the time trying not to get hurt by their father or feel abandoned by their mother. Only Kendra and eventually Mary, Jeremiah, and then Chris had made sure they had food to eat and clean clothes to wear.

They'd all depended on one another — that was for sure. But Naomi had always considered Kendra to be her real mother. She was the one she'd always gone to for hugs or encouragement or if she had a problem. Kendra had gone without so the rest of them could eat.

Even though Naomi knew it had been Kendra's idea to send her to their grandparents, she'd still missed her.

Now, here she was, at her sister's shop that she was about to open, and she was determined to be so helpful and hardworking that Kendra wouldn't be able to do anything but ask her to stay. Being with Kendra felt like being home.

"Nanny, could you do a favor for me, please?" Kendra called out.

Naomi started, realizing she'd been staring out the window instead of organizing the shelves full of letters an artist had carved out of old wood and painted bright colors. "Of course." She turned to find her sister sitting on the ground and glaring at the cabinet she'd been trying to put together. "Do you need me to hold something for ya?"

"Nee." Sighing, Kendra held out a long metal screw. "I think I'm short three of these. Would you walk down to the hardware store and buy some?"

"Sure." She took the screw. "I'll be right back."

"Hold on. Here." She handed Naomi a ten-dollar bill. "Sometimes they sell hot dogs in a cart on the sidewalk. If you see it, get yourself something to eat, okay? I just realized that we worked through lunch."

"Do you want a hot dog, too?"

"Sure, if there's enough money left over. If not, don't worry about me. I'll be fine."

"Kendra, I'm not a baby. I'm not going to get something to eat and leave you hungry."

Her sister looked about ready to argue, but at the last minute, she pursed her lips and nodded. *"Danke."*

Naomi felt like rolling her eyes, but she simply smiled before darting out the door. This was another reason Kendra needed her. Even after all this time, she still was afraid of her siblings going hungry. It broke her heart. All of their hearts, Naomi knew.

After taking note that the food truck absolutely was there and seeing that the hot dogs were just a dollar and a half each, she walked into Walnut Creek Hardware.

Because it was Amish owned and there were no strong fluorescent lights, the old store had a good number of skylights and fans overhead. The faint whirr sounded comforting, and it was slightly dark and blissfully cool inside.

It also smelled good — fresh and clean. The owners must have used a pine air freshener. She stopped for a moment and

67

breathed deeply. Kendra's shop had been stuffy. She hadn't realized just how much until she'd walked out the door.

"Can I help you?"

She turned to find a boy about her age walking toward her. He had red hair, a thousand freckles, and light brown eyes. Though he was staring at her like she'd been acting strange, breathing in the shop's air like it was an oxygen tank, Naomi pretended she didn't notice.

"Sure you can." Holding up the metal screw in between two fingers, she said, "We need three of these. Do you have them?"

"Maybe." He tilted his head to one side. "What are you building?"

Wondering if he was being condescending, she lifted her chin. "What business is that of yours?"

"None. But if it's brick or something, you're going to need good ones."

"Oh. Well, I'm not building anything out of brick."

He looked her up and down, and a faint smile appeared on his lips. "Why won't you tell me? Is it a secret or something?"

"Yeah. I'm building a secret with two-inch screws," she said sarcastically. "Can you help me or not?"

"*Jah.* Sure. Follow me."

She sighed dramatically and followed him down an aisle, made a right turn, and then walked halfway up another. Just as he stopped in front of a large gray metal cabinet filled with clear plastic drawers, Nate Miller walked out of a back room. "Kane, are you finding . . . Wait, Nanny? You are Nanny, right?"

She smiled at him, noticing that he was still as handsome as ever, with his dark blond hair and murky hazel eyes. But more important than his looks was his personality. He'd always been nice to her. "*Jah,* it's Naomi."

He grinned. "Let me guess. You've outgrown your sister's pet name for you."

"Kind of. I think my siblings will always call me Nanny, but it's not the best name to go by, you know?"

"I can see your point, though I've always been fond of the name myself. I thought it was cute." As if he'd just realized his employee was standing with them, he said, "Naomi, this is Kane. Kane, this here is Naomi, who I've known since she was just a little thing."

"Hello," she said.

Kane stepped closer and smiled at her. "Good to meet you. Can I call you Nanny?"

She lifted her chin to show him that she

wasn't someone to mess around with. "*Nee.* All you need to do is help me get those screws, please."

Kane raised his eyebrows. "Wow. You're pretty bossy."

And he was pretty full of himself! "No, I just have things to do. My sister sent me over here to get these screws, and that's what I've come to do."

Nate looked at her more closely. "Wait, are you saying that Kendra sent you down here?"

"*Jah.* She's trying to put together a cabinet and said the box didn't come with enough of these."

"Trying?"

"It's taking a while." She knew the reason, of course. Kendra had terrible dyslexia. It made numbers seem backward. Trying to read the directions and put that information into practice wasn't easy for her. But no way was she going to share that with Nate Miller, and especially not with this Kane fella standing right in front of them and absorbing every word. He might be cute, but he was way too nosy.

Nate took hold of the screw in her hand, looked at it closely, then spoke to Kane. "I'll take care of this." He reached over to a long bank of drawers, each neatly labeled, skimmed his fingertips along the edges, then deftly pulled open the drawer and took out five or six screws.

Naomi held out her hand. *"Danke."*

"No worries. I'll walk them down and help Kendra get that cabinet together. Half the time the pieces of wood in those kits aren't even cut right. It makes it almost impossible to build easily."

Naomi held out the ten-dollar bill Kendra had given her. "Do you want me to pay you or Kane?"

To her surprise, he looked aggravated by her asking. "There's no charge." Walking toward the door, he passed Kane, who was wiping down the counter next to the cash register. "I'll be down at Tried and True. It's two doors down. I won't be long."

"No worries," Kane replied. "I can handle everything here."

"Hope so." Nate winked at Naomi before striding out the door.

Naomi felt a little dismayed as she watched Nate leave. There seemed to be more going on, but she had no idea what it could be. Deciding that it wasn't any of her business, she focused on the new task at hand — their lunch. Should she still get the hot dogs now, or should she wait? She didn't want to bother Kendra, but she had promised her that she'd bring food.

Kane's voice broke through her thoughts. "Tried and True is your sister's place?"

"Yes. Have you been over there yet?"

"*Nee.* It's a girly kind of store, right?"

"I guess." He might have been right, but she wasn't in the mood to stand around and defend her sister's business. "Well, bye."

"Wait."

She turned, ready for him to accuse her of stealing a handful of screws. But instead, he was looking at her intently. "Do you live here in Walnut Creek?"

"I used to." And she might again, if she had any say in it.

"Where do you live now?"

"That's none of your business."

"Why, is it a secret?"

"Why are you asking me so many questions?"

He held up two hands, like he was fending off an attack. "No reason. I was just curious about you."

"I don't know why. We don't even know each other."

"Maybe that's why I was asking you so many questions." Smiling like he knew he was being irritating but didn't care, he lifted one shoulder.

She wanted to frown at him, she really

did. But she also noticed the humor in their exchange. She'd been as prickly as a porcupine!

And now that she thought about it, there was something about him that had caught her attention. Here he was, wearing a pale gray shirt, faded jeans, and tennis shoes, nothing special. With his red hair and pale skin, the light-colored clothes should have made him look even more awkward. But that was the problem. All that gray shirt did was accentuate his eyes, which were really nice.

"Sorry, I guess I have been interrogating you something awful. I can't help it, I've always been curious about things, especially pretty girls who are new to town." Before she could comment on that, he asked another question. "If your sister lives here, how come you don't?"

Oh, but he was irritating. Just as she was about to very firmly tell him that he had to stop asking so many questions, she decided to put him in his place. "I don't live here because our parents abused us and I had to go live with my grandparents." She turned around with a huff, sure she'd just shocked him to death.

"Wait, you're serious, aren't you?"

Turning back to face him, Naomi saw

73

Kane's eyes staring at her intently, and because of that, the smart, sarcastic comment that she'd been intending to say evaporated in her head.

Instead, she simply told him the truth. "I would never joke about something like that," she murmured before walking over to the food truck and placing her order.

It didn't really matter if Kendra wanted to eat now or later. What mattered was that her sister was finally going to have someone on hand to get her food if she got hungry.

Out of all the things Kendra had done for her when she was a little girl, the memory of her big sister giving most of her food to her younger siblings stuck with her the most.

After a lifetime of Kendra doing everything for others and expecting nothing in return, Nanny was going to make sure her big sister was finally going to have someone to take care of her.

Six

"I have four younger siblings, too. So, um, there wasn't a lot at my house. Not a lot of anything." Seeing E.A.'s eyes fill with tears, Kendra pushed her story forward. "The reason I'm telling you this now is because back then, when I was fourteen years old, I didn't tell anyone. Well, I didn't tell anyone about what my life was really like except for Andy Warner."

Wednesday

Nate Miller's impatient rap on the door matched the scowl on his face.

Looking at him through the thick pane of glass, Kendra knew she wasn't a fan of either his impatience or his scowl. Taking her time, she navigated her way through the piles of merchandise on the floor.

He watched her the whole time, managing to look even more annoyed with each second that passed.

"Yes?" she asked when she opened the door at last.

He held out a handful of shiny metal screws. "I've got the screws you needed."

She plucked them from his palm. "*Danke.* But why are you here?"

"Because I heard you have been having a difficult time putting together a cabinet."

"*Nee,* what I meant was where is my sister? I sent her over to get these."

"Naomi is fine. I left her in the shop talking to my new employee. Let me in, wouldja?"

Her feet moved before she was aware of what she was doing. And, of course, he walked right in. "Nate, what are you doing?"

"I'm doing what it looks like. I came over to help you build the cabinet."

"There's no need."

"Sure there is," he murmured as he walked to the pile of parts scattered like leaves all over the floor. "Whoa."

"I know. Why the maker decided this needed to come in a hundred pieces is beyond me."

"It is a mystery," he said as he picked up a rather thick piece of particleboard. "Most likely it's because it's made of such bad materials."

"I knew it wasn't great quality, but the price was right."

"I wasn't criticizing you." He looked irritated. "Kendra, you really need to stop seeing everything I say and do in the worst light. I'm not like that."

Though it was practically ingrained in her to take everything that he said as a put-down, she knew he had a point. She was being far too sensitive. "You're right. I'll try to keep that in mind."

"Thank you." He smiled at her slightly before waggling his fingers. "Now, hand me the directions, and I'll put this together for you."

Smiling back at him, she felt her pulse give a little jump before she got back to the task at hand. "Here they are," she said, slipping the packet into his hands.

His fingers brushed against hers as he took hold of the papers. "Thank you."

Worried that she was starting to notice far too much about him, she smiled weakly. "How can I help?"

"You can relax and work on something else," he said.

"Are you sure?"

"More than sure. I've got this."

Since he was currently on his knees lining up the scattered parts, she decided to take his advice. After looking out the window and noticing Nanny standing in line at the food truck, Kendra walked over to the box she'd just received and started carefully opening the blown-glass vases.

Soon, Nanny returned holding a brown sack. The moment Kendra unlocked the door, she bounded in. "I got us four hot dogs! We had enough money for two each. Isn't that great?"

Her sister sounded just like a little girl again. Grinning, Kendra said, "It is great, indeed. Now, go ahead and eat yours in the back room."

"Wait . . . don't you want to eat, too?"

"I'll eat later."

"But they're hot, and I asked them to put on cheese and onions, just like you like. They're going to be gross if you wait too long."

Naomi was probably right, but there was no way she was going to eat two hot dogs in front of Nate. "*Danke,* but I'm afraid I'm a little busy now."

"I'll watch the door if you want to go eat," Nate said. "I don't mind.

"See, it's all right," Naomi said.

Now she felt even more self-conscious. "Go on back, and I'll be there in a few minutes."

78

"But —"

"Please, dear?"

After the back door was closed, Nate said, "She looked disappointed. You should go on back there with her."

"She'll be fine. I'm really not too hungry."

"But she looked like you let her down."

"She worries about me not eating." Before she realized how it sounded, she waved a hand across her hips. "Obviously being hungry isn't an issue anymore." Of course, the moment the words were off her lips, she wished she could take them back. "Forget I said that."

"Not a chance." He grinned. "For what it's worth, I think you look great."

There it was again, that new sense of awareness that was floating between them. "Thank you."

"And . . . I hate that she worries about you going hungry."

There were a lot of ways she could respond. But only one honest answer. "I hate that, too. But at least *she* isn't worried about being hungry. I would hate that more."

Nate's hazel eyes clouded. "I've got a feeling you went without a lot of meals when she was little."

She had, but it wasn't anything she cared

79

to remember or talk about. "I learned a while ago that everyone has something to overcome. One can't dwell on the past."

"Everyone does, but I reckon you had things a lot harder than most."

He sounded so sincere. She met his gaze, and for the first time, she felt warmer.

A rap at the door broke the moment. She turned abruptly. "Boy, it's busy here today." Then seeing who it was, she grinned. There were Will and John B.

"Hiya, you two."

"Hey, girl."

"What are you doing here?"

"We wanted to see your shop and how you were doing. What do you need help with?"

"Why aren't you two at the trailer factory?"

"We've both got the day off," Will answered as he stepped in farther. "And just to let you know, we heard from more than one of the girls that you have been turning away help."

"That isn't quite true."

"It kind of is," said John, right before he caught sight of Nate kneeling on the ground. "Miller? What are you doing here?"

Nate got to his feet. "Putting together a cabinet for Kendra here."

Will looked offended. "Kendra, you didn't

want to ask us to do that?"

"I didn't ask anyone. Nate just showed up."

"After Naomi came over asking for help."

"She asked for screws," Kendra corrected. "That's all."

Will smiled. "Nanny's here? Where is she?"

"In the back room."

"Nanny! Nanny, come out here and join us."

Knowing her little sister was never going to be able to ignore handsome Will Kurtz, Kendra grinned at the closed storeroom door and started counting to three.

Sure enough, before she even got to two, the door opened and out popped Nanny like a newborn lamb in a freshly mowed field.

"Will! Hiya."

"Hi to you, too. Now come over here and give me a hug."

Without a bit of caution, Naomi walked to his side and hugged him hard.

Kendra felt warmth permeate her insides. This was what she'd always wanted for her little sister. To be surrounded by good people who cared for her. And Will Kurtz? Well, Will was one of the best.

Will chuckled as he patted Nanny on the back. "Say hi to John B."

81

Nanny blinked. "You're dressed English now."

"That's because I married an *Englischer*."

"Not just any *Englischer,* either," Will teased. "He put a ring on our Marie."

Kendra groaned. "Can't wait until she hears you refer to their marriage that way."

"Maybe it's better if you don't repeat that?" Will asked, his cheeks flushed.

"I don't plan to," she teased.

Nanny was obviously still trying to keep up with the latest news. "I must admit that I'm shocked," she said.

"It was a bit of a surprise, but a good one," Kendra said, putting a hand on her sister's shoulder.

"I'm happy for you," Nanny said.

"Thank you. I'm blessed, it's true," John B. said.

"You look just as pleased now as you did on your wedding day," Nate said.

John B. smiled. "That's because I am."

Kendra might have imagined it, but it seemed as if the men had forgotten all about Nate Miller. There was definitely a new tension surrounding him. Some of the ease that she usually noticed in his expression had vanished. In its place was something new. It almost looked like jealousy, but that couldn't have been it. Confusion, maybe?

"You know, there's no reason for you to stay here if you need to get back to your store," Will said. "We can help her now."

"I'm in no hurry. I can finish this first."

John B. looked back at Kendra. "Is that all right with you?"

Nate turned to her. "What have you told them?"

"I've said nothing to anyone," she said hastily. "There was nothing to say."

"Are you sure? Because I've apologized to you more than once now."

"Apologized for what?" Naomi said.

"Nothing," Kendra said quickly. "It's old history."

But instead of doing the polite thing and dropping the subject, Nate's jaw hardened. "Actually, I think we should clear the air, since everyone is hinting around our history anyway."

Looking directly at Naomi, he said, "The truth is I did something I'm not proud of. I made fun of Kendra back when we were in middle school, and she's held it against me ever since." He paused. "I didn't do it just once, either. I kind of put her down quite a bit."

"Why would you do that?" Naomi asked.

"I don't have any excuse, not anything worth mentioning, at least. The truth is that for a while there, I was feeling pretty full of myself and did and said some things that I'm still embarrassed about. I was a jerk and I'm ashamed of myself."

"That's so mean."

Looking at her sister's stricken face, Kendra felt dizzy. She put out a hand to stabilize herself. "Nanny, don't worry about it. Like I said, it was a very long time ago."

But Nanny was standing in front of all of them like a bantam rooster. "Why did you make fun of her?"

Maybe it was the pain in her little sister's voice, or maybe it was that he suddenly realized what he had said, but Nate looked as ashen as she felt. "I . . . it wasn't nothing important."

Nanny walked to stand in front of him. "No, what was wrong with her? Was it her dyslexia or our living situation?"

Kendra could practically feel John B.'s and Will's attention settle on her.

Nate opened his mouth to speak, hesitated, then blurted. "Both." Straightening more, he said, "I made fun of both."

"We don't have to do this," Will said, glancing at Kendra. "Nate, I think you should leave."

"No, wait," Nanny said, her voice cracking. "My parents were awful to all of us, but

84

Kendra took the brunt of it. They didn't give us a lot of food, but Kendra got the least of it so the rest of us could eat. My brother Chris has a learning disability, too, but he had the rest of us to help him. Kendra had nobody."

"Like I said, I'm not proud of what I did."

"Not proud?" She shook her head. "Oh *nee.* You should be ashamed."

"Easy, Naomi." Kendra put her hand on her sister's shoulder. "I've already forgiven him. He was just being stupid. We've all done stupid things one time or another. It's really okay."

"It isn't, though," she retorted. "Home wasn't good. It was bad enough that you had to leave. Bad enough that Jeremiah had to convince Mommi and Dawdi to take me in."

"They wanted you to live with them. It wasn't a hardship. And as for the other? Well, it was a long time ago," she said gently. "I've moved on. I'm better now."

"I know, but you were always so alone." She pointed to John B. and Will. "You always wanted to be one of the Eight. But you weren't because they had their friends and didn't want one more."

Feeling even more awkward, Kendra shook her head. "It wasn't exactly like that.

85

I was alone, but it wasn't the Eight's fault. I never told you that it was."

"You didn't need to. Mary and I knew." Her voice cracked again. "You had so much trouble in school, too. It ain't fair that you had to listen to boys like him, too."

"I don't know what else to say. I can't go back in time," Nate said slowly. "I can only apologize and move on."

Kendra's little sister's eyes were filled with tears. "And you have. Are you happy now?"

"Nanny, stop."

Nate shook his head. "No, it's okay. She can say whatever she wants. And to answer your question, no, I'm not. I feel awful about the pain I caused."

Shoulders shaking, Naomi turned away from him.

Oh, but this was awful. "Nanny, please calm down."

She hiccupped. "But you haven't even eaten the food I brought you. What if you get hungry again?"

"Oh, my." Kneeling at her feet, Kendra whispered. "I'm not hungry. I'm fine! I promise, I am. Darling, I eat all the time. I'm never hungry now."

When Nanny started crying in earnest, it was John B. who came to their sides. Holding out his hands, he reached for both Kendra and Naomi. "Come now. Let me take you both to the back. You can sit down for a spell and eat that lunch. Will and I will fix things up for a bit."

"That's right," Will said. "We'll make sure everything is right as rain."

"Danke," Kendra murmured, all of her attention on Nanny. "I appreciate it." Glancing at Nate before they headed down the hall, she said, "I am sorry."

"It's all right," he murmured.

She hoped Nate was telling the truth, just as she hoped he knew she was being sincere. Everything between them was finally getting better, and she wanted things to continue improving.

Now, though, all that mattered was helping Naomi. Her little sister needed her, and Kendra wanted to be there for her, just like she always had been.

SEVEN

Tricia Clark interrupted. "Really? My brother never said a word to me about you."

"He wouldn't have, you see. Andy was a lot of things, but he was really good at keeping secrets."

Wednesday
When the girls disappeared behind the door with John, Nate sighed. "Let's get started."

Will knelt down, picked up a screwdriver, and handed it to him. "That's all you've got to say?"

"No, but I don't think it's the time or the place."

"I disagree. After what I just heard, I think there's a lot to discuss."

"Will, I promise I didn't know the extent of Kendra's problems back then." Worse, even if he had, he wasn't sure how different he would've acted toward her. Sure, he hoped he would have been more sympathetic, but he wasn't sure if his fourteen-year-old self would've been a whole lot kinder. The fact was that he'd had a fairly idyllic life with his parents. There had always been food on the table, clothes for him to wear, and an ear to listen when he was worried about something. Getting in trouble meant getting grounded for a few days.

"I didn't, either." Will paused, then shook his head. "No, that ain't true. All of us knew Kendra was in a bad way. But back when we were small, we didn't see her all that much. Later, when we were twelve or thirteen, I think it was easier to pretend not to know. Even when I was Naomi's age, I never said anything when Kendra said everything with her was just fine."

Thinking about Allison and the work he was doing on her house, Nate said, "I'm a different person now."

"All of us are a work in progress. Ain't so?" He scanned the directions, then tossed them on the floor. "Looks like we need to put sections A and D together first."

Nate picked up the particleboard. "This is so badly made, I'll be surprised if it holds anything at all."

"Well, that's not our problem. Kendra got

them. All we can do is put them together for her so she doesn't have to worry."

Nate agreed. "Looks like parts F and H attach on the ends."

Will sorted through the pieces, found them, and handed them over. "We'll get this one done in no time."

And so it continued, Nate and Will hunting for pieces, helping each other, working methodically. Twenty minutes later, they had the first shelf done.

Will grunted. "Only two more to go. Maybe if we get lucky, we'll finish by supper."

Nate was about to reply when John B. came out. Noticing that his expression looked strained, Nate walked toward him. "Is everything okay?"

"With Kendra? I think so. I'm not sure about Nanny, though." His voice lowered. "I think it's evident that Kendra didn't shield her as much as she'd hoped. That girl is really worried about her sister."

"I wonder how we can help," Nate said. "Any ideas? Should we try to plan some activity together to help get her mind off her worries?"

"Uh, no offense, but I don't think you should do anything," John said.

"You, too? John, don't block me out for

something I did ten years ago."

"I'm just saying that you don't really know her. We do." Before he could add something, Kane pulled open the door. "Nate, I really need some help. The store's filled, and some of the customers are asking me to do things I don't know how to do."

He jumped to his feet. "Sorry about that. Of course, let's go." He looked back at John B. and Will and raised a hand. He wished he could say something else, but there really wasn't anything else to say.

Nothing that mattered, anyway.

When they were walking down the sidewalk, Nate said, "I'm glad you came to get me."

"I didn't think you were going to be gone so long." Kane ran a hand through his dark red hair. "I kept telling everyone you'd be right back . . ."

"I didn't intend to. It was just that some of my friends came over, and I decided to help them build bookshelves."

"Where were Kendra and Naomi?"

Kane's voice was carefully light, but Nate wasn't fooled. "In the back room eating lunch."

"Oh." Just before they entered the store, Kane asked, "How well do you know Naomi?"

"Well enough. Why?"

"Do you know how old she is?"

"I reckon she's probably around your age." Realizing that his young employee was definitely interested in Naomi, he murmured, "So, it's like that, hmm?"

Kane looked away. "I don't know. I was just asking."

"Well, while you're asking and I'm answering, try to remember that she ain't a girl who you mess with. If you really like her, then you're gonna need to treat her with respect."

Kane frowned at him. "Of course I will. What kind of person do you think I am?"

That was the thing, wasn't it? Fact was, Kane was a much better person than he had been.

Kendra ate every bite of her two hot dogs even though she could practically feel them expanding in her stomach like coarse balls of wet wool. She would have rather not had anything. Her insides were in knots, and a thousand questions were running through her head.

Beside her, Naomi was picking at her food. In many ways, Nanny was Kendra's crowning achievement. Her sister was smart, driven, and well-liked by everyone. She was also fairly even-keeled.

Something was going on in her life, though, and while it was Kendra's nature to choose to leave her alone and maybe ask her about it at a later time, she was afraid to do that any longer.

After cleaning up all their trash, Kendra dived in.

"Are ya ready to tell me what you are thinking about?"

"I was just worried about you. That's all."

"Naomi, I appreciate that, but I'm not a girl your age anymore. I'm a grown woman who has been living on her own for a long time."

But instead of making her feel better, Naomi only looked more upset. "That's the problem. You were my age when you were taking care of all of us."

"That was a long time ago. And, darling, even though I know you, like the rest of us, still have some sad thoughts to deal with, I don't believe that's what is really wrong — or why you're here in the first place."

Naomi released a ragged sigh. "It's that obvious?"

"It is."

"Fine. I don't want to live with Mommi and Dawdi anymore."

Kendra felt as if she'd just gotten a fist

93

punched into her stomach. What had brought that on? Had they hurt her? "What did they do?"

Naomi froze at Kendra's tone. "Nothing. I mean, nothing bad."

"Are you sure? They didn't hurt you?"

"*Nee.* I just want to leave their house. It's time."

"You are too young to live by yourself, Nanny." And yes, she realized the pot was calling the kettle black.

"I don't want to live by myself."

Her words had tumbled out, practically all in one breath. Because of that, it took a minute for Kendra to process what she said, but once she did, her knee-jerk reaction was that her worst fears were coming to life. "Please don't say you're moving back in with our parents."

"What?" Her eyes widened. "*Nee.* I don't want to go back to them." Softening her voice, she said, "I want to move in with you, sister. I want to live with you for the next two years at least."

"Me?"

Nanny nodded. "I can't handle our grandparents anymore. They keep trying to fix Mamm, and worse, I think they're starting to think that all of us ought to try to fix her, too."

94

"That ain't possible." Maybe not that their mother couldn't be fixed. After all, with God's blessings, all things were possible. But there was no way Kendra was ever going to let her little sister take on that burden. "You *canna* fix Mamm." And then there was their father. Sometimes, when the memories got so bad, she would be certain that not even the Lord could change Hank Troyer into anything of worth.

Naomi looked incredulous. "Of course I can't fix our mother. But that's not what Mommi and Dawdi think! They are sure that she just needs more time and one more chance, and that nothing that happened to any of us has been her fault."

Kendra mentally cringed. "They don't want to take any responsibility, either." She shook her head. "Sometimes I feel as if they blame all Daed's abuse on us."

"That's because they live firmly in denial-land. And they don't listen," Nanny said. "So, can I?"

Her sister's expression was so filled with hope, it broke Kendra's heart to disappoint her. "I love that you want to live with me. But I don't know if I'm the best person."

"Why not? You're all grown up. You have your own place and your own business."

Jah, she did. She was real proud of those

accomplishments, too. But she was also broken. "I don't have a lot of extra time, Nanny," she said gently. "It's just me, you know."

"I don't need you to look after me. I can look after myself."

"Then, there's high school. I don't know what to do about that."

"What about it?" Talking quickly, Nanny added, "I can go to the Mennonite school that your friend E.A. went to. She was Mennonite, right?"

"*Jah.* She was. But it's private."

"I had a scholarship at the school in Canton. I'm sure I can get one here. I'm really smart, Kendra."

Yes, Naomi was. She could probably go to a university if she had a mind to do it. "What about your friends? Do you really want to leave all of them?"

"I can make friends here."

Nanny said that so easily, like finding friends was nothing she'd ever worried about.

Just as she opened her mouth to gently tell her that she was just going to have to hang in there a little bit longer, Naomi grabbed her hand. "Please, Kendra? Don't say no. I want to be with you. I've really missed you. You've been more of a mother

96

than either Mamm or Mommi, you know that, right?"

Nanny wasn't wrong. Kendra had been the one who'd changed Naomi's diapers, who'd stayed up all night with her when she'd been sick with croup. Who'd made sure she had food and clothes. Who'd pulled her into bed and hugged her tight when she couldn't sleep or had been scared hearing their parents yell and cry.

What could she say? "All right, then."

"Yes? Really?"

Kendra almost smiled. "*Jah,* but I'm not promising that everything with me will be easy."

"I'm not asking for easy. I just want things to be easier."

That said it all, didn't it? All of her brothers and sisters had grown up not expecting much. Peace at night. Food in the pantry. None of them hoped for things to be easy. No, the most they ever longed for was for things not to be too hard.

Kendra ran a hand down the back of Nanny's head. "I'm guessing that you probably have not told our grandparents."

For the first time in their conversation, Naomi looked a little unsure. "I thought . . . well, I thought you could do that."

Kendra groaned. "Oh, Naomi. All right,

but I'm going to make you be in the same room when I speak to them."

"Are you sure?"

"Oh, *jah*. No way am I going to take their guilting and accusations all by myself. At the very least, I have to have a witness."

"Fine."

If Kendra wasn't so frazzled, she would have laughed.

At least it was better than crying.

EIGHT

"Obviously, I didn't mean to tell him. But one day after, um, a pretty rough night, Andy saw me walking to school. I was having trouble walking, and my clothes . . . they were really dirty."

Friday

"You have football practice in thirty, Kane," his mother called out. "Do you have all your equipment?"

"Yeah!" he answered from the laundry room. He and his mother played this game almost every day. She got his things together, he put them in his duffel bag, and then just as he was getting ready to go, she asked if he remembered to actually take his duffel with him to school.

Since he was sixteen and not six, it was as annoying as could be. But it also made him remember his older brother, who would have forgotten his head if it wasn't attached

99

to his body.

Andrew died when he was ten years old and Kane was six. That was ten years ago.

"Kane, I didn't hear you," his mother called from halfway down the hall.

He exhaled and reminded himself that not only would his father have his hide if he learned he spoke to her like that, but also he knew better. Poking his head out of the laundry room, he said, "Yes, Mom," in a much better tone. "Thank you for getting everything together."

Leaning against the wall, she shook her head. "You always say that. You don't need to thank me, you know."

But he kind of did. Their best boy was gone, and they were left with him. In a lot of ways, he was a mediocre replacement for Andrew. "I'm gonna go. See you later."

"Want me to take you? I don't mind. I have time today."

Sure, a ride would be great, but he didn't want her spending her spare time on him. He knew she was currently swamped with work. "Nah, I've got it." He kissed her on the cheek. "See you tonight."

She smiled at him before walking back into her home office. He hoisted his duffel on his shoulder and headed out.

The high school was nearby, only about a

fifteen-minute walk. Ten minutes if he was running late. Even less than that if he drove his Jeep.

But in between his house and the high school was the shopping center, where his part-time job at Walnut Creek Hardware store was. And where that new girl Naomi was hanging out, helping her sister.

It was official. He couldn't stop thinking about her. She was really pretty, but there was something about her that was so different from any of the girls at his school. She seemed smarter. More driven. More mature.

From the minute he had tried to help her and she looked at him like he was messing up her day, he knew he'd wanted to see her more.

Because of that, he half ran over to the shopping center, then took his time walking by, on the slim chance he would catch sight of her.

And yeah, he knew that was pathetic.

He got lucky, though, because there she was, sitting on the window seat. She was sipping coffee while flipping through a magazine, which he figured meant he shouldn't bother her.

But he was looking for any reason to talk to her again.

He knocked on the window. She jumped,

turned with wide eyes, then exhaled in relief.

Trying the door, he walked in. "Hey. Sorry, I didn't mean to scare you."

"It's all right. For a minute there, I thought . . . well, never mind. What are you doing here?"

"I'm on my way to school. I left a little early, so I thought I'd stop by to see if you were here."

She tilted her head and kind of smiled. "I guess I am."

Since she wasn't asking him to leave, he tossed his duffel bag on the floor. "How come you're here so early?"

"I'm helping Kendra. She's going to open her shop next week, you know."

"I didn't know that. But that's good."

"It is. It's going to be great. We're even going to serve cookies and punch. Kendra's been cooking in the evenings for days. Maybe you could stop by."

The invitation was sweet. "As long as it isn't Thursday; I've got a game."

"What kind of game?"

"Football." She had to be the only person in Walnut Creek who didn't know he was the starting running back for the team. "If Kendra's grand opening isn't Thursday, you should go to the game."

"But I wouldn't know anyone there. I don't want to sit in the stands by myself."

"Yeah, I guess not. Well, there are a lot of games left."

"Maybe."

"Nanny? Who are you talking to?" Kendra asked as she came out of the back room.

"Kane. Do you remember him? He works over at the hardware store sometimes."

"Hi again." Kendra looked at him curiously. "Do you work this early?"

"Oh, no. I'm on my way to school. I just stopped by . . ." He allowed his voice to drift off, because, really, how was he going to be able to explain to Naomi's sister what he was doing here?

Naomi hopped to her feet. "I'll walk him out right now." Lowering her voice, she said, "Come on."

He followed her out, looking at her curiously. When they were alone on the sidewalk, he said, "How come your sister has a *kapp* but you don't?"

"Hmm? Oh, Kendra is still Amish. I started living with my *mamm*'s parents a couple of years ago. Since they're Mennonite, I decided to be Mennonite, too."

"I didn't think that was allowed."

Her chin lifted. "Not everything needs to make sense to outsiders."

103

He grinned. "Since I'm Mennonite, I wouldn't exactly call me an outsider."

"Oh." It was then that she seemed to take a good look at his collared shirt and dark pants. "Sorry."

"Hey, are you going to be attending my school?"

She nodded. "I'm a junior. I start on Monday."

Things were getting better and better. "That's awesome. I'm a senior, so I can show you around. Hey, maybe we can even hang out sometimes?"

"I don't know if I'll have time for that. I'm moving here to be with my sister. Between work and school I won't have a lot of extra time."

She sounded so prissy. It was actually pretty cute. "Understood."

"*Gut.* As long as we're clear."

Everything was as clear as mud. "I better go. I'll see you."

She smiled at him. "Have a good day, Kane." And then she turned right around, as if he hadn't gone out of his way to see her.

On his way to school, Kane couldn't stop thinking about his interaction with Naomi, and as he walked to his first class and smiled back at some of the girls he'd known for most of his life but wasn't the slightest bit interested in, he realized that his mind was set.

Naomi Troyer was complicated, beautiful, and a little prickly. But somehow she'd already claimed his interest.

He had to get to know her better. He didn't have a choice.

NINE

"When I saw Andy approaching, I kind of tried to ignore him. But because it was Andy? Well, he stopped right there in the middle of the sidewalk like I was his long-lost best friend. 'Hey, Kendra,' he said. 'What's wrong with you?' "

Friday

Though maybe she should have given her sister some privacy, Kendra had stood in the middle of the shop and watched Naomi talk to the boy on the sidewalk. Naomi was looking rather haughty, while Kane seemed to be trying to figure her out.

Well, that made two of them, Kendra decided.

First Nanny had shown up out of the blue and started helping her at the shop. Then she wanted to live with her. And now she had boys visiting her. It was all confusing and out of Kendra's comfort zone. She'd spent her teenage years trying to shield her younger siblings from their father, not flirting with boys. She had no experience being monitored and didn't know when was the "right" time to intervene or when it was better to step aside and let a relationship run its course.

She had a feeling Chris, Jeremiah, and Mary would probably feel the same way. But of course, they weren't around. This was all on her.

Worry began to pool in her stomach as she debated the right thing to do.

She still didn't have an answer when Naomi came inside, her face a careful mask. Kendra folded her arms across her chest and waited for her to tell her what Kane had wanted.

But all she did was walk over to a container of tags. "Should I start pricing this box of sewing notions?"

"*Nee.* You can tell me what that was all about."

"What do you mean?"

Oh, brother. "Nanny, why did that boy visit you here? Is there something going on between the two of you?"

"Of course not. We just met."

"Are you sure?"

"Yes. All we were doing was talking, Kendra. Don't make a big deal out of nothing."

She supposed she had been overreacting. "Sorry, I, well, I just figured it's best to ask."

Naomi lifted her chin. "I wanted to move here to be with you. Not date."

"Do you want to date him?"

"He hasn't asked me out, Kendra." Sounding more annoyed, she added, "Don't worry about it. Now, would you like me to tag those notions or not?"

"*Jah.* Go ahead and tag them." Feeling confused, she walked back to her office to think. Her dog, Sweet Blue, lifted her head and thumped her tail a couple of times. "Hey, sweetie," she said as she knelt down. "I'm so glad you're here." Blue, she could understand. She'd found the mixed-breed dog at the pound, and the little thing had looked lonely and dejected, like she'd already given up on anything good ever happening to her, even though she was just a puppy.

Kendra had known that look well. She reckoned she'd felt the same way more than a time or two. She'd taken her right home, but Blue had seemed set on doing everything she could to get taken back to the pound. Kendra had continued to patiently coax her into minding the rules and feeling comfortable. Then, one day, it was like Blue had decided she no longer needed to test Kendra. She'd started doing everything Kendra had been trying to teach her for weeks. Since then, they'd practically become inseparable. Dogs, she could relate to.

"Kendra, Nate is back."

Wondering what he wanted now, Kendra left the door open so Blue could follow her into the main showroom. "Hi."

"Hey there. I came over to see if you needed any help, but it looks like you've got plenty right here."

"I do, indeed. Between Blue and Nanny, I'm well taken care of today."

"In that case, I was wondering if you wanted to go over to Will Kurtz's *haus* this evening."

"Why?"

"He invited a bunch of people over and asked me to see if you could come. Can you?"

"Well, I'm not sure. See, Nanny —"

"Is perfectly able to look after herself," Nanny interrupted. "You should go, Kendra."

Nate grinned. "Well, what do you think?"

Glancing at Naomi, she raised her eyebrows. "I think that sounds *gut.*"

"Will wants everyone to come over around six. Where do you want me to pick you up?"

109

Was he asking her out on a date? It sure felt like it. Nate was looking at her intently, not like there was something wrong with her, but like there was something hidden that he was hoping she'd see. That hadn't happened a lot to her, but it had happened enough for her to be fairly certain that there was something new going on between them.

Realizing that he was waiting on a response, she said, "I could meet you there. It might be easiest."

He shook his head. "Nope, I'm taking you, Kendra," he said firmly. "Shall I pick you up here or at your house?"

This was definitely a date! Catching herself before she told him that he could pick her up anywhere, Kendra glanced at Nanny. She needed to make sure Nanny would be safe at home. "At my *haus,* please."

His expression warmed. "All right, then. I'll be there at five thirty."

Just as he was about to walk out the door, she hurried to his side. "Hold on a moment. You need my address."

"I know where you live, Kendra. Don't worry about that."

"All right, then. I'll see you in a few hours."

Pausing before he left, he cast her a long look. "*Danke,* Kendra."

110

After shutting the door behind him, she leaned against the entryway frame and wondered if they could really go from enemies to more than friends so quickly? They hadn't technically been enemies, though. It had been one-sided, on her part. Nate, at least as far as she knew, hadn't considered her his enemy. She'd been the one who had held that grudge tight to her chest. Not him.

TEN

"Am I the only person in this room wincing right now?" Harley Lambright asked.

"I am," Logan said. "But that was Andy for you. He wasn't exactly the type of guy to sit around and try to think of a diplomatic way to say what was on his mind."

Friday Night

Walking up to Kendra Troyer's small, neat-as-a-pin home, Nate was taken aback by his nerves. Though he hadn't exactly dated a lot of women, he had never had any problems in that area. Most women usually found him agreeable and easy to be with. Some had even commented that they found him handsome.

Then, there was his livelihood at the hardware store. He made his living chatting with all sorts of people, men and women of all different ages. He realized now that owning his store had given him a false sense of security. He'd mistakenly imagined that very few things could make him uneasy.

That was before he'd started talking to Kendra again. Something was different about her. He couldn't quite put his finger on it. Was it her past? His guilt? Or was it something more elusive?

Her door opened before he had the chance to knock. "Is everything all right, Nate?"

"*Jah.* Of course. Why?"

She tilted her head to one side. "Oh, no reason. Only that you've been standing out here looking at my door for several minutes."

He inwardly groaned. Of course she had to see him standing there like a fool. "Sorry, I must have been lost in thought."

"Ah." Humor lit up her eyes — she didn't believe his story for a moment. "Well, I'm ready. If you'd wait a moment, I'll go tell Nanny that I'm leaving."

"Take your time." She hadn't invited him inside. He wondered why before reminding himself that until last week she hadn't even considered him a friend. Nothing about the two of them was going to change in the near future.

When she appeared again, she had on a sweater cloak in a pretty shade of blue. "I'm ready now," she said as she picked up a small purse and a ceramic covered dish.

He noticed then that her dog was looking at him warily. "You've got quite the guard dog, Kendra."

She looked down and smiled. "She's a protective *hund,* for sure. Blue, say hello to Nate here." Blue, who looked like a cross between a Siberian husky and a small poodle, looked up at him curiously.

He bent down and held out a hand. "Hiya, Blue. Good to meet you." After several sniffs, the dog wagged her tail.

Kendra laughed. "That's a good sign. She's skittish around strangers."

"Have you had her long?"

"Eight or nine months, I think. I got her at the shelter. She's a sweetheart but doesn't always take to new people."

"I'm glad she likes me."

Kendra smiled softly at him. "Me, too." After petting the dog again, she stepped onto the stoop and shut the door behind her. "I'm definitely ready now."

He gestured to the dish she was holding. "What do you have there?"

"Oh, it's nothing. Just some puppy chow."

"Puppy chow?"

Her smile broadened. "No, it's not left-overs from Blue. It's cereal, candy, pretzels, and nuts all covered in white chocolate."

"Whew. You had me worried there for a moment."

"Have you really not had it before?" she asked as they walked to the street.

"Nee."

"Well, maybe you'd like to have some when we get to Will's."

"I'd love to try it. But why did you make something? Everyone knows you worked all day. There was no need."

"I always try to bring a dish as a thank-you." Before he could point out that such a thing wasn't necessary, she added, "I enjoy making food, and it's a pleasure to share what I've made."

"I've heard you're a fantastic cook. I'm sure we'll all be happy to have it." Stopping at the street corner, he added, "So, Will's house is a little under two miles away. I hope you don't mind walking. We might be a minute or two late, but no one will mind."

"I don't mind. I usually walk there instead of riding my bike."

"Let's get on our way, then."

Kendra was taller than a lot of other women he knew and she walked with sure strides. He appreciated not having to shorten his steps for her.

She had both hands on her container, so

115

when she slipped on a patch of gravel, he had to reach for her elbow to keep her steady.

She flinched.

He pulled back his hand. "I'm sorry. I was afraid you were about to fall."

"*Nee,* I'm the one who must apologize." She paused, obviously struggling for the right words. "I . . . well, I'm not too used to being helped. Thank you for looking out for me."

Her words were so proper and so sad.

He knew, too, that they also barely covered how she was feeling or what she'd been through. "Don't thank me for caring, Kendra."

She shrank back before visibly finding her backbone. "Don't chide me for apologizing, Nate."

It was all he could do not to grin. She was such a contradiction of vulnerability and strength, mixed with a healthy dose of salt and vinegar. It made him want to learn everything about her. Nate bit back what he'd been about to say, which was to offer to carry the container of puppy chow. Instead, he simply walked by her side.

Kendra wasn't a chatty sort. He'd known that. Though he usually would have been pleased to walk quietly, he didn't want to miss the opportunity to get to know her better.

"How do you like having your sister with you?"

"Nanny?" She smiled softly. "Boy, I don't know."

Surprised by her candor, he said, "Really? I thought you were close."

"We are close, but in a lot of ways our relationship is more mother-daughter than sisters. I'm eight years older, you see. She's sixteen, and I'm twenty-four."

"She seemed more mature than sixteen."

"She does, but then sometimes, she acts just like she should."

"Which is?"

"Like a little girl. Full of silliness." She smiled. "I'm afraid I'm weak where she's concerned."

He loved that she was opening up to him. "Weak how?"

"I find that I *canna* deny her wishes." Just as he was about to ask what kind of things Naomi wanted, Kendra spoke again. "She wants to be normal. You know, not like me."

"Kendra, what are you talking about? You're normal."

She wrinkled her nose. "*Nee,* I wish I was. But I'm afraid I'm too scarred."

Scarred? His heart felt like it stopped. He

117

wondered what she was referring to. Her heart? Her confidence from foolish kids like he'd been, speaking without thought?

Or was she referring to her family?

"Oh, Nate! If you could see your face right now!" Before he could form a sentence, she rushed on, as if she was causing him trouble. "Don't worry. I promise, none of my scars are visible right now."

Right now? A ball of pain hit the pit of his stomach. Was she speaking of actual scars on her skin? What the devil had been done to her?

"Hi, you two!" Katie Lambright called out. "Stop and wait for Harley and me to catch up."

Nate turned to watch the two of them amble over. Katie had to have been seven months along in her pregnancy. She was such a little thing, too, which was why her stomach looked enormous.

Kendra hugged Katie and pressed her hands onto Katie's beach ball tummy. "Look at you. Are you feeling all right?"

"Never better. Just big, *jah*?"

"Never that, Katie," Harley murmured before greeting Nate. "*Gut* to see you."

"You, too. It's been too long."

"At least three days. Ain't so?" Harley joked as they walked the last few yards to

118

Will's house. Harley remodeled houses, so it was a rare week when he wasn't in Nate's hardware store for one thing or another.

When they arrived at Will and E.A.'s new home, they saw Marie's large SUV parked in the driveway next to a pair of bicycles that Nate knew belonged to Tricia and Logan.

"Looks like everyone's here," Kendra said. "That's a blessing."

"Indeed," Katie said as she hurried forward. "E.A., look at your lovely green dress. It's fetching."

E.A., who'd accepted the Amish lifestyle when she'd married Will, looked down at her dress in dismay. "What? It's Plain."

Kendra chuckled. "Katie is teasing you, E.A. You not only look pretty, you look mighty Plain, indeed. It suits you."

E.A. smiled softly. *"Danke."*

Nate stood at the door and allowed everyone to go ahead of him. Watching their interactions, he realized that though Kendra, like him, had never been a "true" member of the Eight, she was far closer to the group than he was. It was a bit of a surprise, though he now realized that it shouldn't have been.

Growing up, he'd been close to Andy, who'd introduced Nate to his friends, and they'd seemed to accept him with open arms. Then, like so many people, they'd grown older and drifted apart.

After Andy passed away last year, Nate hadn't had as much occasion to be around the Eight in social situations. Kendra, on the other hand, had become even closer to them all. He wondered now if Kendra had been the reason why he'd been included in the gathering so easily.

"*Gut* to see ya, Nate," Will said as he held out his hand. "Glad you could join us."

There was something in his tone that told Nate that his guess hadn't been wrong. "Me, too," he said simply.

Yes, he was glad he'd been able to be there. For many reasons.

ELEVEN

"On any other day, and maybe even with any other person, I would've said I was fine and asked him to leave me alone. But I guess God put Andy right there for a reason. Because I looked him in the eye and told him that my father had gotten drunk the night before and beat me because there wasn't any supper on the stove."

Friday Night

"So, you and Nate, hmm?" Marie asked as she grabbed Kendra's hand and pulled her into the kitchen with the other girls.

Kendra let herself be led, but she dragged her feet. "It's not like that," she protested.

"If it's not like *that,* what is it like?" E.A. asked.

Oh, sometimes Kendra really wished E.A. wasn't quite so analytical. "I don't know. We're trying to become friends."

"You aren't sure that you are friends?"

E.A. looked perplexed, and Kendra didn't really blame her. "We are friends, but things between us are complicated. We've got a history, you know."

"Harley and I had some problems that we had to get over, but once we talked, we realized that we'd taken a lot of things the wrong way," Katie confided. "Have you two really talked things through? It seems like there's something special brewing between you."

"We've been talking, and it has smoothed out things." She thought about their recent conversations and how they went much better, but there still seemed to be something missing.

Kendra added, "But as far as us being something more? I don't know. We may never be anything more than simply friends." Noticing Katie's crestfallen expression, Kendra chuckled softly. "Don't look so depressed by that, Katie. If Nate and I are only ever friends, I'll be grateful. Honestly, I think he would be a mighty *gut* friend to have."

"Nate was super close to Andy. I think his death hit him hard," Marie said. "I've worried that he might have kept some of his pain inside. Some men don't express their feelings very openly."

"I had forgotten how close they'd been," Kendra admitted. "Now I feel bad that he might not have had anyone to talk to. I hope that wasn't the case." Thinking back to the last year, she realized that he hadn't been present any of the times they'd all gotten together to talk about Andy and help one another recover from his loss.

"He's part of our group now," Katie said. "Who knows? Maybe one day the sparks that we all see between you will turn into something more."

"Maybe," Kendra allowed. "It's not like I could concentrate on a new relationship anyway. I have my hands full. Naomi asked to live with me."

"John told me that he's seen her around town," Marie said. "How is that going?"

"I have a feeling it's going to be a daily question. She's a teenager, you know. One minute, everything is wonderful-*gut,* the next minute it's not."

Marie chuckled. "I'm afraid my mother probably said the same thing about me. Naomi is a sweet girl, though."

"She is, but she is also willful. I'm not saying that's a bad thing, but sometimes I get the feeling that she still has some secrets she hasn't shared with me."

"There's nothing wrong with secrets," E.A. said. "She is sixteen."

"I hope and pray that her secrets are simply normal teenage things."

Katie frowned. "Do you really think they might be something darker?"

"Maybe. I love her dearly, but she didn't grow up like the rest of us. We all did our best to shield her from our father's violence and Mamm's denial. At one time or another, all of us tried to get Naomi to move into our grandparents' house. When Chris and Mary left, Jeremiah helped convince them to take her in. I think Naomi was only twelve at the time."

"So she's lived with them for years," E.A. said.

Kendra nodded. "*Jah.* I'm glad we all protected her, but because of that, Naomi doesn't always see everything through the same lens as I do." Which was something to be celebrated, she reminded herself. If Naomi became a different sort of person than Kendra, a strong, confident woman who wasn't filled with dark memories and regrets, then that would be wonderful. She would feel like she'd done something right.

Logan stuck his head into the kitchen. "Ladies, would you be able to join us now? Will's about to pop, he's so excited."

"We're on our way," Marie said as she grinned at their friends. "Hmm, I wonder what this is all about."

Kendra shared a smile with Katie. It was obvious that they all had a pretty good idea of what Will's big secret was. The girls filed out, each of them going to her man.

Nate was standing next to Logan and his wife, Tricia, Andy's little sister. She and Logan had a lot of things to overcome: Logan had been Amish, while Tricia had been English; they had an age difference of almost three years; and Logan had been one of Andy's best friends, which meant defying the male friendship code of not dating friends' sisters. But in spite of all that, they'd fallen in love. Tricia had even surprised everyone by wanting to become Amish, and now they were married.

Their story made Kendra realize that if they could overcome all of those things, then it would be wrong of her to put so much emphasis on some thoughtless words said a decade ago.

Gathered together in Will and E.A.'s living room, Kendra knew she wasn't the only person trying not to look at E.A.'s stomach.

"Everyone, before we begin our meal, E.A. and I have something to tell you." Will reached for his wife's hand and gave her an adoring look.

After the room quieted, Will continued. "Today's announcement has been a long time coming. We've experienced quite a few hurdles, but we feel like the Lord was guiding us all along." He took a deep breath. "Just this morning, we got the news that all our prayers were answered."

After Will meandered along for a couple more minutes, Kendra could practically feel everyone's confusion. Beside her, she noticed Harley give Katie a perplexed look. Kendra could relate. This seemed like a lot more information than necessary to announce a pregnancy.

Finally, John B. spoke up. "Not that we aren't all mighty happy for you, but when are you going to tell us your news?"

Will slapped a hand on his face. "I guess I have been dragging my feet, haven't I?"

"He has," E.A. said with a sweet look at him. "What he's trying to tell you all is that our application to be foster parents came through today. Will and I will soon be fostering two *kinner*. We'll be getting them sometime this fall."

The news was such a surprise that all of them looked as dumbstruck as Kendra reckoned she felt.

"Say again?" Logan asked.

"We're not pregnant," E.A. explained. "See, though I imagine one day we'll want a baby of our own, we decided to foster and eventually adopt some children in need instead."

"That's *wunderbaar*!" Katie exclaimed. "Well, tell us more."

"They're a pair of siblings who lost both parents in a car accident. They've been shuttled around to a number of foster homes. They're five and six. *Gut* ages, don't you think?"

"The best!" Marie said, rushing over to give them hugs. "No wonder you wanted us all over here. You've got to get everything ready for them."

Will grinned. "We sure do. We're hoping you all might help us do some painting and shopping over the next couple of weeks."

Immediately, everyone started volunteering their time and offering to buy things for the kids.

Kendra looked at Nate, wondering if he felt uncomfortable, but he was already offering to raid his store in order to help Harley make beds for the kids.

"Hey, Kendra?" E.A. asked.

"Yes?"

"I was hoping you'd make me some meals when they first get here. Would you be willing to do that?"

"Of course I would. You don't even need to ask. But are you sure?"

"You are the best cook we have. And all of your food is tasty and simple. I think that's exactly what these kids are going to need." She frowned. "You wouldn't believe how they've been living."

A lump formed in her throat. She didn't like to see things only in terms of herself, but she couldn't fight her own memories. She had a pretty good idea of how those children were living because she'd lived that way. Though it felt almost hard to talk, she said, "I will be happy to make some meals for you to freeze."

"I can give you some money for the groceries."

"Of course not. It will be my gift."

"*Danke,* Kendra." E.A. hugged her tight.

Kendra hugged her back, then realized that Nate was standing right there, his focus completely on her.

After E.A. was claimed by someone else, he leaned close. "Are you all right?"

"Of course," she said, but despite her best efforts, she was barely holding it together.

Nate leaned closer. "We can leave or even go somewhere to talk for a few minutes."

"There's no need for that. But thank you,

Nate. That's kind of you."

He smiled at her before moving back to the others.

Later, as they all walked into the dining room to eat the meal E.A. and Will had spread out for them, all Kendra could do was wonder how her life would have changed if such a thing had happened to her.

What if someone had tried to save her, just like Will and E.A. were trying to save those kids? Just like she'd tried to save Naomi?

What would her life have been like if she'd known she was cared for and loved?

Things might have been very different, indeed.

TWELVE

"What did Andy say?" Marie whispered.

Kendra smiled sadly. "He said that not only did it look like I was having trouble walking, but that my dress smelled. Then he asked if I'd like to skip school and go to his house."

Sunday

The weekend had been wonderful. Kendra had gone out with Nate and her friends, leaving Naomi in charge of Blue. Kendra probably hadn't thought too much about what she'd done, but for Naomi, it had been huge. Kendra had not only trusted her to be just fine on her own, but she'd also entrusted Naomi to look after her shelter dog.

Since she was sixteen, that really wasn't anything special. But for Naomi, who'd been watched over by her siblings when

130

she'd lived at home and had never been given any responsibilities beyond school when she was living with her grandparents, it had meant a lot.

Naomi had taken advantage of the time alone by cleaning Kendra's house. Her sister had told her once that she always dreaded days off work because she'd have to spend it washing and dusting her home.

When Kendra had woken up on Saturday morning, that had been the first thing she'd mentioned to Naomi — how nice it had been to wake up to a clean-smelling house on a Saturday morning.

They'd spent the rest of the day doing things together. Kendra showed her how to make apple butter, and together they'd put up a dozen jars. Then, they'd celebrated their hard work by going out for pizza. Those were the kinds of things that Naomi had hoped would happen — spending time with her big sister without any difficult discussions or work.

But now that it was Sunday and she was set to start school the next day, Naomi knew she had to face her grandparents, so she'd asked them over to Kendra's house for a visit.

Kendra, of course, knew about the invitation, but it had been obvious that she wasn't looking forward to it. However, she put on a good face and acted like she was happy to be making snacks for what was sure to be an uncomfortable visit.

As each minute passed, bringing them toward the big discussion about her future, Naomi found herself wishing time would slow down. Unfortunately, it did not.

Therefore, all Naomi could do was pray that everything was going to be okay — or at least not too terrible.

Looking at the clock, Kendra reckoned Mommi and Dawdi would be there in ten minutes.

From the moment she'd learned of Naomi's plans, she'd been cooking up a storm. Ham and cream cheese roll ups, pretzel sticks, buffalo chicken dip, and lots and lots of molasses cookies. Of course it was too much, especially since she hoped they wouldn't stay longer than an hour. But she not only had a lot of nervous energy, she was also acting shamefully prideful. There was a part of her that wanted to prove that she could provide well for her little sister.

"Are you sure you're not expecting half of Walnut Creek?" Nanny asked as Kendra loaded up another tray, Blue gazing up at it hopefully.

Looking at the three filled trays, Kendra winced. "I guess it is too much. Do you think I should put part of it back?"

"No way. You know that you cook better than Mommi. At the very least, they'll get to have a good meal before they leave."

At the very least. That said it all. "We can give the extras to some of our friends. Or I'll bring it to the shop when I go in on Monday."

Naomi nodded. "Once word gets out that you've been cooking, I bet everyone will step inside Tried and True."

Wiping down the counter, Kendra sighed. "So, are you ready for this?"

"*Jah.* What about you?"

"I am, but they aren't going to be disappointed with me, Nanny."

"Oh, sure they will. They love to be disappointed about everything. Except our mother, of course."

Kendra hated that Naomi felt that way, but she couldn't really disagree. Their grandparents were kind enough, but they weren't encouraging in the least.

"Let's go put out these trays and get this visit over with. Maybe it will go better than we think."

Naomi picked up a tray but didn't say anything, which said everything.

■ ■ ■ ■

Ten minutes later, Kendra reckoned that no visit could ever be so long.

Mommi and Dawdi had entered her home with wide eyes, looking around at Kendra's small living room and kitchen with interest. After walking down the narrow hallway and peeking into both Kendra's room and the bathroom, her grandmother nodded. "This is a nice home for you, Kendra."

When Nanny looked prepared to protest the rather cool compliment, Kendra shook her head slightly. "*Danke,* Mommi."

"How long have you lived here again?"

"A little over a year now." Blue walked to her side, suddenly seemed to notice the guests, and barked.

"What is that?" Dawdi asked.

"This is my *hund,* Blue." Kendra knelt down by her dog's side and petted her.

"I didn't know you got a dog," Mommi murmured.

"I've had her for several months now. Don't worry, she usually walks out to meet newcomers, then goes back to my bedroom," she said as she got to her feet. "She's rather shy."

And sure enough, after giving Kendra a

look that seemed to say she was satisfied with how things were going, Blue turned around and walked back down the hall.

"Hmm," Mommi said.

Her grandparents remained standing in the living room, surveying the space. Almost as if they couldn't wait to leave.

Naomi jumped in. "Um, Kendra has been cooking."

Kendra chuckled. "Indeed I have."

Dawdi gaped at the arrangement of platters. "Why did you make so much?"

"I don't know. Naomi and I had fun cooking together."

"So much food for two guests seems wasteful to me," Mommi said.

On another day, Kendra might have reminded her grandmother that they weren't guests, they were family. Not that they would have appreciated being corrected. Instead, she waved a hand. "Please, sit down and have something. I'll bring you drinks. Would you prefer coffee or tea?"

"*Kaffi,*" Mommi said. "For both of us."

"*Jah,* Mommi. I'll bring you and Dawdi a cup right now." Turning to go back into the kitchen, Kendra gentled her voice. "Nanny, perhaps you'd like to sit down, too?"

Her eyes widened. "You don't need to wait on me, Kendra."

135

"I know, dear." Lowering her voice, she said, "But it's time to have our talk, I think."

Going back into the kitchen, she prayed for patience. Her grandparents could try the patience of a saint, for sure and for certain. She hadn't exactly expected them to apologize for never visiting until now, but it would have been lovely to hear.

Now it was obvious that she was never going to hear such a thing. So far, her grandfather had hardly said a word and her grandmother was perched on her sofa like she was a visiting queen. It was a mystery as to how they could expect so little of their daughter but so much of her.

After taking a deep breath and saying a prayer, Kendra fixed four cups of coffee and set them and a cream and sugar set on the bright blue tray she'd recently found at the thrift store. There was only one thing she needed to do, and that was make Naomi happy. She needed to remember that.

Walking back into the living room, she noticed that both of her grandparents had their plates piled high with her food. Dawdi, especially, looked taken with it.

"Here's the *kaffi*," she said. "Cream and sugar, Dawdi?"

"Black," he said.

"I take mine black as well," Mommi said

as Kendra handed her a cup.

"Would you like to fix your own, Nanny? Or would you rather I fixed your cup?"

"Could you do it, Kendra?"

Kendra added a spoonful of sugar to both Kendra's cup and her own and then added a healthy amount of milk to each cup. Mommi looked on with dismay.

"It's unhealthy for a girl to have *kaffi.*"

"Perhaps, but I've been drinking it for a mighty long time," Kendra replied. "I started drinking coffee when I was thirteen or fourteen. It hasn't done me much harm so far."

"Nanny is a different sort of person."

As in, her little sister had a lot more promise than Kendra ever had.

Maybe that was true, but it still stung. One day she'd have the nerve to remind her grandparents that part of the reason she'd been up early drinking coffee was because there usually wasn't juice or milk in the refrigerator. And when there was, she'd known that her younger siblings needed the nutrients more than she did.

Of course, she'd also needed the caffeine. She'd been responsible for getting her siblings up, dressed, and fed. Their father, when he was working, was gone, and their

137

mother was usually too depressed to get out of bed.

But today was not the day to go back in time.

Dawdi had been steadily cleaning his plate. As soon as it was empty, he put it on the trunk that served as Kendra's coffee table. "Naomi, we need to head back home. Where is your suitcase?"

"Well, about that . . ." Pausing, she darted a hopeful look at Kendra.

It was time. "I'd like Naomi to live with me," Kendra said.

Their grandfather frowned. "When?"

"Now." When they simply stared, she added, "I mean from now on."

"That seems rather sudden, Kendra." Their grandmother's expression had tightened.

"It's not that sudden. After all, Nanny is already here," Kendra explained. "There's no time like the present. I'll get some of my friends to help us gather her things at your house over the coming weekend or sometime next week."

Both of their grandparents turned to Naomi.

"Naomi, what do you have to say about this?" Dawdi asked.

Nanny flushed. "I want to stay here with

Kendra. And . . . and Kendra just lied. This wasn't her idea; it was mine. This is what I want to do."

"You may not stay here. Go get your suitcase now," Mommi said.

"I'm not going to do that," Nanny said.

Before the argument could continue, Kendra spoke again. "This isn't your decision, Mommi."

"It is. She is just a child. Only sixteen. She needs an adult to supervise her."

"I agree," Kendra said. "But you are forgetting that I'm an adult, too."

"What is this about?" Dawdi interrupted. "Are you feeling guilty for leaving your siblings all those years ago?"

Kendra felt as if she'd just been struck. Was that really how her grandparents had twisted the past? Beyond agitated, she got to her feet. "Don't try to change the past to make yourself feel better. You know how my parents treated me. You know how they treated all of us."

"Your mother did the best she could," their grandmother retorted. "Your departure hurt her deeply. She hasn't been the same since."

"If she isn't the same, then one could only hope she has gotten better. But we all know that is likely not the case," Kendra said. Yes, there was venom in her voice, and she hated it, hated that she had so much hurt and anger buried deep inside her that it could spew forth just like a geyser, pouring out a lifetime of pain.

Their grandfather crossed his arms over his chest. "I know you haven't gone to see your parents in years, *and* you've encouraged Jeremiah, Mary, and Chris to also stay away."

"We all stayed in that house as long as we could bear it." Except for Nanny. They'd gotten her out.

"Rehashing the past doesn't do any of us good. Naomi, you belong with us." Their grandmother lumbered to her feet. "Go get your things, child. We are leaving now."

"*Nee.* I am staying here," Nanny said. "Mommi, Dawdi, the truth is that I asked you to take me to Walnut Creek so I could talk to Kendra about moving in. I love you both, but I want to live with my sister."

Mommi swung her head back to Kendra. "Is this true?"

"Mommi, look at Naomi. She's all grown up now. She knows her own mind and doesn't lie."

"She *canna* be so close to her parents and not live with them. People will notice. What will everyone say?"

140

Kendra could hardly speak, she was so angry. That was what they were concerned about?

But before Kendra could say a word, Naomi jumped to her feet. "Listen! Your daughter, Rosanna, and her husband, Hank, had five children. They abused Kendra." She sucked in a breath. *"Nee,* they hurt *all* of us. We didn't have food. We didn't have heat. They didn't do much for us *at all."*

Their grandmother shook her head. "It wasn't like that. Your mother —"

"My mother takes all sorts of pills so she doesn't have to deal with her husband or the memories of how she neglected us," Nanny said.

"She has prescriptions," Dawdi said. "Doctors gave them to her."

"Well, she has a lot of them," Nanny said. "And the sad part is that you are both sticking your heads in the sand as much as she is. It's as if you pretend that Kendra didn't get beaten as much as she did or that Chris hadn't half starved or that Jeremiah didn't almost die. Then . . . then you don't have to feel any guilt."

Their grandmother turned deathly pale. "We did the best we could for her and for you. We took you in, child."

"But what about everyone else?" Naomi

said. "I'm grateful for you taking me in for the last four years, but it doesn't change the fact that you never stepped up for Kendra or Mary or the boys."

"We didn't know how bad things were, Naomi," Dawdi said stiffly. "Besides, it wasn't as if we could have done anything. You were with your parents."

It was such an obvious lie that Nanny paled.

Kendra jumped to her defense again. "If saying such things helps you sleep at night, then I hope you sleep well," Kendra said as she walked to the door and opened it. "But unless you are willing to accept Nanny's decision, I think it's time you left."

Her grandfather walked to the door, his whole body stiff. "You are going to regret this, Kendra. You are going to regret turning her against us."

"I regret a lot of things, but I'm fairly sure I'll never have as many regrets as you. I did my best for my brothers and sisters. And I'll never, ever regret being here for Naomi."

Dawdi turned, and Mommi walked out without a backward glance.

Seconds later, the door closed. Kendra walked to the window and watched their grandparents march to their car, slowly get inside, then drive away. She sighed.

"Well, that went well," Naomi mumbled. "Good thing you made all that food."

Surprised by the sarcasm, Kendra turned to her little sister, who had her arms folded over her chest. "Are you okay?"

She shrugged. "I have a feeling in a little while I'm going to feel worse. I love Mommi and Dawdi, and I'm sad they're acting like I don't. But . . . well, right now, all I feel is free." She exhaled. "Kendra, have you ever felt like that?"

The day she walked out of her parents' house for the last time, she'd been hurting, almost penniless, and burdened by guilt. But above all that, she'd known that no matter what happened in her future, she'd never have to worry about being yelled at or beaten again.

"Yes, darling, I have felt like that. Freedom is a mighty *gut* thing. It feels like none other."

THIRTEEN

"Tricia was at school, and his parents were gone for the day, you see."

Sunday

"What's this thing called?" Allison asked Nate, pointing to the socket set.

"It's a socket set. You use it to tighten bolts."

"I know these are screwdrivers, but one is pointy and one is flat."

Nate pulled his head out of the cabinet under the bathroom sink. "One's called a Phillips-head screwdriver; the other is a flat-head."

"Huh." She sat back on her heels. "I thought the names of all these tools would be easy enough to memorize, but I don't know."

Nate grinned. He wasn't sure why Allison cared about the tools at all, but her ignorance was eye-opening. He'd taken his grandfather's and uncles' lessons about fixing things for granted. He actually couldn't remember a time when he didn't know what a flathead screwdriver was. "Anytime you want a lesson on tools, stop by my shop."

"No one will mind?"

"Of course not. Besides, you'll probably just run into me anyway. I do own the hardware store, you know."

"I haven't forgotten that." She sat down on the ground, watching Nate go back under the sink to finish switching out the corroded pipe with a new one.

"I wouldn't be too hard on yourself," Benjamin said as he continued patching the wall. "Think about all the different tools one needs to make a meal in the kitchen. Sometimes one needs a wooden spoon, other times a spatula, other times a big ladle for soup. They're all spoons of one kind or another, but they do different tasks. It takes different tools for different jobs, *jah*?"

Allison nodded. "That's a good point." Looking up at the ceiling that was now almost ready for drywall, she sighed. "You all have done so much work in our house, I'd be surprised if you had any tools left in the store."

She didn't lie. Ever since that first visit, he'd made a point to spend an hour work-

145

ing at her house every couple of days. Ben had done the same thing. However, today, the two of them had decided that it was time to actually make a difference for Allison and her mom.

When he'd arrived at the house at seven that morning, the first thing he and Benjamin had done was put on masks and pull down the last of the rotten wood. And there'd been a lot of it. The first time he'd knocked out some plaster, he'd discovered that the damage inside the house was worse than they'd thought. Ben had even joked that it might be easier to tear down the whole structure and start from scratch.

After such a long morning, Nate was now really thankful he'd asked his friends Harley and Kyle Lambright to help them for a couple hours as well. They were due to arrive any minute.

"By the time we leave today, I promise that you're going to feel better about your house."

Allison stood up. "That means I better get out of your way and stop asking so many questions about tools. I'm going to go help Miss Becky across the street now. She likes me to read to her and help her sweep her back porch and clean the kitchen. If you need anything, just call."

"Will do." Nate had to smile. Allison was such a nice girl.

"She's worth waking up at six this morning," Benjamin murmured.

"I was just thinking the same thing."

The door opened again, this time bringing in Harley and his younger brother, Kyle. "Aren't you two a sight for sore eyes," Benjamin called out.

"I'd take that as a compliment except for the mess you got going on in here," Harley said.

Nate had already told him the extent of the damage. "I appreciate you stopping by." After briefly explaining what he planned to do, he said, "What do you think? Will that work?"

Harley climbed on the ladder, touched a few of the remaining joists in the ceiling, then climbed down. "Your plan will work, but you're gonna need help." He looked around the room. "Where are the girl and her mother?"

"Mom's at work, and Allison just went over to the neighbor's."

Harley peered at the ceiling again. As was his way, his expression was serious. "It's gonna rain this afternoon, and I don't think that patch is gonna hold. We'll need even more help." Turning to Nate, he said, "Hand me your work cell phone."

"You sure?"

"Uh-huh." He held out his hand.

Nate handed him the phone and listened as Harley started calling their friends. Ten minutes later, he had rounded up another three men to come over within the hour. Looking pleased, Harley turned to Kyle. "Clear out the rest of this debris. John B. is going to bring his truck. He said he'd take a load to the dump."

"On it."

Benjamin grinned. "Remind me never to sit too still around you, Harley Lambright. You don't mess around."

Harley smiled for the first time. "We got no time for that. Besides, my Katie has a houseful at the inn."

That was all they needed to know. After dividing up the chores one more time, they got to work.

By three o'clock that afternoon, the roof had been repaired, boards replaced, and the ceiling patched. In a couple of days, either Nate himself or Ben would come over and paint the ceiling. John B., Logan, and Will had come over for a couple of hours, bringing along fifty dollars' worth of groceries as well.

Only Nate was still there when Allison and her mother returned. Though she'd always been appreciative over the past week, Monique Berry appeared shell-shocked when she saw all the work the men had done. She touched each surface with a look of wonder on her face.

"I don't know how to ever thank you."

"No thanks are needed. We were glad to help."

"I've told my daughter this, but I still don't quite understand how this all happened."

"I told you, Mom. I wrote a note and explained our situation. Nate read it, stopped by, and then said he'd help us."

Her mother shook her head. "I know what happened, but it still amazes me. I mean, things like this never happen."

"Usually I'd agree with you, but in this instance, Allison isn't far off. Her letter touched my heart, and I wanted to help."

"But all these materials — they had to cost a small fortune." Allison's mom eyed him closely. "Are you sure you can afford to donate so much to one pair of women?"

Nate didn't mind her questions and surprise. If their situations were reversed, he knew he'd have had a very hard time accepting so much so easily.

So he said the only thing he could — and had to hope she would understand where his heart was. "God was working with us, Ms. Berry. I feel sure of it. Everyone who I called had time to spare today. That ain't always the case."

"Maybe I should try to argue with your generosity or even come up with a payment plan, but I'm too grateful to do that. So, I'm just going to tell you that I'm really thankful for you and your friends. You all have changed our lives."

He smiled. "You're welcome."

She blinked away a tear. "Now, I don't know if you've realized but the weather turned pretty nasty out there. It's time for you to get on home before your loved ones start to worry."

"It sounds as if I'd better get on my way then." Nate put his hat back on and tipped it in Allison's direction. "I hope you two have a good evening."

"We will," Allison said with a smile.

"Then I'll see you in a few days. I'll give you a call to see when I can come back."

"Sounds good," she said, walking to his side. "I'll walk you out."

She opened the door and stepped out on the stoop, frowning at the dark skies and his backpack. "How are you going to get home?"

"My bike. I leaned it against your fence over there."

"Do you want me to ask my mom to give you a ride?"

"Nope. I'll be good. I like to ride it when I can." He pointed to his head. "Riding helps clear my head."

Allison hesitated, then said, "I just wanted you to know that I really appreciate everything."

"Allison, this is the honest truth: helping you helped me."

She looked up at him and smiled.

Which was a blessing, indeed.

FOURTEEN

"Maybe some of you would have refused. Maybe some of you might have at least thought about it for a while, weighing the consequences of being alone in a boy's house when you were supposed to be in school." Kendra shrugged. "But that day, right in that moment, I felt like I had nothing to lose."

Monday Morning

"Do you think you'll be all right today?" Kendra asked her. Again.

Naomi glanced at the clock, then at the massive lunch her sister had made for her and put in a small cooler. Then at the pile of notebooks and pencils — *pencils*! — she'd placed on the counter early that morning. How she was supposed to carry all of this around, she didn't know. "I'll be all right, as long as I get out of here soon. I need to leave."

"I'm not going to ask if you want me to go with you to the high school office."

"That's *gut,* especially since you've already offered and I've already turned down your offer. Several times." She edged toward the door.

Kendra sighed. "Go ahead, now. I hope you have a good day. Stop by the shop after."

"*Danke,* sister." After reaching down to give Blue a pat on the head, Naomi kissed Kendra's cheek and pulled on the door's handle. Maybe she could just "forget" to grab everything?

"Wait! Silly, you almost forgot your lunch and your supplies."

She picked up the cooler — it had to weigh close to fifteen pounds — one of the pencils, and a notebook. "*Danke,* Kendra. You are a *gut* sister."

"I try." She looked at the pile of pencils Naomi had left on the counter.

"There's no need to try anymore. You are an *excellent* sister," she said before heading out.

The high school was fairly close to Tried and True, but not all that close to Kendra's house. If things had been different, Naomi would have asked to get a driver at least for this first day. She didn't have the nerve to do that, though. Her poor sister had already been through so much, what with their grandparents acting so foolish the night before.

She had been far more naive than her big sister. For some reason, she'd thought her practical grandparents would have been just as practical and understanding in Walnut Creek as they were in Canton. But that hadn't been the case at all. They'd treated Kendra callously and hadn't been understanding at all when Kendra had spoken her mind about their parents. Actually, they'd done a real good job of acting oblivious, even though nothing Kendra had said had been a surprise.

If Naomi hadn't been 100 percent sure that she'd wanted to distance herself from them, that conversation would have done it. She would never side with anyone against Kendra. She didn't think any of her siblings would. Their big sister had been through too much — and had done so much for them as well.

She'd just shifted her heavy cooler from one hand to the other and had even considered stashing the cooler while she was at school when an old black Jeep slowed down beside her.

"Naomi? Is that you?"

Warily, she glanced to her right, then grinned. "Kane, I know only one person at the high school: you. And here you are."

"What a coincidence, huh?"

He was speaking too lightly for it to be one. "How did you know I was walking to school?"

"Someone might have told me when I stopped by your house to pick you up."

Naomi almost rolled her eyes. "Kendra?"

He grinned. "She *might* have looked a little worried. So, want a ride?"

"Thanks." Hefting up her cooler into his backseat, she said, "Kendra is under the impression that each school day is a week long. There's a ton of food in that thing."

"What did she make you?"

"Oh, just a roast beef sandwich, two pieces of leftover fried chicken, an apple, some kind of carrot salad, a container of trail mix and — just in case I never want to fit into my favorite dress ever again — four brownies."

After making sure she was buckled up, Kane whistled softly as he pulled back onto the road. "Do you think she's going to make you lunches like that every day?"

"I don't know — wait. You're looking like you hope she will."

"Uh, yeah. Can I help you eat that lunch today? I mean, if you don't think you can finish it all?"

"There's no way I'm going to be able to eat even a fourth of it. She already made me a monster breakfast, saying I needed good food for 'brain power.' "

Kane grinned. "No way."

"Believe me, I wouldn't make something like that up. So, I promise, you can have as much as you want." Yes, she might have also realized that if he ate lunch with her, then she wouldn't have to worry about eating lunch by herself.

"My day just got better," he said as he stopped at the light in front of the school.

Gazing up at the high school, she felt her toes curl with a fresh batch of anticipation. It was big, almost twice the size of the school she'd attended before. She was sure she was going to get lost a lot.

"Are you *neahfich*?"

"Nervous? No. I mean, I wasn't until now."

He smiled. "But now?"

"Now, well, I'm not really sure." On the one hand, she was a little scared about actually walking into the big school. But on the other hand, she was going to be walking in with Kane at her side, and he was so cute

156

and kind.

"Hey, you've got nothing to worry about. Everyone's going to like you."

"How do you know? You hardly even know me."

"I know enough." His smile was thoughtful, making her heart beat a little faster. After a second, he added, "Plus, lots of people know *about* you. You're the new girl. We don't get a lot of those. Especially not at the end of September."

"I guess not."

"You'll do fine, though. I heard you're really smart."

She didn't mind him saying that, but it did seem kind of strange for him to say. "Who did you hear that from?" she asked. Then suddenly — "Oh, goodness. Please don't tell me that Kendra told you that, too."

"*Nee.* It wasn't her."

"Who then?"

"Fine. Nate at the hardware store. It seems he has friends who know Kendra well. Well enough that they talk about one another's families as if they're part of them." He drove into the back parking lot, slowly eased around a group of students standing near a truck, then parked in slot number 432. "Weird, huh?"

"Not if Nate's friends are part of the Eight. They're like a big family, and Kendra is real close to most of them." She got out of the Jeep and looked around at all the cute girls sporting small backpacks or handbags. Not a one of them was so much as carrying a paper sack. "Kane, I can't bring this in."

"I know." After tossing his backpack over one shoulder, he said, "The principal would probably think you were smuggling in a weapon or something if you tried to bring that in. But . . . I can store it in my Jeep until eleven thirty."

"That's what time lunch is?"

"Yep. We're small enough that the whole school eats at the same time."

Just as she was about to take Kane up on his offer, two guys and a really pretty girl with long black hair stopped in front of his Jeep.

"Kane!" one of them called out. "Where've you been?"

He turned to them. "Hey. I picked up my friend Naomi. Naomi, this is Lauren, Baker, and Ted."

"Hi."

"Hi to you, too," the taller of the two guys — maybe Ted? — said. "Who are you?"

"She's transferring here from a high school over in Canton."

"And you're Mennonite?"

"Yes."

"Oh."

She noticed Lauren exchange a glance with the other boy before pasting an obviously fake smile on her face.

Naomi smiled back, but she knew it was just as fake because inside, her stomach was beginning to flutter. She'd never thought she was particularly insecure, but maybe it was because she'd always been in her comfort zone. She'd been confident because her family had put her into situations where she had no reason to be anything but confident.

She'd been fooling herself into thinking she could face any situation easily, but now, feeling Kane's three friends study her and come up wanting, she realized she was very wrong.

"Well, we've got to go," the boy she figured was Ted said. "See ya, Kane."

"Yeah. See ya."

Lauren and the other boy followed him.

Naomi glanced at Kane. His expression was blank. She wondered if it was because he was embarrassed by his friends or by her. Had she said something wrong? Maybe they just did things differently back at her old school?

"Hey, you know what? I should probably

get over to the office and get my schedule."

"I'll walk you there."

"You don't have to," she said in a rush. "You've already helped me out a ton. Plus, I'm sure you've got plenty of things to do."

He started walking. "Like what?"

"I don't know. Whatever boys like to do." See his friends. Not have to walk her around.

Amusement lit up his eyes. "I don't know about other boys, but this guy wants to walk you to the office."

"All right."

They walked through the parking lot. She looked straight ahead while several guys and girls — a lot, really — called out to him or waved at him. Kane responded in kind but didn't show any inclination of wanting to join any of them.

"Here," he said, pushing open the main door to the school.

Walking through the doors, it was all she could do to not stop and gape. The place was huge. The school's foyer was two stories, two large trophy cases took up an entire wall, and there were pennants hanging down from the ceiling, proclaiming different championship wins and titles the school's sports teams had earned.

There were people everywhere. Groups of

160

kids, some obviously freshmen, others seniors, teachers, who knew who else. All of them seemed to be watching her and Kane.

He kept walking, saying hi to one or two, but otherwise staying by her side.

"Here's the office." They'd stopped in front of the door, and she hadn't realized it.

"Oh. Thanks again for walking with me. I'll see you later."

He shifted his backpack onto his other shoulder. "What are you talking about?"

"Hmm?"

"I'm not going to drop you off here." He shook his head, like he couldn't believe she'd think he would do something so stupid. "Go on in, and I'll wait for you."

"Kane, there's no need. I mean, you have so many friends."

But instead of looking relieved, he just looked even more annoyed. "Do you know your way around this school?"

"You know I don't."

"Then stop worrying about me and go get your schedule."

She felt like they were fighting, but she didn't even know what they were fighting about. "Fine." She pushed open the glass door, sidestepped around a pair of girls about her age wearing tank tops and short shorts, and almost ran into a lady with frizzy gray hair, a harried expression, and readers perched on the end of her nose. "Sorry," she said.

The teacher barely spared her a glance as she strode out of the room.

"Can I help you?" a petite woman with a chin-length blond bob asked as she thumbed through a pile of papers.

"*Jah.* I mean, yes. I'm Naomi Troyer. I need to pick up my schedule."

The lady looked at her directly for the first time. "You're our new girl."

"Yes. My sister and I registered last week?" Worry settled in. What if they'd forgotten? What if she was supposed to have gotten to school earlier? Kane had to get to class. "Is there a problem?"

The lady paused. "A problem? Oh, no, dear. I just realized that I need to get you a buddy for the day."

"A buddy?"

"Yes. Someone to stay close to you. Help you get acclimated and find your way to all your classes." She scanned the office. "Not to worry. I'll find someone for you. Maybe —"

"I don't need a buddy. I've already got a friend here."

"Are you sure? Because we pride ourselves on helping new Mustangs."

162

Mustangs, the mascot of their school. "It's Kane." She pointed through the window at Kane. He was currently standing with another boy.

"Oh! Well, go get him!"

"I'm sorry?"

She waved a hand. "Hurry, now. The first bell will ring soon. Kane's going to need to help you find your locker and such."

"I could just show him my schedule when I get out."

She slid a hand on top of the sheet of paper she'd just printed out. "That's not our way, though."

Naomi could practically feel the secretary's impatience. She didn't want to go bother Kane, but what could she do? The woman was holding her schedule hostage. "All right."

With a feeling of foreboding, she walked toward him. Kane's eyes darted in her direction, then warmed. "Hey." The other guy stopped talking and stared at her. "Stone, this is Naomi. Naomi, Carl Stone, but everyone just calls him Stone."

"Hiya."

Stone's eyebrows rose. "Hiya to you, too."

"Got your schedule?" Kane asked.

"Not exactly." She lowered her voice. "Can you come into the office with me?"

163

His brows snapped together, but he nodded. "See ya, Stone." Walking toward her, he lowered his voice. "What's up?"

"I'm so sorry, but I think you're my buddy."

He paused. "What?"

"They were going to assign me someone standing around in that office, and she wouldn't let me have my schedule until I came and got you. I'm so sorry."

"Oh. Sure." He opened the glass door and strode through with hardly more than a brief glance her way.

The blond lady was smiling at him. "Hi there, Kane. I heard you're being a real help today. That's so sweet."

Kane shrugged. "What do I need to do, Mrs. Cabrilo?"

"Show Miss Troyer here around, help her find her locker, make sure she gets her lunch all right. Can you do that?"

"It's not a problem."

Mrs. Cabrilo smiled at him just as the bell rang.

"I need my schedule, please," she said.

"Oh, yes. Of course. Here you go, dear. Welcome to Walnut Creek."

"Thank you."

Holding on to her schedule, Kane led the way out. "Hey," he said to her when they

164

stopped in the middle of the hall. "It says your first class is honors calculus."

She nodded. "Do you know where that class is?"

"I know where five A is. Honors calculus is usually a senior class, I mean, for anyone who usually gets that far."

She didn't know what to say about that. She'd never been embarrassed about her grades, but she was starting to hope that everyone wasn't going to just see her as the nerdy new girl.

Looking at her curiously, he added, "I knew you were smart, but you're really smart, aren't you?"

"I wouldn't say that."

"I would. Well, come on. Let's get you to your smart class before they mark you tardy."

"I'm sorry about this. It's taking forever."

He looked at her, then slowly shook his head. "If you learn anything about me, Naomi, it's that I don't do anything I don't want to do. Ever."

She smiled. She couldn't protest that, so she remained quiet as she walked through the halls by his side. They walked upstairs and down a long hallway, passing open doors with students standing around desks or teachers talking with other teachers or lone students. Something was announced over the intercom, but it was so garbled that Naomi couldn't make heads or tails of it.

All the while Naomi wondered why God had decided she needed to make this change in her life. At the moment, not a bit of it made a lick of sense.

FIFTEEN

"I didn't want to walk around in a smelly dress, so I said okay. And Andy? He grinned like I'd done the right thing."

Monday

"What's the deal with you and the new girl?" Erin asked over his right shoulder in the middle of government class.

Kane mentally groaned. He should've known that gossip would have spread like lightning about Naomi Troyer's arrival and the fact that he was showing her around.

Naomi was really pretty. That alone would have caused notice. But the fact that he was paying a lot of attention to her made her even more interesting to his peers. It wasn't that he was that popular, but he had a reputation for never putting himself out there.

"Nothing is going on," he finally answered. "Naomi needed someone to walk her around today, and I didn't mind."

"That's not what I heard." Erin pretended to lower her voice, but in actuality, it had risen to a pitch that encouraged everyone within a two-foot radius to lean in a little closer. "I heard Naomi told Mrs. Cabrilo in the office that she had you so she didn't need anyone from student council to help her find her classes."

"She said that because we know each other. It's not a big deal." If he knew anything about high school, it was never make a big deal out of something that could be fodder for gossip — and everything was fodder for gossip in high school.

"Are you going to sit with her at lunch?"

He could practically feel the rest of the class waiting for his answer, even though he was sure nobody but Erin even cared. But gossip was gossip, and for a class of graduating seniors, it alleviated boredom. It was time to go on the offensive.

After double-checking that Mr. Howell was still going over something on his laptop with Diane, Kane turned to look Erin in the eye. "What's up with you? Why do you even care who I walk with or eat lunch with?"

As he'd expected, twin spots of color tinged her cheeks. "I don't care."

"If you don't care, then why are you acting like you do?" he pressed. "All I'm doing is helping someone out, and you're acting like that's a crime. I mean, you're on all those committees and student council and stuff. Shouldn't you be trying to help people like Naomi instead of gossiping about her?"

"There's no need to get so defensive," Erin shot back.

"I'm not defensive. But I'm not going to act like your interest in my relationship with a girl you've never met before is normal."

Three people near them snickered. Erin shot him a death glare and pursed her lips but didn't say another word.

Kane leaned back in his chair. He wasn't exactly proud of himself, but putting Erin in her place was worth it if she stopped talking about Naomi.

"Mr. Law, is there a problem?"

He looked up at their teacher. "No, Mr. Howell. Erin just was confused about something, but I helped her clear it up."

"Oh, good job."

"Thanks." He grinned. The guy behind him made a sarcastic remark, but Kane pretended he didn't hear.

After scanning the room again, Mr. Howell cleared his throat. "All right, gang. Last week, we were discussing a bill that is currently lingering in the House. Who can explain what the ramifications will be if the bill dies on the floor?"

People started raising their hands. Kane flipped open his notebook and pretended to listen, but all he could think about was Naomi. He hoped she was doing all right and that not too many people were pulling an "Erin" on her and asking her a bunch of questions that didn't need to be answered.

After class an hour later, Kane headed toward Naomi's English classroom. He wanted to catch her in case she'd decided to not wait for him and sit by herself for lunch.

"What was up with you and Erin?" his buddy Billy asked as he reached his side in the crowded hall.

"You know how Erin gets. She's always into everyone else's business. She wouldn't stop, so I decided to put an end to it."

"She was ticked."

"I was, too. What I do isn't Erin's business. You know, just because she asked me a hundred questions doesn't mean I had to go and answer them."

Billy shrugged. "Yeah, I guess not." But he didn't sound all that convinced.

What was it with everyone and their interest in him and Naomi? "You ready for the game

Thursday night?"

"Sure. All of us should be, since Coach is making us stay late for practice every night this week." He grinned at him. "Having a Thursday night game under the lights is cool, though."

"Yeah. Friday morning is going to be awful, but it will be worth it."

"Especially if our quarterback does his thing."

Happy to be talking about football instead of his personal life, Kane grinned. "Of course he will. Shawn's going to get us to state."

"I heard that college scouts will be there."

"That would be cool, though Shawn told me he's already committed to play for Dayton."

"I heard they were looking at you, dude. Oh, hey, I've gotta go. See you later."

Him? In spite of his best intentions, he started imagining the possibilities. He was a good player and was having a good season, but he hadn't let himself believe that he had a shot. "Yeah, later."

Walking up the stairs, he gave in to the impulse. If he got recruited, he could go to college, which meant he would have more of a future than his grades had afforded him. Maybe his parents would even be proud and realize they hadn't lost everything when they'd lost Andrew.

He was still thinking about his brother and the possibility of going to college when he spied Naomi walking out of her classroom. She was smiling at a pair of junior guys who looked like they were trying real hard to impress her. When she caught sight of Kane, her shy smile widened. "Hi, Kane."

It was obvious that she'd already forgotten about the pair of guys standing next to her. That was all the encouragement he needed. "Hey, Naomi, everything going okay?"

"Everything is great. Better than I expected."

Casting the guys a look that silently said to move on, Kane moved closer to her side. "Ready for lunch?"

"*Jah.* I'm starving. Now I'm really glad my sister made us so much," she replied, not even seeming to notice that the other guys had walked away. Suddenly, worry clouded her face. "Oh. Do you still want to eat lunch together? It's okay if you don't."

"I've been thinking about that food all day. I'm starving. Come on," he said, grabbing her stack of books and leading her out the parking lot door.

They decided to sit in his Jeep with her

giant cooler between them. That way he wouldn't have to worry about everyone talking about the two of them eating together. When she started passing him food, he grinned. After trying a bite of everything, he sighed in contentment. Naomi might have been embarrassed about the amount of food she'd brought, but as far as he was concerned, she could bring it every day.

"It's all really good, Naomi."

"Thanks. I don't know what to do about Kendra. I think she's either trying to make me feel better about living with her, or she's wishing so bad that she was me, trying to imagine what being in high school would be like."

"Do you think she's jealous of you?"

"*Nee.* Maybe wistful? Or, I don't know." She slumped. "It's just that she never even had a choice, you know? She sees my future, and it's so different from what hers was. Boy, I bet I'm not making a bit of sense."

Thinking that he might actually get the chance to go to college when he'd been sure those doors were closed to him, he said, "Actually, I understand everything you said. It's crazy when you're confronted with the opportunity to make a dream a reality."

"What dream of yours might come true?"

"A buddy of mine just told me that he

heard a college scout might be watching me at the game Thursday night. Don't tell anyone, though."

Her eyes widened. "Wow. You must be really good at playing football."

"I'm all right. I didn't think I was scout-worthy, but maybe they're still trying to fill their roster. Hey, don't say anything about the scout to anybody, okay? It's probably just a rumor."

"Kane, you're sitting with me in your Jeep, eating my sister's lunch after walking me to half my classes this morning. You also introduced me to tons of your friends, who are all seniors, so all the kids in the junior class think I'm okay now. I owe you big-time."

"You don't owe me anything."

"Well, how about this, then? I know how to keep a secret. I promise, you can tell me anything, and I'll keep it to myself. You can trust me."

"Thanks." Taking another piece of fried chicken, Kane grinned at her. While he didn't really know her, he had a good feeling about their future. She was different from any other girl he knew. More mature, more serious. He could be wrong, but he had a feeling he could trust Naomi Troyer with just about anything. She was that kind of person — a trustworthy one.

Sixteen

"Now, since then, I've been in a lot of *Englischers'* houses. But that day, back when I was fifteen, awkward, and shy? I never had. So, seeing Andy Warner's fancy house, all clean, bright, and filled with so much stuff . . . and seeing that swimming pool in the backyard? I felt like Alice in Wonderland when she went down that rabbit hole."

Monday Afternoon

"Thank you so much for coming in," Kendra said as she handed her very first customer a large bag filled with yarn.

The middle-aged lady smiled. "I'm delighted you are here. I'm going to tell everyone I know about your store. You've got an excellent selection of yarn and gift items."

"I'd appreciate that. Thank you again," Kendra said as she watched her leave.

When the door shut with a merry ringing

of the door chimes, Kendra gazed again at the credit card receipt. Her very first transaction in the store had been over a hundred dollars! She hadn't expected anything so big. To think she almost had decided to forgo getting a credit card machine!

After carefully putting the slip into the right envelope, she toured the store and straightened the yarn display. It didn't really need fixing, but she couldn't just stand in one place. She was too excited.

When the door opened again, she turned, ready to welcome her second customer into the shop, but then she saw who it was.

"Oh. Hiya, Nate."

"Hi, Kendra. It's really good to see you, too."

She winced at his sarcastic tone. "Sorry, I guess I didn't sound too gracious, did I?"

Luckily, he laughed. "I get it. You're on the lookout for customers, aren't you?"

"Maybe. Or maybe I'm still floating on my success. My first paying customer just left!"

"You've had a purchase. Good for you."

"She used a credit card. I was a little worried about not using the machine right, but it worked just fine."

"Let me guess . . . you practiced?"

"Only about a half dozen times. I felt foolish, practicing for something so simple, but now I'm glad of it. I was afraid I would push the wrong button and overcharge someone."

"I've gotten the impression that you don't leave a lot to chance."

"I try not to. My life goes easier if I plan for everything." Realizing that she still hadn't tried to figure out why he had come in, she walked toward him. "Did you need something?"

"Yes, as a matter of fact. I came over to see if *you* needed anything, on account of your sister being at school today."

"I don't need anything yet. Thank you for checking on me."

"No reason to thank me for trying to help." He paused. "I also wondered how you are doing, now that you've had Naomi home with you for a while."

She leaned against the counter. "I'll be better when I discover how she did on her first day at *shool.*"

"You look nervous. Are you really that worried about school?"

"I can't help it. Starting a new school has to be difficult. And then there's the fact that she's not an *Englischer.* Kids like everyone to be the same, you know."

"Kane told me he was going to look out for her today." Nate's voice warmed. "I bet

178

he sat with her at lunch and made sure she got through the lines okay in the cafeteria."

"She didn't have to buy anything. I fear I might have packed too much in her cooler."

"Wait, are you telling me that you sent your sister to school with a cooler of food?"

"*Jah.* Naomi told me there was no way she was going to be able to eat it all, but she's the type of girl who likes to eat often. I wanted to make sure she had enough food for snacks."

"Um, how big was this cooler?"

When she approximated its size with her hands, he raised his eyebrows. His silence was worse than making fun of her. "Uh-oh. What did I do wrong?"

Nate's lips twitched. "You didn't do anything wrong, exactly. But . . ."

"But what?"

His voice softened. "Kendra, where did you think she was going to put that cooler when she was at school?"

To be honest, she hadn't even thought about that. "In her locker?"

"No high school locker is going to be big enough to hold a giant cooler, Kendra."

She supposed he was right. "Oh. Well, then she could have carried it with her. It wasn't too heavy." Of course, now that she thought about it, she realized that cooler

179

hadn't been exactly light, either.

"You expected Naomi to carry a giant cooler to all of her classes?"

Just as she nodded, Kendra started to think about how she would have felt as the new girl carrying a giant cooler from class to class. She winced. "Naomi wouldn't have wanted to do that, would she?"

"Would you? I mean, she probably had a purse and schoolbooks, too."

Kendra had given her a bunch of school supplies, as well. And Naomi didn't know where any of her classes were.

She closed her eyes, imagining her little sister wandering around the big school with her hands full. Ugh. Why hadn't she just given her five dollars? She could have grabbed whatever she wanted. "I'm starting to realize that I should have worried about how Naomi would be feeling on her first day of school as much as I did about her not going hungry. I really hope she's not mad at me."

He smiled at her. "I'm sure she's not mad because you were trying to help. I bet she appreciated your thoughtfulness."

"Nate, Naomi tried to leave that cooler, but I made sure she took it out the door with her. I gave her no choice! I sent her off with ten sharpened pencils, too."

180

"Just in case she didn't know how to sharpen one of them?" he teased.

He was right. She'd been ridiculous. "She's sixteen, not six. Ugh. I bet she hates me."

"You know that isn't true."

"Okay, I just made her lug around a giant food cooler on her first day of school."

"At least you suggested I call Kane. He was glad for the heads-up and said he was going to try to find her before school. I bet he probably helped her stash it somewhere."

That was true. At least she'd asked Nate to have Kane look out for her. "He *did* come to the house right after she left." She sighed as she looked at the clock. "She said she was going to stop by here on the way home. Hopefully she won't be in tears."

Nate reached for her hand and gave it a little squeeze. "Kendra, you need to calm down, *jah*? You're imagining all sorts of things that we know just ain't true. Naomi isn't going to hate you for trying to do something nice for her. She's not going to cry because she took a cooler to school for her lunch."

"But —"

"No buts. She's a resourceful girl and a junior in high school. I'm sure she figured

181

out how to find her classes and eat her lunch."

He was right. Naomi might not have had the childhood that she had, but she'd had her share of hardships. And even if she hadn't, she was a sweet girl. She wasn't the type to yell at Kendra for attempting to help her.

"There it is," he murmured.

"Hmm?"

"That smile." He reached out and ran a finger along her cheek. "I've been hoping to see it for a good five minutes. I'm glad it's back."

He'd been waiting on her to smile? Right then, she noticed that she'd even leaned into his touch. What was happening? She took a step away.

His eyes widened, then he dropped his hand to his side. "Sorry. I didn't mean to do anything you're not comfortable with."

"You didn't. I . . . well, never mind."

"Of course." He took a step back. "Is it all right if I stop by later? You know, just to see how Naomi's first day was?"

She stopped herself from only nodding. Nate deserved more from her. "I'd like that."

He tipped his hat. "I'll see you then, Kendra."

Just as he left, an older Amish woman walking with a cane came in.

Kendra approached her with a friendly smile. *"Wilcom,"* she said in Pennsylvania Dutch. "Please let me know if I can help you at all."

SEVENTEEN

"I used to love swimming at his house," Logan said.

"I used to love everything about that house," E.A. said.

Monday Afternoon

"So, how about you let me pick you up tomorrow morning at your house?" Kane asked as he pulled into the parking lot a few spaces down from Tried and True.

"Are you sure you wouldn't mind?"

"I wouldn't ask if I did."

Naomi wasn't going to argue. It had been such a relief to have him by her side today. And she really liked being around him. "In that case, thanks. I'd really appreciate it." She reached for the door handle. She knew Kane had to get back to school soon for practice.

Resting an arm on the back of the bench

seat, he turned toward her. "Hey, wait a minute. If I pick you up, are you going to bring lunch again?"

"I honestly don't know if you're joking or not."

"Of course I'm not. Your sister's fried chicken is amazing. I wouldn't joke about that."

"Then of course I'll bring you lunch." She'd make it herself if it would make him happy. It was the least she could do.

He grinned. "Hey, that was easy. I was sure you were going to make me beg."

She was really starting to have a big crush on him.

"Bringing you *middawk* isn't hard. Plus, I owe you. I don't know how I would've gotten through today without you."

His gaze warmed. "I have a feeling you would've done just fine." He shook his head. "I still can't believe the crazy classes you're taking."

She shrugged. "We're all good at something. You're the one who might have a college scout coming to watch you play."

His eyes lit up, but seconds later he looked wary. "Don't say anything to anyone, okay? I don't want to jinx it."

"I won't. Now, I really better go so you aren't late." She opened the door and

185

hopped out, then was surprised to see he'd gotten out, too, and was reaching for the cooler in the cab. "Thanks."

"See you tomorrow at seven fifteen."

"I'll be ready. Thanks again." Wanting a minute before she walked to her sister's shop, she stood on the sidewalk until he drove out of sight. Then, when she realized she was actually feeling a little giddy, she reminded herself that Kane Law was just a friend. That was all.

But wouldn't it be something if she were wrong?

Still thinking about Kane and what it would be like if he were her boyfriend, she walked into the shop.

And was practically tackled by her sister.

"Oh, Naomi!" Kendra cried out. "I am so sorry about this morning. Are you all right?"

Putting her things down on a nearby display case, Naomi hugged Kendra back before pulling away. "I'm fine. At least I think I am. What's wrong?"

"I feel terrible about sending you off to school with that cooler and all those pencils. And you let me do it."

Naomi grinned. "Kendra, the things you worry about."

"Come on, tell me true. Was it awful, lugging that cooler around?"

186

"Well, it would've been if I'd had to do that. But Kane Law picked me up and let me store it in his Jeep. And he helped me eat all the food."

"He did? And that was okay with you?"

That was her sister, always ready to fight her battles. "It was more than okay. He's really nice. But, ah, Kendra, how did you know he would help me so much today?"

She looked taken aback by the question. "I didn't know if he would or wouldn't. I was just worried about you walking around by yourself. I only asked Nate to ask Kane to look out for you if he could."

So Kane had done so much for her on his own. Not because he had to, but because he'd wanted to. That was a pretty significant difference.

Feeling lighter than air, she said, "You are the best *shveshtah,* Kendra."

"Hardly that."

Looking around the shop, she said, "Now you have to tell me all about your day. How was it?"

Kendra smiled brightly. "I had customers! And some of them even bought things."

"Really? Start from the beginning. Tell me everything."

Just as Kendra was about to speak, the door opened and a group of ladies walked in. "I guess we'll have to chat later, *jah*?"

Naomi nodded as she picked up her things and took them to the back room, determined to be of as much help as possible to Kendra.

It was late by the time Kane got home. Football practice had been grueling, especially since he'd barely made it out to the field on time. His coach had noticed. No, *everyone* there had noticed, and Kane had to put up with the consequences. Being on time for practice meant getting on the field ten minutes early.

He had to do extra repetitions of just about every play, all while listening to the coach talking about how "some people" didn't seem to think Thursday night's game was important.

When he walked in the door, all he wanted to do was take a shower, grab something to eat, and fall into bed. He couldn't care less about homework. There was a pretty good chance he wasn't going to be able to stay up long enough to do it anyway.

His father met him in the kitchen after Kane showered and threw his practice uniform in the washing machine.

"Hard practice, huh?"

"Yep." Kane walked to the refrigerator and

grabbed the plate his mom had left for him. "I didn't think it was ever going to end."

"Coach was in a mood, hmm?"

"Yeah, but it was my fault, too." He looked at the plate of lasagna and broccoli and considered heating it up in the microwave. Deciding it would be too much trouble, he grabbed a fork and started eating.

Dad raised his eyebrows but didn't comment on his cold supper. "Why do you say that?"

After swallowing another bite, Kane said, "I dropped off Naomi Troyer at her sister's shop after school. It made me late, which made the coach mad. I had to run two extra miles." He'd hated every minute of it, too.

"Kane, that's not like you."

"I know." But what was really weird was that he had known it wasn't a good idea to drop Naomi off and he still had. "She needed the ride, though. You know, today was her first day there. She needed someone looking out for her."

His father nodded, watching as Kane shoveled another monster bite of lasagna into his mouth. "You know, son, I actually knew about your practice because Coach Emerson called me."

He put his fork down. "Really? Daed, I promise, I wasn't that late. I just wasn't early. And I didn't give him any back talk, either."

"I'm sure you didn't." He paused. "Actually, he didn't call me to tattle on you. He called to tell me about the scout coming to Thursday's game."

So the rumor was true. Carefully tamping down his excitement, he said carefully, "Why did he call *you*?"

"Because you're one of two players the scout is coming to see, son." He smiled. "Coach Emerson sounded like you have a real good chance of getting a scholarship. That's exciting, isn't it?"

It was. But it was also so far from his expectations, that he wasn't sure how to act about it. "Yeah." Feeling awkward, he said, "Are you happy about the scholarship?"

His *daed* placed the glass of water he'd just picked up back on the table. "Me? It's not me they're looking at, Kane. This is your good news."

"I know, but . . ." His voice drifted off.

"But?"

"Well, it's just that it would be great if you were glad about a college scholarship."

"Of course I would be glad. Both your mother and I would be real happy. It's a wonderful thing. But it's only wonderful if playing football in college is what you

190

want." He studied Kane a moment longer, then said, "There's something else going on here, isn't there?"

Kane looked down at his plate. He didn't want to bring up his brother, but he was starting to think he didn't have a choice. "Kind of."

"Son, just spit it out."

"It's just that Andrew was so perfect. But he's gone. I know that you wish he was here . . ." Kane couldn't say the last of it, that he was afraid his parents wished he'd been the one who died.

"Kane." His father's voice was hoarse. "Is that how your mother and I have made you feel? Like Andrew was perfect and you aren't?"

"*Nee*. It's just true. He was good at school, good at a lot of things." Kane was sure that if Andrew had gotten to live, he would have done a great many things to make his parents proud. But instead, they only had him.

Still looking shell-shocked, his *daed* continued. "You're exactly who we want you to be, son. I promise that there's never been a day when we wished for anything other than that you would be happy."

There was a lump in his throat. Realizing that there was no way he was going to be able to eat another bite, he got up to rinse off his plate.

"If you don't want to play football in college you don't have to, Kane. We don't want you to be anything but yourself. That's enough."

"No, I want to play football. And I'm really excited about the scout, too." Finally allowing himself to dream, he said, "It would be really cool if he liked what he sees on the field."

"If you're excited, then your mother and I are, too." He took Kane's plate, dried it, and then put it carefully away. "Oh, before I forget, your mom wanted me to ask if you needed some money for lunch."

"No, Naomi's bringing me lunch."

"She is?"

Kane grinned. "Daed, you should've seen the cooler her sister fixed up for her today. It was huge. The food was really good, too. Naomi shared it with me."

"And she's going to bring you more tomorrow? That's nice."

"I think it's because I'm picking her up."

"You are? Hmm."

Kane shrugged. "Her house is on the way." It wasn't really, but what else could he say?

"I see." His father's expression warmed.

"If you're picking her up, you better get on to sleep, then. See you in the morning."

"Night, Daed." As Kane walked down the hall to his room, he felt like everything in his world had just changed. He wasn't sure what was going to happen next, but he felt optimistic.

And if the last thing he thought about before going to sleep was Naomi and not college scouts, he figured that was okay. It wasn't like anyone else needed to know about that.

EIGHTEEN

"The first thing we did when we got inside after, you know, I stopped staring at everything, was head up to Andy's room.

" 'No offense,' he said, 'but we need to wash your clothes.' He handed me a pair of gym shorts and a T-shirt. 'Go in the bathroom and change and then bring your dress down to the kitchen.'

" 'How come the kitchen?' I asked.

" 'Because the laundry room is right next to it,' Andy replied, just like I should have known."

Friday

Naomi thought she'd never seen her sister look so doubtful. "Are you sure you want to continue to take all that to school?" Kendra asked for the second time. "The cooler is almost overflowing."

"Kane had a game last night. I'm sure he's going to be starving." Plus, there was the visit from the college scout. Naomi wasn't really sure what a college scout's visit entailed, but she was pretty sure it meant that Kane had probably played harder than he usually did.

"I hope he likes his brownies."

Feeling a little guilty, Naomi looked over at the pan on the counter. She'd made brownies last night and then had neatly put half of them in the cooler for Kane. "Are you upset I'm giving so much of our food to him?"

"Of course not. We have plenty of food, darling." Kendra only ever called her "darling" when she was worried about her.

"I guess I did get a little carried away. I'll bring everything he doesn't eat home. I promise."

"You mean 'we don't eat,' yes?"

"*Jah,* Kendra." She barely refrained from rolling her eyes.

Her sister's voice turned hesitant. "Naomi, I don't really know Kane, but try not to expect too much of him, okay? He might get busy and not have so much time for you in a couple of weeks."

"I know. And don't worry. I'm not pretending he and I are going to become a couple. He's just being nice." She was being honest, too. She didn't have any big dreams about Kane wanting to pick her up from school and eat lunch with her every day. But she would take his attention now.

Kendra blew out a sigh of relief. "I *canna* tell you how relieved I am to hear you say that." When they heard a faint beep, she chuckled. "We'll talk more later. Your ride is here."

Naomi grabbed her backpack in one hand and the cooler in the other. "*Danke,* Kendra. Thank you for understanding. I'll see you at the shop tonight."

"Don't hurry. I'll be all right if you want to do something fun after school."

There was no way she was going to blow off her sister. "I'll be there," she promised again before rushing out the door.

As she'd hoped, Kane was standing outside his Jeep. He had on a pair of faded jeans, tennis shoes, and a slightly wrinkled long-sleeved T-shirt. He was also wearing a smile, which widened when he saw she was carrying her cooler.

"Hey," he said as he met her halfway and pulled the cooler out of her grasp. "Oh, wow. This thing is pretty heavy. I think your lunches are getting bigger."

196

"I might have packed some extra food for you."

He put the cooler in the back of his Jeep. "You did, huh?"

Her sister's warning rang in her head as she climbed in her seat. "If you want to do something else for lunch, that's okay. I mean, I bet you want to sit with your friends."

After he buckled his seat belt, he backed out of Kendra's driveway. "I don't need to do that. I was with most of them for five hours last night." He looked over his shoulder, wincing slightly with the motion. "Plus, I'm so sore, all I want to do at lunch is sit in here with you and relax." He raised an eyebrow. "That okay with you?"

"*Jah.* Now, don't keep me waiting any longer. Did the college scout show up?"

"Yep."

"And? What happened?"

Slowly, the biggest smile appeared on his face. "It was awesome. Coach Emerson let me start after all, and I played my heart out."

Naomi wished she could have seen it, but she knew Kendra would have worried about her being there on her own. "And?"

He chuckled. "And he stayed after the game and talked to me and our coach. And

197

my parents, too. He didn't make any promises, but I think things are looking really good."

"Kane, that's great."

"Yeah, it really is. I can hardly believe it. I never thought I'd get to go to college." He shook his head. "Has anything so hard to believe ever happened to you?"

"Jah." Getting picked up by one of the cutest boys she'd ever met fell into that category for sure. "I'm really happy for you."

"Me, too. I mean, I'm relieved. I didn't want to fumble and embarrass myself, you know?"

"Since I don't really know what *fumble* means, I'm gonna say no. But I get the gist of it."

He smiled again. "That's good enough for me."

"Where are you headed, Law?" Shawn asked.

"Out to my Jeep." He didn't want to say any more. He knew Naomi was going to be heading that way in a couple of minutes, if she wasn't there already. "I'll see ya later."

"Hold on." Shawn sidestepped so he was blocking Kane's way. "What are you doing? We're all going over to Jackson's house to watch the tapes. Don't you remember?"

"I remember. I'll be there in about an hour."

"An hour? Wait, are you going to be with that girl again?"

"Her name is Naomi, and yeah. I've gotta go." When he started walking toward the double doors leading out to the senior parking lot, Shawn kept pace beside him.

"Don't you think you're going a little crazy about that girl?"

"All I'm doing is driving her home."

"And picking her up. And eating lunch with her." Shawn smirked. "What's her deal?"

"There isn't a 'deal.' I just like her. That's all." Seeing that Naomi was now walking across the parking lot from the opposite direction, Kane said, "I've got to go."

"Fine, but I hope she knows you're not going to be around for her much longer. I mean, you've got plans, right? You don't want to have a girl messing that up."

Kane merely raised a hand as he kept walking. Shawn's comment wasn't worth a reply, especially since he didn't agree with him. He didn't know what exactly was going on with Naomi and him, but he was sure that he wasn't in any hurry to stop seeing her.

"Nanny!"

She drew to an abrupt stop, giving him a look that was so horrified, he laughed. "Kane, don't call me that."

He picked up his pace, darting through a pair of parked cars, and was by her side in less than a minute. "Why? It's adorable."

"It's awful."

"That might be your opinion —"

"It is."

"Well, I think you're wrong. I like calling you that." He unlocked his Jeep and flicked a switch so Naomi's side unlocked, too. "Come on, let's get going."

When she slid in beside him, he said, "I know you've got to get to your sister's, but you want to get a Coke or something?"

Her blue eyes widened. "Do you have time?"

"Time for a pop. What about you?"

"I have time for a pop, too." She smiled. *"Danke."*

He smiled back as he drove her out of the parking lot, determined not to think about his future or Shawn's warning. It was warm, the sky was bright blue, and he had Naomi by his side.

As far as he was concerned, that was all that mattered.

NINETEEN

"I wasn't real happy to be putting on Andy's clothes. They were too big, and it felt weird to show so much of my legs. But I wasn't really thinking about modesty too much. See, the real problem was that I have a bad scar on my leg, and I had some pretty bad bruises on me, too. But I decided I'd rather have Andy Warner see my cuts and bruises instead of thinking I smelled."

Monday

Kendra was so glad she'd decided to start closing the shop on Mondays. She needed a day to do laundry and clean her little house from top to bottom, and now that she had a younger sister to look after, she liked to spend a few moments being home alone, just relaxing with a cup of hot tea and a book.

She'd always done her best to be organized, but her new venture meant that she always had paperwork to check and banking to do. Yes, it was a lot, but she was doing her best, that was for sure and for certain. And today? Well, so far, it was proving to be a mighty good day. She'd made banana bread early that morning and had even managed to send off two big slices with Naomi and Kane, who seemed content to pick Naomi up every morning.

Kendra also had fresh laundry hanging on the line outside, had already cut up a chicken that was soaking in buttermilk before she would fry it that afternoon, and had changed the sheets on both her and Naomi's beds.

Pleased with all of her accomplishments, she decided it was time to relax for a bit, especially since a new library book was calling her name. After cutting a slice of bread and placing it neatly on a plate, she sat down, feeling a sense of peace that had eluded her during her childhood.

Of course, she wasn't even sure if she'd longed for peace in those days. Mostly, she'd just tried to take care of her siblings, avoid her father, and keep everyone fed. More often than not, she'd failed at all three things. Her younger brothers and sisters would go to bed hungry, she'd be sporting a welt from whatever her father had decided to hit her with, and she'd be overwhelmed with schoolwork.

No, back then, her sense of peace had come from being around her friends or in the pages of a book.

Annoyed with herself for letting those sad memories intrude on her sunny day, she motioned for Blue to hop up next to her, opened up the book, and slowly read the first page of the next chapter. She'd never be a good reader, but she did enjoy a good story.

She'd read only a few pages when two raps on the front door interrupted her.

Blue ran to the door, barking.

"It's all right, Blue. No need to get excited." Sure one of her girlfriends from the Eight had come to visit, Kendra opened the door without looking through the window.

And immediately regretted that decision.

Her brothers, Jeremiah and Chris, were standing on her stoop. And in between them was their mother, wearing a faded gray dress hanging on her slight frame and old black tennis shoes.

Kendra blinked. She hadn't seen her mother in years. Unfortunately, those years hadn't been kind to her. Her hair was already gray, her skin looked sallow, and there were too many lines on a face that hadn't even seen forty-five yet.

As if Blue sensed her mood, she growled.

Kendra picked her up and cuddled her close. "It's all right," she said, though she wasn't sure if she was reassuring herself or her pet.

Jeremiah stepped forward. "Kendra, are you all right?"

No, she didn't think she was. But she was old enough now not to let her discomfort show. "I'm fine, Jeremiah. Just surprised to see you. Hello, Chris."

Chris's expression warmed. "Hello, sweetheart." Before she knew what was happening, he enfolded her — and Blue — into his arms. "It's been too long."

She leaned close and hugged him back. "You are such a man now," she said with a laugh. "Whenever I think about you, I only see a boy who was impatiently waiting for his growth spurt."

Chuckling, he pulled back, keeping his hands around her waist. "I should've listened to you, girl. I don't know how many times you told me to be patient."

"Too many to count," she said with a smile. "You look *gut,* Chris. Happy." He was an *Englischer* now, and wearing a black sweater, jeans, and tennis shoes. Most importantly, he looked comfortable with himself. That was all she'd ever prayed for them. To survive their childhood and eventually lead happy, healthy lives.

"You look good, too. As pretty as ever."

"Hardly that."

"Always," Chris countered before glancing at Jeremiah and then their mother.

It took everything Kendra had to finally meet her gaze.

Rosanna Troyer licked her bottom lip. "Are you ever going to acknowledge me?"

"All right. Hello, Rosanna."

"You can't call me that. I'm your mother."

"*Nee.* You might have given birth to me, but you did not mother me or my brothers and sisters. I promised myself I'd never call you mother or *mamm* ever again."

Jeremiah, ever the peacemaker, sighed. "Kendra, we came over for a reason. May we come in?"

Peeved that they had shown up at her house unannounced and then acted surprised when she wasn't more gracious, Kendra turned around and strode down the hall. "I'm going to put up Blue," she called out, not caring what they thought. She needed a moment to grasp what was happening. Her brothers had brought their mother to her door and were now escorting

205

her inside. She felt like screaming. She'd never wanted her parents to even know where she lived.

She did deep breathing exercises as she set Blue on her bed, then closed her bedroom door. When she felt composed again, she returned to her family, who were all standing around her small living room.

She folded her hands together. "What is going on?"

"Sit down, Mamm," Chris said.

With a weary sigh, their mother sat down on the sofa. Chris took a seat in the lone chair, and Jeremiah took the spot next to Rosanna, leaving Kendra the only one without a place to sit. Usually, she would pull over one of her kitchen chairs, but she remained standing. She was too agitated to sit down.

"Now would be a *gut* time for one of you to tell me why you are here."

Chris answered. "I got a call from Jeremiah yesterday. He told me Daed was in the hospital."

Their mother remained silent, so Jeremiah continued. "Mamm stopped by the lumberyard to tell me, so I called Mary from work."

"Did you get hold of her?" Though she saw Chris and Jeremiah every now and then, they rarely saw Mary, who had moved up to Cleveland.

"Jah," Jeremiah replied. "We talked."

She noticed that he didn't mention that Mary would be rushing into town to see their father. Kendra would have been shocked if she was, for Mary's life hadn't been any better than hers had been in that house.

Kendra waited to feel something — a sense of loss, sadness, even worry. Instead, all she felt was irritation that they'd brought this news to her living room, her private space. "I don't know why you brought her over here to tell me this, Jeremiah."

Her mother inhaled sharply, but it was Chris who gave her the information she'd asked for. "Because Daed, who'd been losing weight, started developing sores on his body that wouldn't heal. He collapsed two days ago and was taken to the hospital. His whole body is riddled with disease."

"The *doktah* doesn't know if he'll make it more than another day or two," Jeremiah concluded. "His liver has shut down, and his heart doesn't look good, either."

Her father was about to die. Soon.

Once again, Kendra waited to feel something. But she couldn't feel anything but relief that she'd never have to see him again. "I see. Thank you for telling me."

"That is all you can say?" Rosanna blurted.

Each word felt like pins being stuck into her bare skin. "It is not. But it's unlikely you're gonna want to hear anything else that's on my mind," Kendra replied. "Now, if you will all excuse me, I have other things to do."

Chris stood up. "Kendra, we came here because we thought you might want to go to the hospital to see him. I've got my car. I could take you."

As far as she was concerned, he might as well have just asked her if she wanted to go to Hawaii to learn how to hula dance. "Chris, have you gone?"

He nodded.

"And you have, too, Jeremiah?"

"I did. Mary said she is going to go to-night."

"I see." She took a deep breath. "Let Mary know that she's welcome to stop by if she has time."

Her mother surged to her feet. "That is it?" she asked incredulously. "That is all you can say? Kendra, he is your father."

The last of Kendra's tight clamp on her emotions broke free. "I still have a six-inch scar on my thigh from when I was locked in the shed for two days," she said, her voice

208

trembling. "Do you remember that, Rosanna? Do you remember that I was seven and that I was locked in there as punishment for not doing all the dishes good enough?" She laughed darkly. "At least, I think that was the reason. Or was it? Was there ever a reason? I was scared. I was hurt. That gash, it got dirty and infected, and I got so sick. I was so *very* sick."

While her brothers stared in shock, Kendra stepped closer to her mother. Rosanna still smelled the same — slightly musty, like old laundry and cheap soap.

"Do you remember that, *Muddah*?" she asked, letting the word ooze with sarcasm. "Do you remember how sick I was? How I got a terrible fever and my leg swelled to almost twice its size?" She lowered her voice. "Or do you only remember what you did?"

Her mother swallowed hard.

Kendra swiped a hand over her leaking eyes. "*You did nothing.* You let me cry in that shed in the dark. You didn't help me clean up when I finally got out. You surely didn't take me to the doctor. It was only when I went to school that I got care. My teacher took one look at me and brought me to the clinic. The nurse ended up taking me to a doctor's office to get shots and medicine."

Her voice trembled. "She let me sleep in her little office because she knew I couldn't go home. She knew my father was evil and my mother didn't care about me."

Chris walked to her, tried to hug her. She knew it wasn't fair, but she pulled away. "Christopher, I know you were little. I know you don't remember that. But I do."

Turning to her mother, she shook her head. "No matter how hard I try, I can't forget. I had to live in that house for another six years because *someone* had to take care of my four younger siblings."

She turned to Jeremiah. "I wasn't the only one who got hurt. Don't you remember when you broke your arm? *Nee,* when *he* broke your arm?"

"Of course I remember," Jeremiah said. "But we should forgive, Kendra."

"If you can forgive, I'm happy for you. I cannot forgive either of them." She took a fortifying breath. "At least, not today."

"You don't know what my life was like," Rosanna said. "I did the best I could."

Though both of her brothers' expressions softened, Kendra only got angrier. "I don't believe that. You never helped me, Rosanna. All you did was give up . . . on all of us."

The tension in the room tightened. Feeling it, hating it, Kendra released a ragged sigh. "I'm sorry, boys, but the fact of the matter is I know I'm supposed to care that our father is in the hospital, but I don't understand why you would ever think I would want to see him again."

"All right, then," Chris said. "Now, where's Naomi? Mommi and Dawdi said she's living here now."

"She's at school."

"She's too old for school," their mother said.

"Naomi is Mennonite now." Unable to help herself, Kendra added, "She's also very smart. She's taking all honors classes. She even has a chance to get an academic scholarship for college."

"Tell her about your father," Rosanna said. "I'm sure she'll want to see him."

"I will let Nanny know."

Her mother's face was pinched. "Daughter, forgiveness is a virtue."

"Indeed it is. I hope our father will find a way to ask God for forgiveness."

"Let's go, Mamm," Jeremiah said, escorting her out the door.

Chris lagged behind. "Kendra, I know Mamm feels really bad about how she treated you. For what it's worth, we all know you were the one who really raised us."

"Chris, don't you understand? I'm not seeking acknowledgment — or praise — for that. I know I raised you. I loved you, and I am glad I helped you all as much as I could. But the problem is I still can't be okay with how that impacted my own childhood. Too much happened."

Looking sad, he nodded. "I love you."

"And I love you back. Jeremiah and Naomi and Mary, too."

Chris pressed a kiss to her brow. "I'll call you soon." And with that, he walked out the door.

She shut it right behind him, locked it tight, and then went upstairs and lay down.

Although she had promised herself she wouldn't shed another tear over her parents, Kendra cried like she hadn't in years. Cried like she had the night before she'd finally left that house for good.

TWENTY

"When I found my way to the kitchen, Andy was making BLTs. He dropped the knife he was holding onto the cutting board when he caught sight of my leg.

" 'Did your dad do that to you?' he asked.

"When I nodded, he met my eyes. 'That sucks.'

"And though it wasn't a particularly nice phrase, and I was a little shocked, I couldn't help but nod. Because he was right, and sometimes only an ugly word can describe an ugly situation."

Tuesday
"Hey, Nate?"

Nate leaned back on his heels. He'd been attempting to inventory some bins filled with various dimensions of tubing and had

213

almost finished counting when the interruption made his mind go blank.

Looking up, he was surprised to see Naomi peering down at him. "Sorry, I was counting pipes."

"Yes. I, um, noticed that."

She seemed hesitant.

"What can I help you with?"

"It's okay." A line formed on her brow. "I could come back later . . ."

"Of course not." He got to his feet. "What can I help you find in the store?"

"Nothing." Looking frustrated with herself, she paused. "I mean, I don't need anything from here."

He scanned her face. "Is everything all right?"

"With me, yes." She hesitated before continuing. "The problem is with Kendra."

Tension rose up his spine. Taking a step toward the door, he said, "Where is she? Is she sick?"

"Nee," she replied in a rush. "I mean, it's nothing like that." She scanned the area. It wasn't all that crowded, maybe only ten customers were in the shop at the moment. "I know you're mighty busy, but could we speak privately for a moment?"

"Of course. We'll go to my office."

His office had once been his grandfather's.

It was hardly bigger than a storage closet, but it did sport windows on one of the walls, allowing anyone inside to look out at the shop floor. His *dawdi* had enjoyed catching employees taking breaks. He, on the other hand, simply enjoyed not feeling boxed in.

After signaling to Benjamin that he would be off the floor for a few moments, Nate led Naomi inside.

The moment he closed the door behind him, he said, "Talk to me. What's going on with your sister?"

Her stoic expression crumbled. "It was so horrible. Yesterday before I got home from school, my brothers, Jeremiah and Chris, showed up at her door."

"What's wrong with that? I thought she got along with them. All of you are close, *jah*?"

"We are close. We all love Kendra dearly. But this wasn't just about them." She reached out and gripped his arm. "Nate, they brought our mother along with them."

If he had been outside, bees could have flown into his gaping mouth. "I don't know if I'm more surprised that they brought her to Kendra's house or that your mother agreed to go in the first place."

"It gets even worse. My father is in the

215

hospital. He's dying, and they wanted Kendra to pay her respects."

"Really? Did she go?"

Naomi's scowled. "Oh, Nate. *Nee!* She can hardly even speak of our parents, let alone pay respects to our father. Anyway, from what Chris told me, they attempted to guilt her into going, and that's when she lashed out and told them all about her leg and how it got so bad when she was a little girl and almost died."

Nate's head was spinning. He took a deep breath, trying to weigh his conversational options. He wanted to know more about Kendra's injury and wondered why her brothers would ever bring their mother to visit Kendra, why any of them would want her to visit her evil father, and most of all, how Naomi ended up coming to see him.

Since Naomi looked like she was on the verge of tears herself, he decided to tread carefully. "While I'm sure Kendra is mighty upset, I'm not sure how I can help. This seems like it would be better handled among all of your brothers and sisters."

"That's where you're wrong," she said impatiently. "Kendra doesn't need our help. She's so used to putting the four of us first, it's almost impossible for us to do anything for her." She tugged lightly on the sleeve of his shirt. "Nate, Kendra needs someone outside of the family to cheer her up."

Cheer her up? They seemed to finally enjoy being in each other's company. But was he good at making her smile? He didn't know about that. "Naomi, no offense, but I don't think I'm who she needs to see right now."

"I promise, you are. I wouldn't have come here if I wasn't certain of it." Looking at him directly in the eye, Naomi's voice hardened. "Please go over there and help Kendra feel better. It's really important, Nate." She stepped toward the door. "Please? I'll watch the shop."

But he couldn't just up and leave. Could he? "Benjamin is alone. I'll need to call Kane to see if he can come up for a spell. I don't know, though," he added, half to himself. "He might have practice right now."

"He doesn't. He's at home."

"And how do you know this?"

"Because he dropped me off here."

"He did? Boy, I didn't know you two had gotten that close."

"Kane and I aren't important right now, Nate. Kendra is! Please, Nate? I moved here to take care of her. If we don't fix this, I'll know I've been doing a poor job of it."

"All right, then. Give me fifteen minutes

and I'll be over there to pick her up."

Naomi flung her arms around him. "*Danke,* Nate. I knew I was right to come to you."

Before he even had a chance to pat her back and let her know he would try his best, Naomi was out the door, hurrying through the hardware store and leaving him stunned in her wake.

His mind spinning, he called Kane. The moment he answered, he said, "Kane, I know this is late notice, but I'm in a bit of a bind. Would you be able to work a few hours this afternoon? Ben's alone, and we're expecting a couple of contractors to stop by. They're going to have big orders."

"Sure thing, Mr. Miller. I'll be over in fifteen minutes."

Hanging up, Nate realized Naomi had already prepped Kane as well. She was a smart one, that Naomi. He reckoned that young lady could probably manage a whole town.

He shrugged off his work apron, washed up, and then went out to the showroom to tell Benjamin what was going on. Luckily, Ben had just finished with a customer, and the store had emptied out considerably. "Ben, Kane is on his way over to fill in for me. I'll be taking the rest of the afternoon off."

"Is everything all right, Nathan?"

"I don't know. I just learned that a friend of mine needs some help. I couldn't say no."

Benjamin's worried expression turned knowing. "Don't worry. We'll have things covered."

"*Danke.* I appreciate it." His mind running a mile a minute, he said, "If you need anything —"

"We won't. We'll be fine. Give my best to Kendra."

Nate nodded before wincing. "I guess Naomi was a giveaway, huh?"

"She wasn't the only clue," he said cryptically. "Go on now."

Nate walked out the door, but after a few steps, he slowed to a stop. What was he going to do with Kendra? What would make a girl like her happy?

After a few seconds passed, he suddenly knew. It wasn't fancy, and maybe it wasn't even the best idea, but he was fairly sure it was going to be a new experience for her.

Feeling full of himself, he strode right into Tried and True.

Kendra was standing with Naomi and a group of three women, looking at fabric remnants. The minute he saw her, he knew

Naomi had not exaggerated the gravity of the situation. Kendra had dark circles under her eyes, and she was paler than usual.

She really was upset.

When she saw him, she broke away. "Hiya, Nate, did you need something?"

No, but she did. She needed something fun, something to take her mind off her sister, her family, even her new business. "I do. Kendra, I came over to tell you to grab your things. It's time to go."

Her brown eyes widened. "I don't understand. Go where? Did . . . did something happen?"

"Not at all." He tipped his hat. "Miss Troyer, we're going courting this afternoon. Grab your cloak and your purse."

"Courting?" She almost smiled. "What are you talking about?"

"You're twenty-four years old. I'm twenty-five. I think by this time in our lives, it's fairly self-explanatory. Don't you?"

"Well . . ."

He lowered his voice. "Come on, girl. For once, don't worry or think about the consequences. Just do what you want."

Her eyes widened.

"Go, Kendra," Naomi called out. "Things are fine here."

220

"Naomi knows about this?" she whispered.

"Kind of." He figured that answer was honest enough. After all, he wasn't even sure what he was doing.

Twin spots of color stained her cheeks. "I don't know what's going on, but I'm going to trust you on this, Nate Miller."

He held those words dear to his heart. "That's what I'm counting on. Now, don't make me beg. Go get your things and come on."

Feeling extremely satisfied, Nate winked at Naomi while Kendra scurried away to do as he bid.

TWENTY-ONE

"But after that, Andy led me to the washing machine, helped me put my dress and detergent inside, and then turned it on.

" 'Would you do me a favor?' he asked as it started running.

"I was wary, but I honestly would have done anything for him at that moment. So I said, 'Sure. What do you want me to do?' "

Tuesday

Kendra felt a bit like she was moving through a fairy tale. Nothing else in her life had felt like this. Just as she was walking back down the hall — Nate had asked her to grab a sweater and a quilt to wrap around her in case she got cold — he'd been hanging up her kitchen phone, as if he used her kitchen phone all the time.

"Who did you call?" she asked.

"My *mamm.*"

"You decided to call your mother while you sent me to go get my sweater?"

Nate's eyes sparkled. "It wasn't quite like that."

"What was it like? How come you decided to give her a call?"

"I needed her to ask my father to help me do something. Don't worry, it's taken care of."

Kendra raised her eyebrows. "Don't worry? I don't even know what I'm supposed to be worried about."

"That's a good thing, I think." He looked at the quilt she was holding and the light blue sweater she'd tossed around her shoulders with approval. "Those will work. We should get going. Are you ready?"

"*Nee.* Nate, I have no idea what we're doing."

"That's because it's a surprise." He held out a hand. "Now, hand me that quilt so we can get on our way."

"Our way to where?" She was beginning to get annoyed. She wasn't the best with surprises.

Looking determined, he pulled the quilt out of her hands. "First, we're going to my house."

"And then?"

"You know, I'm beginning to think that you've got a lot to learn about surprises."

"I don't like not knowing what is about to happen, Nate." During too much of her childhood she was always on edge, never knowing what was going to happen next.

"I know it's hard, but you're going to have to trust me, Kendra." His voice softened. "Please. Trust me not to hurt you — or to let you down."

His words were sweet. And he looked so sincere, too, like a little boy who had a big secret he could hardly wait to share. It was so unusual for him that it made her heart soften and maybe even encouraged her to do as he asked and trust him a little bit more.

She opened the door and led the way outside. "I hope I won't regret this," she teased. Okay, maybe only half teased.

"If you regret it, then I'll know I'm doing something wrong." Nate turned to face her. "Do you have everything you need?"

"*Jah.*"

"*Gut.* Come along, then."

Nate didn't live that far from her, less than three miles. As they started walking, Kendra peeked at him. "You know, I know where you live, but I've never been inside."

"It's time you came over, then. My *haus* ain't nothing too special, to tell you the truth. But it's home."

She liked the way he said *home,* like it really meant something. "Well, if all of us lived in houses like the Lambrights', we'd have a difficult time seeing one another."

"I reckon so, what with those hundred acres."

It was true. Harley Lambright was from one of the wealthiest Amish families in the area. For decades, multiple generations had lived on his property, and every bit of the rambling, oversize house was filled with finely crafted woodwork and custom-made cherry and maple cabinets. The whole thing looked like it was out of a magazine. It was such a far cry from the way she'd grown up that Kendra had been a little scared the first time she'd gone inside. She'd been sure she was going to accidentally break something.

Harley wasn't a man who showed much emotion. He was a bit self-contained and sometimes came across as distant. She'd been afraid his whole family was going to be like that, or worse, they'd know she'd come from far different circumstances. To her relief, though, his family had been wonderful and made her feel welcome from the minute she'd stepped into the kitchen.

All of that made her start thinking about Nate's home. She wondered if it was as grand and picture-perfect as Harley's. "What's your *haus* like? Did your parents build it?"

"*Nee.*" He chuckled. "My father worked at the hardware store from time to time, but my uncle was the one who ran it. My *daed* ain't what you'd call real handy with inanimate objects."

"I don't understand."

"He's a farmer, you know. He has a way with heirloom tomatoes that make some of his customers weep. And we've raised fancy chickens, too. Those chickens follow him around like he's their mama."

"I'm not sure what an heirloom tomato is." When Nate gaped at her, she shrugged. "I'm sorry. I'm not much of a tomato fan, you see."

"Heirlooms look a little different. Some are green, others more orange than red. They've got a distinctive taste."

"And fancy chickens?" she asked as they continued to walk. "What does that mean? That they're really clean?"

"*Nee.* They're breeds. Polish chickens, Mottled Houdans, the Blue Cochin . . . they're special."

Who even knew there were so many kinds

of chickens? "They sound exotic."

"Oh, they are. We have Araucana chickens, too. They lay blue eggs."

She giggled. "You are lying."

"Not at all. They're robin's-egg blue. They're beautiful, really. They cost a pretty penny, too." He grinned. "Course, when you crack one open, it looks like any other egg yolk, I suppose. It's just in fancy wrapping."

"People want to pay a lot of money for blue eggs?" She couldn't wrap her head around it.

"*Nee,* people want chickens that *look* fancy and lay blue eggs. There's a difference you see." Shifting the quilt to his other arm, he continued. "My father gets all kinds of gentlemen farmers who want pretty chickens they can take pictures of."

"Why?"

"So they can post them on Facebook or on their Instagram pages."

"Truly?"

He grinned. "Oh, yeah. They're fine-looking birds, for sure and for certain."

"I don't imagine their appearance matters too much when they're cooking in a pot."

Nate looked horrified. "Kendra, Daed's customers don't eat them! They eat the eggs and care for them like pampered pets. They even get special organic corn and grain."

"Sounds like I should have been born one of your father's hens."

He laughed. "Your life might have been easier . . . but no one is happy simply strutting around and looking good all day."

She thought it sounded pretty idyllic herself. Liking the sound of his laugh, she said, "I promise, I won't ask myself over for a chicken supper."

"Oh, I eat chicken. Just not my *daed*'s."

"I can't believe I didn't know all this about you."

He shrugged. "Not much to tell, really. As much as I like to eat tomatoes and can appreciate the prancing of a Polish hen, I've always preferred to work in my uncle's hardware store."

"Your parents never minded you working there?"

"Nope. It's a better fit for me. I like being around people, not bugs and birds. I really wouldn't mind if I never had to clean up a henhouse again, either." He shrugged. "All this is to say that while my parents make a good living with birds and tomatoes, they're not rich. Our home is tidy and comfortable, but a far cry from the Lambrights' mansion."

She looked up and noticed they were approaching Nate's house at last. It was painted white and had a neatly shingled black roof. He was right. It looked just like a regular house — single story, maybe two or three bedrooms at the most.

But, oh, the yard! It was beautiful. Even in the fall, his parents had mums and pansies of every color, red and orange leaves on the trees, a porch swing painted a glossy black, and a little chicken-shaped sign next to the front door that read MILLER'S POULTRY AND GARDEN IN THE BACK.

"I like your sign."

"My sister Maggie made it when she was twelve. To be honest, my *mamm* wasn't real fond of having a chicken-shaped sign by the front door, but Maggie explained that she was tired of telling customers to go around back. So, it stayed."

"I don't know whether to ask to see your house or these famous chickens first."

Nate shook his head. "We are not here to look at birds. If my father discovered you were interested, we'd be stuck walking around the henhouse for two hours."

"We?"

"There's no way I'd leave you alone with my father and his chickens. He'd talk your ear off."

"I wouldn't mind." Did he not realize how nice it was to have a father to be proud of?

229

Just as he looked about ready to argue that point, his eyes lit up. "How about we come back here another day? I give my father a hard time, but he's a *gut mann.* And he'll love getting to know you."

"If you want."

"I do."

His invitation felt like so much more, though, like a promise that had nothing to do with tomatoes or chickens or his father. "What do you want to do here?"

"Go to the barn, of course," he replied.

Just as they walked around the back of the house, she saw a lovely brown quarter horse attached to a courting buggy. When the gelding spied Nate, he whickered softly.

"Hi there, Ten." He patted the horse's flank.

"Ten?"

"It's short for Tennessee."

"Because you got him from there?"

He smiled. "*Nee.* Because he's a Tennessee walking horse."

"He's handsome."

"*Jah,* he is, indeed." Setting the quilt on the bench, he said, "Are you ready?"

"Wait. We're going on a buggy ride?"

"We are. And a picnic." He sounded delighted.

"A picnic, too?"

230

"We've got to eat, *jah*?"

"You're not going to get to eat much if you don't go inside and get the basket, Nate," Maggie called out as she approached. Smiling at Kendra, she said, "Hiya, Kendra. It's been ages since our paths crossed."

"It has. I was in Columbus for a while."

"So I've heard. Good to see ya."

"And you, as well," Kendra replied. "How have you been?"

Maggie shrugged. "*Gut* enough, I suppose." Crossing her arms over her green dress, her voice grew warmer. "Are you looking forward to your big date with Nate, Kendra?"

Before Kendra could reply, Nate frowned. "Maggie, why don't you go in and get the basket?"

"Nope, you're going to have to go inside and get it yourself. And before you start complaining, I think you know why, too." She grinned as Nate's expression turned resigned. "At least I ran out here to warn you."

"Fine. Kendra, it seems my parents want to say hello. Come on."

On another day or maybe even a week ago, Kendra would've been nervous to meet them. But between her conversation with her mother and brothers and all the sweet

231

stories Nate had just shared about his father, she realized she didn't have anything to fear anymore. "Don't worry. I'm looking forward to meeting them."

He smiled softly and pressed a hand on the small of her back as he guided her into his house.

The first thing she noticed was that it was very plain, especially for a New Order Amish home. Though she hadn't expected any decorations, the interior was filled with fine wooden floors, ice cream–white walls, walnut-colored woodwork, and a few pieces of simple furniture. Nothing adorned the walls, and the only color came from a beautiful rag rug in the center of the living room and a large basket filled with knitting supplies.

Before she was even aware she was doing it, Kendra walked to the basket and ran her hand over the yarn. It was silky soft and finely made.

"Kendra, here are my parents, Peach and Atle Miller."

She turned abruptly. "I'm pleased to meet you, Atle and Peach." She blushed as she stumbled on Mrs. Miller's name. She'd never heard of such a thing.

Peach Miller grinned. "I know. It's an awful name, ain't so? My real name is Mary, but it seems I loved peaches when I was a tiny *boppli.* My grandfather started calling me Peach, saying I was going to turn into one, and the name stuck."

Peach was only a little over five feet. She was rather plump and had brown eyes and light brown hair that was fading to gray. Dressed in her pale orange dress and black tights and shoes, and treating them to a bright smile, Kendra thought the name was perfect. "I like it, Mrs. Miller. It's *gut* to meet you. And you as well, Mr. Miller," Kendra said, turning to Nate's *daed,* who had a shock of blond hair just like Nate's.

Mr. Miller, dressed in worn pants, black suspenders, and a white shirt that had been washed so many times it was rather gray, smiled at her, too. "Hello, Kendra. I hear you're keeping our boy in line."

Thinking about how he'd managed to surprise her with this outing, she shook her head. "Not so much, I'm afraid."

He chuckled. "You'll just have to try harder then, *jah*? Our Nate's a wily one."

Kendra laughed as Nate's cheeks turned red.

"Daed, we need to go. We only came inside to get the picnic basket."

Suddenly realizing that in order for Nate to take her on a picnic, someone had to make the food first, Kendra turned to Nate. "Who made the food?"

"I did, dear," Mrs. Miller said.

"Oh! *Danke.*"

"It's nothing fancy. Roast beef sandwiches, pickles, potato salad, and frosted oatmeal cookies."

It sounded delicious, especially since she hadn't made any of it. "It sounds *wunderbaar.*"

"It was my pleasure. I hear you're a good cook, Kendra. I hope you'll find my cookies to be acceptable."

"I'm sure they'll be delicious," she said, thinking there was only one person from whom Mrs. Miller would have heard about her cooking skills — Nate.

"Daed, Kendra here is interested in your chickens, so she'll be back another time. But now we're off. Ten's waiting."

"Have a good time," Atle said. "And don't worry, Kendra, I'm sure we'll see each other again soon."

Kendra smiled at Nate's parents, but her insides felt like she'd swallowed a handful of bumblebees. She tried to tell herself that it was her fear of surprises making her body feel that way, but she had a feeling it was something else entirely . . . the sweet, foreign feeling of anticipation.

TWENTY-TWO

" 'Don't ever tell my mom that I know how to work this, okay,' Andy said. 'As far as she's concerned, I'm the laziest boy she knows.'

" 'I won't tell anyone,' I replied, as if I were making a promise about something that was actually important."

Tuesday

Kendra would've said it was almost over-whelming, the effort that Nate had made to make their date perfect, but it had passed "almost" about the time he'd told her about his father's chickens.

There'd been something about that story that had touched her heart in a way that little had in a long time. It wasn't just that Nate had a good relationship with a kind father, either. No, for her, it was the fond way he talked about his parents' businesses,

235

never finding fault with their choices, and instead, simply deciding their paths weren't the ones he wanted to go down, and so he'd made his own.

It was . . . well, it was sweet.

"I never knew you were such a romantic," Kendra said as they clip-clopped down the road, Ten looking very proud as he led the way.

"I'm not."

"You don't see this courting-buggy-picnic as romantic?"

Nate chuckled. "I do, but that's not who I am. I mean, I'm usually not this way," he corrected, the words tumbling over each other. "I mean, I don't do things like this."

If he didn't . . . why did he do it for her? "Well, for someone who doesn't do things like this, I think you're doing a *gut* job. I'm going to give you an A plus."

"That high a score?"

"Oh, *jah.* I'm impressed."

"Kendra, you are impressed too easily." Nate did look pleased with her praise, though.

Watching him guide Ten to a stop at an intersection, Kendra noticed him smile. "You are a good driver, Nate. Though I must say I don't recall you driving a horse and buggy much."

236

"That's probably because I don't care for it." His face went slack. "I mean, I like this, a ride in a courting buggy, with nothing to do but enjoy the evening and such. This, I like. But hitching it up to run errands or get to church? Guiding Ten along the highway in the traffic? It's not my favorite thing to do at all."

"I don't think it's anyone's favorite thing." There were far too many obstacles out of their control when driving a horse on a busy road.

"I reckon you're right." After a pause, he said, "I don't recall your parents driving a horse and buggy when we were younger."

"That's because they didn't. We couldn't afford to keep a horse. The feed and upkeep was too expensive, let alone the cost of a buggy. We walked everywhere." She still had never driven a buggy.

"My parents like to take the buggy, but I've been more of a bicycle man myself."

She leaned against the hard back of the bench seat, liking the feel of him next to her. "I guess this evening is a bit of a novelty for both of us, then."

"I think so. I'm glad for it, too. It puts us on more even ground."

Though she was trying hard not to be sensitive, the comment stung. "Because you

237

have so much and I don't?"

"What?" His hazel eyes widened. *"Nee."* He shook his head. "Honestly, Kendra. First of all, even if I thought it, I would never say such a thing. I hope one day you'll learn to think better of me." He turned his head to meet her eyes. "But I don't, okay? I was meaning the opposite."

"Okay . . ." She didn't want to fish for compliments, but she couldn't see what he was referring to.

"Look at all you've accomplished on your own! You got schooling. You are taking care of your sister. You are starting your own business. You were even able to buy a house."

"Well, the bank helped with that. But thank you. I . . . I guess I've been so intent on reaching my goals and simply existing that I hadn't ever thought to look at my life through another person's eyes. You made me feel good."

"I'm glad, but you are far too hard on yourself. I guess I'll need to make it my job to remind you how special you are," he murmured as he directed Ten to the edge of a meadow. There was a pond nearby and a couple of trees that were bright with fall foliage.

"This place is *shay* — so beautiful. I can't

238

believe I've lived here all my life and never knew such a place existed."

"That's likely because it's private property. It's my uncle's land."

"The hardware store uncle?"

"None other. Anyone in the family can use it. My mother told me once that Uncle Marvin saved the land, hoping he would have *kinner* who would want to live here one day. But he and Aunt Josie were never blessed with children."

"That's sad."

He nodded. "I've always thought so, too. But today, his loss is our gain, because it's a mighty nice place to have a picnic. Ain't so?"

"I couldn't think of anyplace better."

Nate parked the buggy under an old maple tree. After they got out, he handed her the quilt he'd asked her to bring. "Go find us a *gut* spot while I take care of Ten."

"Do you have a favorite place where you like to sit?"

He scanned the area. "I like off to the side myself. But I ain't picky. If there's a spot that suits your fancy, just let me know."

Walking toward a patch of oak trees, Kendra looked down at the hem of her dress. It was gliding along the tops of the grass. Underneath, her flats peeked out. Sometimes the grass would tickle the tops of her feet, making her smile. Such a little thing, but it lifted her spirits even higher. She knew that days, even weeks, from now she would remember the feel of the cool grass brushing her skin as she walked toward the edge of the field to have a picnic with Nate.

Perhaps years from today, she would remember it as the first of many picnics together.

This spur-of-the-moment date was going well. Nate knew it, from the way Kendra was smiling to the way she had arranged their food on the blanket to the way he'd noticed her blush when he'd given her a compliment. Kendra was enjoying their first "real" date very much.

Now, all they had to do was keep things nice and easy. He needed to avoid her past and any mention of her parents. And no matter what, he had to stop thinking about kissing her.

He wasn't even sure where that notion had come from. Though he was no saint, he wasn't exactly the type of man who went around kissing women. Actually, he'd only kissed two other women, and one of them had been eight years old to his nine. That kiss had been filled with giggles and a sense of danger, and as soon as they'd kinda sorta pressed their lips together for all of two seconds, they'd run back to their friends.

His second kiss had been when he was far older. He thought he was in love and had been filled with all the nervous energy a teenager could have. He'd second-guessed everything, from his sweaty palms to his fear of bumping her nose to worrying about bad breath. Kissing Sally had been sweet, but it had also been apparent that there wasn't a spark between them. They'd broken up soon after.

But now? Well, all he could think of was holding Kendra close and showing her how much he liked her. However, if he did that, Nate was fairly sure Kendra would either push him away or be offended.

"What's got you thinking so hard? You look like you're trying to solve all the world's problems," she murmured.

Kendra was lying on her side. Her head was propped up on her hand, a position he always thought looked comfortable but never actually seemed to be.

"I was just thinking about the way you're lying down."

"Oh?" Immediately, she moved to sit up.

"No, don't do that. I like seeing you that way."

"You do? Why?"

Because she looked especially pretty like that. "I was just thinking what an uncomfortable position that is for me."

Her brow wrinkled. "So you like seeing me in an uncomfortable position?"

"That's not exactly what I was thinking." He cleared his throat. "But it's part of it."

"Nate, what are you trying to say?"

"I don't think you want to know." He hoped she kept it at that. He was a miserable liar.

"I think I do." She sat up slowly and circled her arms protectively around her knees, like she was shielding herself from more hurtful words from him.

He paused, hating to make himself so vulnerable, but then the expression on her face, so wary, made him decide that pride was overrated. "All right. The truth is that I was thinking just now that you looked really pretty and that I wanted to kiss you."

"*That* is what you were afraid to mention?"

He couldn't tell if she was amused or offended. "*Jah*. Don't be *bays*."

She didn't look mad. Actually, her brown eyes shined with humor. "Why didn't you want to tell me that you wanted to kiss me?" she whispered.

242

This was turning into one of the most humiliating conversations of his life. "I didn't want to tell you because I didn't want you to think my intentions toward you weren't pure."

"Ah." She looked away.

Which told him nothing. "I don't know what you're thinking now."

When she met his gaze again, her expression was light and, perhaps, carefully controlled? "This time, I think you're the one who needs to be kept in the dark."

"And I think I really need to know, because I'm afraid I've just gone and ruined everything."

"Nate, you planned a picnic, arranged for the food, took me out in a courting buggy, and have been nothing but kind and amusing. It's been one of the nicest evenings of my life. You couldn't ruin a thing about it." After a pause, she smiled. "Not even if you went and kissed me."

His stomach dropped. He might have been nervous, but he was old enough to know a shy invitation when it was given. He scooted closer. "In that case . . ." He leaned close and carefully brushed his lips against hers.

To his surprise, she raised a hand to his shoulder and kissed him back.

He sat back and smiled at her. No, grinned.

Kendra raised her eyebrows. "What is that for?"

"I, well, I was just thinking that this went a whole lot better than when I was nine and sixteen."

Kendra pressed a hand to her face and giggled softly. "Well, you are older. I believe that experience does make some things better."

"Indeed it does." He held up a hand. "Look at this. Why, *mei hannt* is not sweaty at all. By the time I'm thirty, I might even get real good at this kissing thing."

"I reckon you might be a pro well before you get that old."

"Do you really think so?" He raised a brow.

"Oh, *jah.* I'm not an expert by any means, but I think it only takes practice, you know?"

Looking pleased, he grinned. "I reckon so." He figured that was all the encouragement he needed to lean closer and kiss her again.

TWENTY-THREE

"Next thing I knew, I was sitting outside in the sun, drinking pop, eating an enormous BLT, and listening to Andy talk about you."

Tuesday Evening

Naomi thought everything about the cozy restaurant was perfect. She liked the beautiful pink and green tablecloths adorning each table. Liked how one wall was completely made up of books. Liked how the servers were wearing simple blue T-shirts and jeans with white aprons. Really liked the big bowl of broccoli cheese soup she'd ordered. But what she liked the most was that she was with her brother Chris. He always had a hug and supportive words for her.

Well, until today. Today, he'd seemed intent on spouting his opinions and not exactly listening to anything she was saying. It was beyond irritating.

"Naomi, are you sure the right place for you is with Kendra?" Chris asked from across the table.

He'd picked her up from Tried and True in his Jeep and taken her over to Millersburg for supper and a trip to the Walmart. Naomi had been excited to spend some time with her English brother. He was so different from the rest of them that it was sometimes easy to forget how things were when they'd all lived at home. With Chris, she could simply concentrate on their present, not the mistakes or worries of their past.

That was why she wasn't too happy with his comment. "I'm sure, Chris. I like living with Kendra."

After a pause, in which she could practically see him weigh his words, he blurted, "Kendra has a lot of demons, you know."

"No, I don't." What was he talking about, anyway? He knew as well as she did that Kendra was the most unselfish member of the whole family. She was kind, too.

"Come now. Think of how she talked to our mother the other day."

"What did you expect her to say? Mamm wanted Kendra to visit our father in the hospital. You knew that was never going to happen."

"See, that's what I'm talking about. She is

246

so angry. She calls Mamm Rosanna. That's disrespectful, don't you agree?"

"She has her reasons, and you know what they are."

"Of course she does. Of course, all of us have reasons not to trust our parents. But, that said, she's a grown woman now."

"Doesn't that mean Kendra gets to decide how she wants to live her life?" Naomi countered. After all, she was doing the same thing, choosing to move in with Kendra and attend a different school.

But instead of acknowledging that Naomi's point was valid, her brother only looked even more out of sorts. He pushed the roast beef sandwich he'd only half eaten to one side. "Naomi, I know you think the world of our big sister, but she isn't perfect. She's never moved on. She's refused to let the past go, and it's making her bitter. Jeremiah and I are afraid she's influencing you, too."

But weren't they all marked by their life in that house? "She's angry about our childhood, but that's not a shock, Chris. All of us bear scars from the things that happened." Feeling knots in her stomach instead of the hunger pangs that had been there an hour earlier, Naomi studied her big brother. "I'm kind of surprised you are saying all of this. I mean, Daed wasn't good to you, either." Their father had attempted to beat him with a belt the night Chris had announced he was leaving in the morning.

Chris looked troubled by the reminder. After another pause, he said, "Naomi, that's my point. All of us were abused. But while Kendra has held close to her bitterness, Jeremiah and I have moved on."

Naomi swallowed hard. He hadn't been exactly right when he said all of them had been abused. She'd had a different experience than her older siblings. Their mother had mainly ignored her, and their father's anger had been far more focused on her four older siblings than on herself. Then, of course, they'd all shielded her and even moved her out so she wouldn't have to live in that house without them.

But what if no one had ever stepped in to shield her? That was the point, of course. No one had ever been there to help Kendra.

"I might be eight years younger than Kendra, but even I remember how much harder things were for her. You know that, too."

"You're right. She did have it worse. But what can we do? When all of that was happening, we were all victims. It wasn't like we could save her." He cleared his throat.

"That isn't the point, though. What I'm trying to say is that you can't change the past. All you can do is make peace with it."

Everything he was saying was probably true, but it also seemed awfully neat and tidy . . . and improbable. "You are expecting the person who was hurt the most to do the most forgiving and peace-making." She raised a brow. "Or is that what you already told Mamm? Or maybe you advised Daed to make amends and beg Kendra for forgiveness?"

He grunted. "You know I didn't do that."

She folded her arms over her chest as she lowered her voice. "You can pretend that you've moved on, but I think you are living in denial."

"Whoa. Sounds like you've learned all kinds of fancy terms with your higher education."

"Feel free to be as sarcastic as you want, Chris. But Kendra is still Amish and living in Walnut Creek. You abandoned everything about this place. You are living as an *Englischer* in the big city. Do you even tell any of your *Englischer* friends about your past?"

"Just because I've taken my own path and don't choose to tell strangers about my baggage doesn't mean it's wrong."

"If you really believe that, then you

249

shouldn't be finding fault with Kendra's choices." Naomi looked around the beautiful dining area and felt sick. They weren't getting anywhere, and all Chris was doing was making her want to leave the table as soon as possible.

"Just tell me this. Has she been sober?"

The question came out of nowhere. "What are you talking about, Chris?"

"She had a drinking problem. A serious one." He raised an eyebrow. "Nanny, you look surprised to hear that."

"That's because I am."

"Really? Kendra never told you about the way she used to live her life?"

Her brother's voice had turned hard. Chiding. The change in tone felt like sandpaper grating on her skin, and she ached to get away from him.

But as much as it hurt, she knew she needed to hear it. Reluctantly, she shook her head. "What did she do?"

"Well, back in Columbus, she had a terrible drinking problem and she even started taking pills."

"Pills? Like medicine?"

"*Nee,* pills that are bad for ya. Opioids. They are real addicting."

"Kendra was addicted to drugs?" She could hardly wrap her mind around that.

250

"Oh, *jah.* She had to go to rehab to get better."

"I didn't know about any of this." She was shocked, and hurt, too. She had thought she and her sister were close, but maybe they weren't as close as she'd thought. How could Kendra go through something so big and never tell Naomi about it? It just didn't make sense.

Chris pressed his palms on the table. "Everything she did? Well, it was bad."

He might as well have been talking in riddles. "What do you mean 'bad'? Was she sick? Did she hurt herself?" All kinds of worst-case scenarios began running through her head. Had Kendra gone into the hospital? Had she almost died?

For the first time since they'd started talking, Chris looked unsure. He shifted in his chair, then took a sip of his iced tea. "I'm not exactly sure about all that."

"Why not? How did she look when you saw her? What did the people say who were looking after her?"

"I never went up to Columbus to see her."

"Who did? Jeremiah? Mary?"

"None of us did." When she gaped at him, his voice turned defensive. "Oh, come on, Nanny. That was eight years ago. I was still at home, taking care of you. All of us were."

251

She blinked. Chris was giving her more questions instead of answers, and she didn't understand any of it. She wasn't that much younger than the rest of the family. Had everyone kept it from her . . . or had they just pretended it didn't concern them?

Instead of giving her any real, concrete information, Chris murmured, "Now, I'm not saying that she could have a relapse, but things could happen."

"Why would you think that? I've been with Kendra a lot. She's never even been tempted to have a sip of beer. I know that."

"You are getting off track, Nanny. What I'm trying to tell you is that if you don't want to leave our sister's *haus,* then at least promise me you'll call me if you start to suspect she's drinking again."

Though he wasn't saying Kendra was going to relapse, he sure was insinuating that, which made her feel slightly sick. "Chris, I think instead of saying all this to me, you should be talking to Kendra. You know, see if she needs your help or anything . . ."

"She wouldn't appreciate me bringing it up."

"She might. Sure, she might be embarrassed, but don't you think it would be better if this were out in the open? I mean, if you offered to help her now, at least she'd

252

know you cared . . . ."

He sighed. "Will you just promise to call if she gets bad again? Please?"

It was real obvious that he wasn't going to let her out of his sight until she did. "Fine. I promise."

"Danke." Just as she was about to tell him she was ready to leave, he said, "Now, we're not far from the hospital. Will you go with me to see our father?"

"I don't know."

"I think you should. He's dying, you know. If you don't see him, you're always going to regret this choice. I've already got one sister who has done things she can't ever undo. I don't want that to happen to you, too."

Chris's words were awful. He'd also completely manipulated her. He'd offered her supper and a quick shopping trip in order to put down Kendra — and take her to see their father — which she didn't want to do.

She didn't want to do that at all.

Unfortunately, Naomi knew Chris wasn't going to give up until she relented. And what if he was right? What if their father was at death's door? She would have to live with her refusal to see him for the rest of her life. "Fine. I'll go."

His gaze warmed. "I think you're going to be real glad about this."

She might feel relieved. She might even feel disappointed their father never changed his ways before he met the Lord. But glad she visited him? No, she was fairly sure that wasn't how she was going to be feeling, especially since she was already regretting having a meal with Chris.

"Let's just get it over with so you can take me home."

"Wow, Nanny. That's pretty harsh."

"Call me Naomi, Chris. I'm not a little girl anymore."

"Don't get upset with me. I'm only trying to help."

She didn't say anything more, but she sure was wondering *who* he was actually trying to help.

She was fairly certain that it wasn't her.

TWENTY-FOUR

John B. looked around. "Who? Which one of us did you talk about?"

"All of you," Kendra said. "Andy told me stories about the Eight."

Tuesday Evening

She was practically floating. Kendra couldn't think of another way to describe how she felt. Try as she might, no other word came close.

From the moment Nate had picked her up, she'd felt like she had stepped into another woman's life. A luckier, happier, more treasured woman's life.

Though such an idea was fanciful, it sure felt like the truth. Such evenings as the one that had just taken place didn't happen to Kendra Troyer.

Men didn't go out of their way to court her. They didn't plan picnics and take her

255

to private fields or treat her with such care. Not a lot of people went to so much trouble just to make her happy or feel special. No other man ever had.

Instead, she'd become used to simply being everyone's friend. The girl who helped out, tried hard, but only existed on the fringes. The kind of person who was asked to do things at the last minute, like an afterthought, never the sole reason for a romantic evening.

But tonight, Nate Miller had proved her wrong. And that kiss! *Nee,* those *kisses*! No matter what happened with the two of them, she would never forget their first very sweet embrace. It had been everything she'd ever hoped it would be.

And then some!

Still in a daze even though she'd been home for almost an hour, she put the kettle on to boil and made herself a cup of mint tea. Then she realized it was rather late at night to be home alone. She frowned. Naomi had plans with Chris, but surely it hadn't lasted this late? Walking down the hall, she knocked softly on Nanny's door. "Nan? Nanny, are you in there?"

She waited almost ten seconds, then knocked again. Yet still, there was no answer.

Just as she was about to peek inside, the

front door opened, and Naomi appeared.

"There you are," Kendra said as she hurried back to the front of her little house. "I only now realized how late it was and that I had seen neither hide nor hair of you. I was just about to peek in your room to see if you had fallen asleep early."

"I wish that's what had happened."

"Why?" Walking closer, she got a better look at her sister. Nanny's eyes were red, and her cheeks were blotchy. She'd been crying, and not just a little bit, either.

Which made every protective instinct she'd ever had increase tenfold. "What's been going on? And where are your bags? Chris told me he was going to take you shopping at Walmart."

Looking even further crushed, Naomi groaned. "Oh, Kendra, I don't even know where to start."

Alarm bells were practically ringing in her ears, but Kendra forced herself to sound calm. "Well, maybe you can start at the beginning? I've always found that to be the best place to start." When she noticed Naomi's expression pinch, she added, "I mean, if you want to talk about it with me."

"You would sit here all night by my side, wouldn't you?"

"Of course I would. You know that though,

257

don't you?" She'd sat with Nanny lots of times when she was small. Did she not remember?

"I guess."

That statement felt charged, though Kendra didn't know why. "Nanny, I know you're almost an adult. I'm not going to make you do something you don't want to do."

Her little sister burst into tears.

Kendra rushed to her side and wrapped her arms around her. When Naomi rested her head on her shoulder and cried even harder, Kendra felt tears forming in her own eyes. What in the world had happened?

Half talking, half murmuring nonsense words, Kendra guided Naomi to the couch and sat down beside her. Nanny kicked off her flats, curled her legs under herself, and cuddled close to Kendra. Just like she used to do when she was a little girl.

The whole thing was so pitiful that Kendra was really starting to regret not pushing her for details. Every worst-case scenario she could think of flickered through her head — the worst being that something had happened to her after she saw Chris.

Becoming almost too afraid to even voice her fears, Kendra simply sat as Naomi's tears ebbed and finally ended with a sniff.

"I'm sorry about that." Naomi swiped at

her cheeks.

"Nothing to be sorry about. We're *shvesh-tahs,* and sisters can be themselves with each other."

"I think you made that little saying up."

She had, but because she was so bound and determined to be steadfast, she raised her eyebrows. "What, you think I'm telling tales to ya?"

Nanny gave her a watery smile. "Maybe. Mary never said those things to me."

"Well, that was Mary's fault. Not mine." Missing her cup of tea, she got to her feet. "Want a cup of hot mint tea? I'd just made myself a cup when you walked in."

"Not yet. But you go get yours."

Kendra took her time to retrieve her cup and get Nanny one, too. She needed the moment to collect her thoughts, and it was obvious Nanny did, too. When she returned to her side, her suspicions were confirmed. Nanny was looking clearheaded once again. "Here you go," she said as she placed the mug on the table next to Naomi. "Now you'll have your tea whenever you're ready."

After taking a sip, Naomi said, "Kendra, are you ever going to tell me how your date was?"

She didn't really want to talk about her night at the moment. "Yes, but maybe another time?"

"Come on. Please?"

She smiled. "Fine. It was a mighty fine date."

"What did you do?"

Realizing that her sister needed something good to think about, Kendra said, "He took me out in his courting buggy, and we had a picnic." And yes, she was still smiling, and her voice was all soft.

A slow smile lit up her sister's face. "How very . . . Amish."

"Stop. It was perfect," she said. "Even for an old girl like me."

Naomi wrinkled her nose. "You're not old."

"Oh, I'm old enough. Certainly too old to be mooning over a man."

"So, you *do* like him now." Satisfaction oozed with each one of Naomi's words.

"I do. And I do believe that he likes me back. What do you think about that?" she joked.

But Naomi didn't adopt her teasing tone. Instead, she looked to be on the verge of tears again. "I think that nobody deserves a good relationship more than you do."

The comment was sweet. It would have been sweeter if she wasn't so worried about her sister, though. "Are you ready to talk now?"

"I guess." After taking another sip of tea, she spoke again. "Chris took me to the hospital, Kendra. He set up this meal so I would have no choice but to go see our *daed*."

She didn't even attempt to hide her dismay. "Did you know about this visit, too? I mean, is that what you'd intended, but you didn't want to tell me?"

"*Nee!* I really thought we were going to have a meal and go to Walmart. But he only said those things in order to get me to say yes."

Kendra was ready to pick up her kitchen phone and call her brother, but she pulled herself together. "So you went."

After a brief hesitation, Naomi nodded. "Chris wasn't going to let me get out of it."

"He forced you to go against your will?"

"No, but he kept pressing me about something else. By the time he got to bringing up the visit to Daed, I was worn down. I was ready to do just about anything to get out of that restaurant."

"Oh, Nanny." Her mouth felt dry. "Well, um, how did the visit go?"

Naomi's lips pursed. "Not well. Daed, I mean, our father . . . he's lost a lot of

261

weight. He looks a lot smaller, lying there in a hospital bed."

Kendra couldn't imagine that. He'd always been a big man. Strong and unafraid to use that strength to bully them. Even though each word felt like a sharp stone in her mouth, she murmured, "I bet he was glad to see you."

"He looked surprised." Naomi curved her arms around herself. "Mamm kept saying things like I was being a good girl."

That made Kendra's stomach turn in knots. "And Daed, what did he say?"

"He didn't say much. I guess it hurts him to talk."

There was a small, evil part of Kendra that was glad about that. Which of course made her feel terrible. "What was Chris doing while you were in that room?"

"Well, when we were at the restaurant, he had acted like it was real important for me to be there." She paused, obviously trying to explain herself. "Like he wanted me there with him so much that I was sure he was going to be practically sitting on the edge of Daed's bed."

"But he wasn't?"

"Not at all. He stayed by the door. Actually, he looked as uneasy as I felt. So maybe he's not close to Mamm and Daed, either?"

"I hadn't thought Chris was, but I would have never expected him to make you go to see our parents, either."

"Well, anyway. I did it." Naomi picked up her mug and took another sip.

Kendra nodded. "You did and you survived, too!" Determined to make her sister feel better, she added, "And you know what? Maybe Chris was right. Maybe you did need to go to the hospital so you could feel at peace with yourself."

Remembering something her counselors had said back in Columbus, she added, "Closure is a good thing. Now, if our father does go to his maker soon, you won't feel guilty about not visiting him."

Naomi shrugged. "Maybe, I don't know." She fidgeted with the hem on her skirt. "Hey, Kendra?"

"Hmm?"

"Daed did ask if you were going to see him."

"Me? Really?" Kendra was shocked.

"Oh, *jah*. Daed asked if I was living with you now, and when I told him yes, he asked how you were."

"He asked how I was? What did you say?"

"I said that you were perfect. I told him about your store. He seemed surprised about that."

Kendra imagined he was. He'd never kept his low opinion of her a secret. Fighting back an urge to cover her ears so all those hurtful words wouldn't replay in her head, she took a fortifying sip of tea. "I'm glad you're home."

Naomi nodded. "Me, too. But, um, Kendra? Chris told me something that was kind of hard to hear."

"What was that?" She tried to keep her expression neutral as she tried to guess what story about their parents Chris had shared.

"He told me about your past."

"My past?" She put her mug of tea down. "What about it?"

"He told me about how you drank a lot when you were in Columbus and that you did even worse things, too. Like drugs. He said you took drugs, Kendra." Looking at her with big blue eyes, Naomi asked, "Is that true?"

"Jah." Boy, even that one word was difficult to utter.

Nanny curved her arms around herself again. "Are you mad at me for asking you?"

"Nee. I'm glad you are asking me instead of keeping all your questions to yourself." But was she mad at Chris? Oh, yes.

There was something new in Naomi's expression now. "Why didn't you ever tell me about what you did?"

Each word was harder and harder to hear, but nothing stung as much as Naomi's judgmental tone. "Why do you think?"

"Because you're embarrassed?"

"Yes. That. I am embarrassed. But it's a lot of other things, too. It was a bad time in my life. I was scared and hurting and alone." She'd been so very alone, and those dark days had pulled her down so deep that she'd wondered if she would ever see light again. "I don't like to talk about those years. I don't like to remember them."

"Chris said you went into rehab for your problems." Naomi wasn't looking at her now, and that hurt almost as much as the memories she tried so hard to keep from resurfacing.

"That's true," she replied slowly. "I had a bad problem and had to get help to get better. I was there for almost six months."

"You kept that a secret, too." Her sister was glaring at her now.

Kendra squirmed. "You're right, I did."

"You should've told me. I had a right to know."

"*Nee,* you did not."

Naomi's eyes widened in shock.

Kendra would do almost anything for Nanny, but she wouldn't apologize for keep-

265

ing that portion of her life to herself. Weighing her words, she said, "One day you are going to feel the same way I do. Not everything about me needs to be an open book."

"That isn't just any old thing. Your addictions were important. Really important to me."

"I realize that." But those addictions and the way she'd had to work so hard to overcome them were far more important to her.

"If you do, then you know I shouldn't have had to hear about it from Chris."

Kendra stood up. "Chris shouldn't have shared my personal business with you. It wasn't his story to share."

"But we're family."

That look in her sister's eyes, so full of judgment, so full of hurt — well, it was enough to send her over the edge. "Have you met our 'family,' Nanny? It's made up of a lot of hurting, damaged people. And just about every single one of us is in denial about it, too. Unless you've learned something about family and love somewhere else, I don't think you're the person to teach me how to act like a real member of one."

"You aren't the person I thought you were. I thought you were perfect."

"I never claimed to be. The truth is that

I'm flawed. I'm also a recovering addict. I'm not someone to be proud of, but that's who I am. I'm sorry if you can't handle that."

"Kendra." Naomi was breathing hard and looking unsure of how to continue. Then she shook her head and ran to her room.

Before she even realized what she was doing it, Kendra backed up against the wall for support, a childhood habit. *Nee,* maybe it was just a habit. She'd learned long ago to rely on objects for support. They were the only things she'd found she could trust to hold her up.

The church let me down — all its rules made my men!

Jesus said "You'll know my followers in how they love one another" — Blood on the hands of every so called Christian church —

Only in Jesus have I found peace!

TWENTY-FIVE

"Now, Andy acted like I didn't know any of you. I didn't correct him, but I knew who all of you were. Even though we weren't really friends, I knew all about the Eight."

Thursday

"The new girl is proving difficult to get to know," Kane's buddy Aiden said on their way out to the field house. "She hardly gave me the time of day when I tried to talk to her before school."

"The new girl's name is Naomi."

"I know. Anyway, she's way more standoffish than I thought she'd be." He grinned. "I guess she's going to make me work for her number."

"Why were you talking to her in the first place?" Kane asked. And yes, his tone was a little bit surly.

Aiden's footsteps slowed as he gaped at him. "Uh, because I'm friendly and she doesn't know anyone?"

"I didn't know you went around greeting new people at school."

Aiden raised his hands. "Whoa. I didn't know you were so touchy about Naomi. Why is that?" A knowing look appeared on his face. "Hey, did you finally ask her out?"

"No. We're still getting to know each other." But since he was giving her rides to school, he thought that would've given all his buddies the hint to back off.

"You might want to get to know her a little quicker. She's real pretty, Kane. If you don't make a move, someone else is going to."

He didn't like how Aiden was talking, like Naomi didn't know her own mind. "I don't need you to give me dating advice."

He grinned. "Um, yeah you do."

Kane was just about to tell him to cut it out when he noticed where Aiden was looking . . . at Robert Overholt, standing over by the fence talking to Naomi.

Worse, Kane couldn't even say that Robert wasn't a good guy. Captain of the football team. Vice president of the student council. Did tons of volunteer work at church. Already had a scholarship to Ohio University.

Naomi would be real lucky to have a guy like him as her boyfriend, and that would ensure that she would be accepted by just about everyone in the school. He'd treat her nice, too. But Kane wasn't okay with that. He might not have been ready to make his move, but that didn't mean he wasn't going to.

"I'll see you at warm-ups," he said.

"You're going over there?"

"Don't even start, Aiden." He threw his gym bag over his shoulder as he picked up his pace and dutifully ignored his buddy's laughter filling the air.

Whatever Robert was saying to Naomi ended abruptly when Kane approached. Lifting his chin, he said, "You need something, Law?"

Robert was shooing him away! As if he and Naomi were an item. Which they definitely were not.

All of Kane's good thoughts about the guy evaporated. "I do. I heard Coach is looking for you." Yep, he lied, and he wasn't proud of it.

"What does he want?"

"I couldn't tell you. I'm just the messenger. But I'd get going if I were you."

Robert pursed his lips. "I'm real sorry, Naomi. I better go."

"I understand."

After giving Kane an annoyed look, Robert shifted so he was half blocking Kane. "Can I have your number? I'll call you later."

"I'm sorry," Naomi replied. "I would give it to you, but I don't have a cell phone."

"Really?"

Naomi shrugged. "I live with my sister, and she's New Order Amish. She has a phone in the kitchen, but I don't want to give out the number until I check with her first. I'm sorry."

"I understand. There's nothing to be sorry about," Robert said in a gentle tone, a tone Kane hadn't even realized he possessed. "I'll see you tomorrow in class."

She smiled. "Okay. I'll see you then."

After giving Kane another long glance, Robert started jogging to the field house. Kane watched him with satisfaction, hardly feeling bad that he would soon find out the coach hadn't sent for him at all.

"Did your coach really want Robert?" Naomi asked, practically reading his mind.

"I heard he did."

Naomi's eyes lit up with humor. "You made that up, didn't you?"

"I didn't say that." Before she coerced him into admitting that he was a liar, he asked, "Since you didn't want me picking you up this week, I've hardly seen you. I haven't even seen you in the halls."

"Well, I do know my way around now."

That wasn't what he'd meant, and she knew it. What was going on with her? "Naomi, are you sure you're okay? How were your classes today?"

Some of the light that had been shining in her eyes dimmed. "Oh, they were all right."

"You sure? You don't sound like it." Thinking about Aiden attempting to talk to her, Kane added, "Is anyone bothering you?"

"What, here?" She looked surprised.

"Well, yeah . . ."

"Nee. No one's bothering me *here."*

At last she was giving him a hint. "Naomi, what's going on?"

Looking more flustered, she gripped the fabric of her periwinkle-colored dress. "I mean, it's nothing."

"Sure?"

She nodded. "It's just some trouble at home."

Getting information out of her was like getting blood out of a rock. Usually, he would let it pass, but Naomi looked really upset. "Who's the trouble with? Your sister or the rest of your family?"

"I don't want to talk about it. Actually, I think I better get going." But she didn't budge.

272

Maybe he was getting somewhere. "Hey, would you like me to stop over tomorrow? I've got a game tonight, but tomorrow afternoon I'm free. I don't mind." Realizing that didn't sound too good, he said, "I mean, I'd like to come over after school. I could drive you home and stay awhile. We could catch up. Can I?"

"Nee."

"Oh, okay."

Looking frustrated with herself, she lowered her voice. "I'm sorry, Kane. It's not you. I, I really messed up everything with my sister and I think I might have to move."

"Like, move away?"

Looking even more dejected, she nodded. "Kendra's really mad at me."

"I bet she'll get over it. You wouldn't believe the stuff I've said to my parents when I've gotten mad. They just blow it off, though. They know I don't mean it."

The muscles in her face seemed to tighten. "I bet you take that for granted, too. I bet you don't even think about how lucky you are that you can just say and do what you want and not worry about what's going to happen."

"That's not what I said," Kane replied. "I don't go around saying jerky stuff to my parents all the time."

"Oh. Just only sometimes, when you can't help it?" she pushed, sounding even angrier. "And then what do you do? Do you lie to your friends? What kind of person are you?"

Afraid to reply to any of that, he held up his hands. "Naomi, I guess I'm the type of guy who should've known better than to come over here and try to talk to you. I guess I'm the type of person who shouldn't care about how you're feeling. I better go." He walked away, not looking back. As he heard her walk in the other direction, he realized that he had lost her.

Fifteen minutes later, when he was warming up on the field, Robert strode over to him.

"Thanks for telling me about Coach."

Huh, looked like he got lucky. "No problem. Is everything all right?"

"Yeah, sure. He just wanted me to help him figure out who was starting for today's game. Sorry, but you're not."

Kane opened his mouth to argue, but he knew he deserved Robert's bit of revenge. "That's too bad. Thanks for letting me know."

"Anytime," he said sarcastically.

"Oh, and Robert? I think Naomi really likes you."

274

Robert blinked. "You think so?"

"Oh, yeah." He even tried to smile and act like that didn't bother him at all.

"But wait a minute. I saw the way you were looking at her. I thought there was something between you and her."

"Nah, we're just friends. Barely that. I hardly know her."

"I've got to get to know her better." Readjusting the helmet on his head, he had the grace to look shamefaced. "Sorry about getting pulled off the starting lineup."

"It's no big deal. I didn't deserve it today. Maybe next time."

Robert nodded slowly. "Yeah, maybe next time."

Jogging to the locker room, Kane pulled out a piece of gum and started chewing, trying to think about nothing but the game.

He was pretty sure that was going to be impossible to do. All he could seem to think about was Naomi and the pain in her eyes. How she'd said he hadn't known how lucky he was. And how he was pretty sure that she was right.

TWENTY-SIX

"Anyway, before long, we finished the sandwiches, cleaned up our plates, and put my dress into the dryer. And then we sat by the side of his pool and stuck our feet in. The water felt cool and fresh. It looked a little blue and so very clean. It made me feel clean, too. I don't think I'll ever forget that feeling."

Thursday

The more time that passed since she and Naomi had spoken, the harder it was to smile.

"Miss, where exactly is your source for the alpaca yarn?"

"Hmm?" Kendra asked, trying hard to focus on what the lady in the gray tweed suit asked.

"I asked where the alpacas live. Are they local?"

"I don't know."

276

The woman pulled back her hand from the yarn she was practically caressing. "What do you mean? Could the animals be from a foreign country?"

After taking a deep breath and reminding herself not to tell the woman that alpaca fleece was alpaca fleece, no matter where they lived, Kendra replied, "I get the yarn from a weaver in Middlefield. She makes the yarn in her workshop on her property. So, *nee,* I don't reckon that the alpacas are living in another country."

The woman smiled again, which made Kendra even more confused about what was important and what wasn't. Or, perhaps, she simply didn't care about such things.

"I'll take a dozen skeins of that yarn, then." She pointed to the basket. "Would you mind getting them for me while I look at those vases and flower pots by the window?" She smiled brightly. "There really is so much to see in here."

"*Nee.* Of course not." Feeling as if she was on autopilot, Kendra bent down to count the skeins.

On another day, she'd be practically turning cartwheels in excitement. The alpaca yarn was by far her most expensive. Selling a dozen packets of it was going to not only make her feel as if her gamble on stocking the high-end merchandise had been the right decision, but it would also help her profits for the week.

But all she could think about was how she'd failed her sister and was likely going to lose her, just like she'd lost her other siblings.

The lady walked over with a vase and a bowl that Kendra had made over a year ago and had put in the store on a whim. "I love these!"

"I'm glad. Are you interested in one?"

"I'm interested in both, dear." She set each carefully on the countertop. "Do you have any idea who the artist is? Is he or she local?" she asked, just as the shop's door opened and Katie and Harley Lambright entered.

After glancing at her friends, Kendra nodded at the lady. "The artist is local. Very local. As a matter of fact . . . I made them."

"Did you really?"

"Um, *jah.* I enjoy throwing pots, you see."

The woman ran a hand down the curve of the vase that Kendra had glazed in an unusual shade of green. "This is far more than simply throwing pots, dear. This is a work of art. You're very talented."

She spoke so loudly that her friends walked closer.

"You really made this, Kendra?" Harley asked. "It's very fine."

"Danke."

The woman had turned her attention to the bowl. It had a fluted rim, was rather short and stumpy, and had been glazed a shiny black. "Tell me about this."

"Well, um, I thought the black color made it look kind of fancy. Less homespun."

"You were right. It would look great in anyone's kitchen or dining room." She held it up. "It's the perfect size to give as a gift, too."

Kendra held out her hands to take it. "I'm glad you like it. That makes me happy."

"May I order some more? Do you take special orders?"

"I don't have any on hand. But I suppose I could make more."

"How about ten more? Could you do that many?"

Ten? She'd priced each at twenty-five dollars. Ten more would earn her two hundred and fifty dollars. "Yes, um, I could do that." Remembering that Naomi might not be working at her store anymore, she said, "It might take some time, though. It's just me here, you see."

The lady looked crestfallen. "Oh dear. How long is 'some time'?"

"Well . . ."

"We could help you with the shop," Katie offered in a bright voice. "I'll ask all the girls, even Gabby, Kyle's wife."

"I couldn't ask you to do that."

"I know, which is why I'm offering." She turned to the woman. "Can you wait two weeks?"

The lady grinned like Katie had just offered her the moon and the stars. "I like how you think. Yes, of course." Opening up her purse, she said, "I'll buy the yarn and these two items. And if I gave you a deposit for the other ten, would that be sufficient?"

Kendra nodded. "How much would you like to put down?" She was starting to feel flustered.

"Half? That's, what?"

It was easy math, but at times like this her dyslexia kicked in. "Um . . ." She reached for her drawer, hoping against hope that she'd actually remembered to put a calculator inside.

"That will be a hundred and twenty-five," Harley said, stepping to her side. After quietly moving into her spot, he picked up her pencil, computed the rest of the woman's purchases, and gave her the total. "I'll take care of this for you, Kendra. I know how you like to wrap up your pottery with care."

"Oh. *Jah. Danke.*" Too grateful for her friends' help to be embarrassed, she pulled out some tissue paper and started carefully wrapping the bowl and vase.

Fifteen minutes later, the lady was out the door and Kendra was staring at a big check to deposit. "This is the biggest sale I've had since I opened the store."

"I don't think it's going to be the only one," Katie said. "She told me she was going to tell all her friends to come to your store."

"Boy, wouldn't that be something?"

Harley smiled at her. "You need to keep thinking positively. She'll come back, and she'll bring her friends. She really thought everything about Tried and True was wonderful — *gut.*"

"*Danke* for helping me with the math. I don't know what happened. I mean, I guess I panicked."

"Don't even worry about it. I'm glad I could help you out in a pinch," Harley replied as the door opened and Nate walked in.

Nate grinned at the sight of Harley and Katie. "Hi, you two." Walking up to Katie, he lowered his voice. "You look mighty pretty, Mrs. Lambright."

Katie wrapped an arm around her very big stomach. "You mean for a woman carrying around a basketball?"

"Carrying around basketballs looks *gut* on you," he teased before clasping Harley's hand. "On both of you."

"Danke."

Kendra bit her lip as she noticed that their usually very buttoned-up friend looked pleased as could be.

"So, what's going on?"

"We're recovering from one of Kendra's customers," Katie said. "The lady looked ready to practically buy out the store."

"Truly?" Nate smiled at her. "What happened?"

"She bought a lot of expensive yarn and a couple of pots."

"And ordered another ten more bowls that our Kendra made," Katie said. "Isn't that *wunderbaar*?"

Nate's gaze warmed. "It is, indeed."

Kendra felt as if his warm gaze had made its way directly into her center. She'd felt so empty before her friends and Nate had come over.

Suddenly realizing that none of them had come over to watch her sell things, she blurted, "Katie, Harley, I'm sorry, I haven't even asked what you needed."

"We did come over for a reason, but you already took care of it," Harley said. "We came to see how we could help you in the store."

"I'm so glad we did, too, since you're now going to be busy making pottery," Katie said. "By the beginning of next week one of us girls will stop by with a schedule for you."

"You will? Well, um, thank you."

"You need more help, Kendra?" Nate asked.

"I might. The shop is busier than I thought it would be. There seems to always be a lot to do. Some days, I don't think I'm going to be able to keep up with everything," she finished honestly.

"But what about your sister? I thought Nanny was going to be working here when she wasn't at school."

Though sharing the truth hurt, Kendra couldn't think of a way around it. She was going to need all the help she could get in order to make the shop a success. If she tried to do it all alone, she could lose everything she'd worked so hard to attain.

"Naomi was going to work a lot, but I don't know if that is going to happen anymore."

"How come?"

Kendra had to remind herself that Nate was simply curious and that she didn't have to tell him or Harley and Katie about her conversation with Nanny. However, everything inside of her was encouraging her to tell them the truth.

She was even hoping they could give her some advice.

"Well, um, it seems that my brother Chris told Naomi about what I did when I lived in Columbus. She was pretty upset about it. I mean, she was upset with me."

Katie's eyebrows rose so high they practically reached her hairline. "Kendra, Naomi had no right to judge you. I mean, doesn't she remember what you went through?" Continuing in a rush, she added, "And that Chris. I have to say that I'm fairly shocked. I *canna* believe he is throwing stones. Why, even I know how much you put yourself in between your parents and your little sisters and brothers. If it wasn't for you, his life would have been different."

She snuck a look at Nate. He was staring at her. She didn't need to know why — it was fairly obvious that he, like her little sister, had no idea what she'd done in Columbus. "Settle down now, Katie. There's no need to get so riled up."

"Someone has to!"

284

Looking pointedly at her stomach, Kendra said, "I think you should sit down and relax."

Katie shook her head. "My babe is fine."

Harley chuckled as he rubbed a hand along his petite wife's back. "She's just upset on your account. Nothing wrong with that. I'm pretty surprised about Chris and Naomi, too. What did they say?"

The words started tumbling out of her mouth before she could stop them. "Naomi said she couldn't believe I didn't tell her. She acted like that was the worst of it, but I know better. Harley, I know Naomi was upset with me. I think she's embarrassed about my past."

"Surely not."

"I'm afraid it's true. She was pretty upset about what Chris told her. Nothing I said seemed to do any good."

"What happened in Columbus, Kendra?" Nate blurted.

Maybe if they were alone, she would have hesitated. But here, with Katie and Harley, there was no reason to hide. They already knew about her dark past, and they still cared about her. "I started drinking and taking pills, Nate." When his expression went slack, she realized that she needed to put it all out there. "Um, the truth is, I was an addict. I had to go to rehab and get clean."

"When was this?"

It might have been her imagination, but it seemed like all of the muscles in his face had tensed up. "When I was seventeen and eighteen. About six years ago." For some reason, it was important to mention both of those years — two very bad years of her life.

Nate still looked like he didn't believe what she was saying. He waved a hand. "But . . . but look at you now."

Harley stepped closer to Kendra's left. "*Jah,* look at our Kendra. She's a successful businesswoman."

Katie gripped her right hand. "*Jah,* she is." Smiling at Kendra, she winked. "She's one of the strongest people I know . . . and she bakes like a dream, too."

Still aware of Nate studying her, Kendra deflected the compliments. "You two are too much. You're going to make my head swell."

"We didn't give you compliments, we told the truth."

"Oh, brother. May we please talk about something else now? You all are embarrassing me."

"If you're embarrassed, it's because you might be one of the humblest girls I know," Katie said.

286

Harley chuckled. "I think it's time we let you go. I need to calm my wife down, and it's time for you to end your day, *jah*?"

Surprised, Kendra looked at the time. Sure enough, it was five thirty. "*Jah.* It is time I put everything to rights and got on home."

Katie hugged her goodbye. "See you soon."

"*Jah.* See you soon. And thanks again for your help."

Harley, ever the protective one, paused. "Want to walk out with us, Nate?"

"*Nee,* the hardware store is open for another hour, and Ben and Kane have things under control."

After giving Kendra a long look filled with worry, Harley escorted Katie out.

When the door closed, Kendra braced herself for another difficult conversation. Gathering her courage, she turned. She needed to do this, needed to face him. But, boy, was it hard!

Feeling like she was about to face a firing squad, she exhaled. "You might as well say what you want to say, Nate. I'm listening."

She thought she might die if he rejected her right at this moment. *being Catholic*

He calmly walked to the front door, quietly turned the OPEN sign to CLOSED, and then walked back to her. "I'm going to hug you, Kendra," he murmured, just before he pulled her into his arms.

She stiffened in surprise.

"Hush now," he murmured. "Just relax for a second, Kendra."

It took a couple of cleansing breaths, but she was finally able to do just that. His chest was solid with muscle, and he smelled like fresh laundry and the lemon drops he had for sale on his store's counter. Sweet and clean and like Nate. It was an irresistible combination.

"Nate, what's this hug for?"

"For everything," he murmured as he brushed his lips against her cheek.

She closed her eyes and felt everything she'd been holding on to edge out of her.

This hug, this acceptance? Well, it was everything, too.

TWENTY-SEVEN

"And I couldn't believe it, but I started talking, too. I didn't talk about home or school. I told him about how one day I was going to be different, that everything about my life was going to be different."

Friday

Twenty-four hours had passed since Nate had held Kendra in his arms and had tried to comfort her. Twenty-four hours had passed, yet he was still furious.

For the life of him, he couldn't understand how Kendra's siblings could treat her the way they did. Though he knew there were usually two sides to every story, for the life of him, he couldn't imagine a situation in which Naomi would think it would be all right to side against her big sister. Especially in any way that would benefit their parents.

What really broke his heart was the way Kendra had accepted their decision. He knew that had stemmed from a lifetime of not expecting much from anyone else — no, from getting little to nothing from anyone else.

He couldn't believe that she had been born that way, either. He felt sure that she'd once been a little girl filled with hope.

He must have been scowling when he walked back into the hardware store because two customers took one look at him and walked in the opposite direction. Benjamin, who was working at the counter, paused for a moment in his conversation before continuing.

"Everything all right here?" Nate asked.

"Oh, *jah.* Everything's grand," Ben quickly replied. "No need to help me at the counter, boss. I'm doing just fine without ya."

That was Ben's not-so-subtle way of telling Nate he should go hide in his office until he could stop scaring the customers with his bad attitude.

Nate turned toward the back, deciding to do exactly that, but then he caught sight of Kane and had a better idea. Kane hadn't been scheduled to work, but Ben shared that the boy had called during his lunch to see if they needed any help. Ben had been pleased with the offer and told him to come on in.

290

That made Nate wonder if maybe Kane knew something, too. Maybe the boy could even give him some insight into the Troyer family that he hadn't been aware of.

When Kane saw him approach, he stopped chatting with old Mrs. Moss about the paint samples in her hand and stood up straighter. "Hiya, Mr. Miller."

"Hi, Kane." When he noticed that Mrs. Moss was eyeing him closely, he stepped closer. "Good day, Mrs. Moss."

"Nathan."

"I trust you are well?"

She gestured to the cane in her hand. "Well enough, I suppose. Your young man here is doing a *gut* job."

"That's good to hear."

He took a deep breath, hoping to calm himself down. "Kane, when Mrs. Moss is all set, come to my office for a moment, please. I need to speak to you."

"*Jah,* Mr. Miller. Will do."

"Good to see you, Mrs. Moss."

"Indeed." Her faded eyes peered at him closely before turning to Kane. "I need a gallon of Snowcap, or whatever that shade of white is, young man."

Nate heard Kane reply to the elderly lady as he walked into his office.

Opening the door, he was besieged with

291

the faint smell of tobacco, leather, and a variety of other scents that seemed to have embedded themselves into the woodwork over the last thirty years. But it wasn't just the scents that were so familiar, it was everything about the office. The leather chair that wasn't quite stable but brought back so many memories of his grandfather and uncle that he knew he'd never sit in anything else. The scars on the long wooden counter, evidence of the tools, gadgets, books, blocks, and change from a thousand pockets left scattered on top.

Smiling at a stray nickel, Nate picked it up and carefully put it into the change jar he'd given his grandfather one year for Christmas. The old man had very nicely thanked him for the gift then continued to leave his pocket change all over the counter. Only when he was older did he realize that Dawdi had left it out so Nate would have a reason to visit with him every day. He could still remember the way his grandfather used to prop him up on his lap and help him count the coins as they put them in the jar together.

Yes, the room made him feel at ease and his heart feel full. It symbolized a lifetime of being loved so much, of being given so many opportunities simply because he was family.

For some reason, it seemed fitting that Kendra was making a place for herself just two doors down. She was starting from scratch, while he was caretaker of two generations of hard work, dreams, and success.

The disparity between their two situations never failed to make him feel empty inside. He didn't understand why the Lord had given him such an easy life and Kendra such a hard one, but he was determined to lighten her load as best he could from now on.

Two light raps signaled Kane's arrival.

"Come in," Nate said, hoping against hope that he was going to be able to do the right thing now.

After the door closed behind him, Kane asked, "Is there a problem?"

"There is."

"Really?" Kane's voice practically went up an octave. "What did I do wrong?" A line formed in between his eyebrows. "Are you upset that I came in ten minutes late yesterday? I explained what happened to Ben . . ."

The boy's worried tone made him realize he needed to be more direct — and get a handle on himself. "Forgive me, Kane. I spoke out of turn. My problem, it ain't with you. It's about something else. I'm hoping you might help me gain some insight."

"Oh."

Kane looked completely perplexed, which wasn't really a surprise. Nate knew he was talking in vague riddles.

"Have a seat, wouldja? I just had a question, though now that I think about it, I probably shouldn't even be asking you."

Still looking wary, Kane sat down in one of the comfortable leather chairs that Nate's great-uncle had made. After staring at him a good long second, he said, "If I can help, I will, Mr. Miller. Ask me anything you want."

"That's mighty kind of you. But, well, it's not about the store. My question is about Naomi Troyer."

Back up went Kane's guard. "What about her?"

"I just needed to know something, but I don't want to pry too much. So I decided to ask one of her good friends."

"Oh." Kane shifted uncomfortably.

"I mean, you are friends with her, yes?"

"*Jah.* We're not real good friends yet, though. We just met." He stared at Nate. "But you already know that. What do you want to know?"

294

"It's nothing too personal. I promise you that. And, well, if you don't want to answer, you don't have to." Nate looked at him intently. "There aren't any strings involved. I promise."

"Okay."

"Has Naomi said anything to you about her sister or moving?"

The boy paused. "She said something about that the other day. Just a little bit." When Nate stayed quiet, giving Kane time to weigh his words, he added, "Naomi said she might be moving because she did something to upset her sister."

"That's what she said?"

Kane nodded. "She didn't tell me much, but I didn't ask a lot of questions, either. I got the feeling that her family is pretty complicated."

Nate almost felt like smiling. Saying they were complicated was a pretty kind way of describing the Troyers. "I think you're right," he said slowly. "They, well, they certainly are <u>complicated</u>. Thanks for speaking with me. You better get outside and help Ben now. Tell him that I'll be out to finish up the day in a minute."

"All right." Just before Kane walked back into the shop, he looked in Nate's direction. "Um, for what it's worth, I got the feeling that Naomi is pretty upset because she feels like Kendra will never forgive her. But I told her she needs to put her doubts to the side and start trusting more, you know? We are all imperfect, but God still loves us. I could be wrong, but I don't think we're supposed to forget that."

"I don't think you're wrong at all. In fact, I think you're very right."

"I could talk to her, if you'd like. Try to convince her to talk to her sister and put everything out in the open."

"I think that would help Kendra, but I don't want you to feel obligated."

"I don't, Mr. Miller. I offered, *jah*?" Looking determined, he said, "I'll go this evening after work."

"If you're willing to talk to her, then you can leave whenever you're ready. I'm sorry to put you in a tight spot, Kane, but I appreciate you helping me out. *Danke.*"

Kane smiled at him before walking out the door and closing it behind him.

When he was alone again, Nate realized he had an answer for Kendra at last. God already forgave a pure heart. And since that was the case, he felt sure Naomi would come to her senses soon and Kendra would forgive her.

They'd forgive each other.

TWENTY-EIGHT

"That's when Andy looked a little sad and said he wasn't sure what he wanted to do. He shared that he didn't have any big dreams. When I asked him how that could be, he said it was because he already had everything he ever wanted."

Friday

Kane knew he was going to have to find Naomi and talk to her. The minute Mr. Miller told him that he could leave as soon as he was ready, he pulled out his cell phone and texted his mother, saying he was going to be an hour late.

Since his mother knew he was at work, she texted him right back and said she'd keep supper warm, obviously thinking he was working late.

Kane decided it was a good idea to let her believe that. It was a whole lot easier than trying to explain why he suddenly felt the need to try to fix things between Naomi and her sister.

Now all he had to do was find Naomi. First, he went to Tried and True and peeked in. The sign on the door said closed, and it was completely dark inside. So, Naomi hadn't come back to the shop.

Kane didn't think she would have gone home so early. It was only seven, so she had to have gone someplace where she could wait for the time to pass.

After giving it some thought, he walked over to the bleachers at the high school. Naomi didn't know a lot of people and she probably didn't want to wander around Walnut Creek by herself.

He soon found out that his hunch was right. She was sitting on one of the metal benches, three rows from the bottom. She was hunched over with her elbows resting on her knees. When she saw him, instead of sitting up straighter or greeting him, she just looked away. With most people, he would have taken that for what it was — a sure sign to leave her alone.

He approached her anyway. His tennis shoes crunched on the gravel. During the day or during a game, it made only the faintest of noises, but on a clear night like tonight, when they were the only two people around? His footsteps seemed to echo around them.

"Hey," he said when he got close enough that he wouldn't have to yell.

"Hi, Kane."

He paused, half waiting for her to gesture for him to sit down and join her.

She didn't.

He sat anyway, taking a spot two rows below her. "You know, I'm kind of congratulating myself right now. I thought there was a pretty good chance you'd be here, and I was right."

"Good for you."

He turned, bracing his arms on either side of him so he wouldn't fall backward. "So, aren't you gonna ask why I was looking for you?"

"All right." Looking even grumpier, she said, "Why are you here, Kane?"

"Because I just talked to my boss about you."

"Why?" For the first time since he arrived, she looked alert.

"Because he likes your sister Kendra. And Kendra's upset because she thinks you're mad at her."

Her whole expression fell. "Kendra talked to Nate about our conversation?"

"Well, yeah," he said. "And don't act so

offended. I told you they were close. But you had to know that anyway, right?"

"I knew they were friends . . . but I didn't know they were that close."

"Come on. I'm a guy, and I've noticed there's something going on between them." Grinning at her shocked expression, he added, "Naomi, you had to have seen the way that Nate's eyes follow Kendra whenever they're in the same room?"

"Well, yes. I know that they've gotten closer." Looking uncomfortable, she added, "I've also learned not to think too hard about men looking at my big sister. Sometimes guys stare at her. I don't know why."

Oh, he knew. Kane almost shared that he reckoned every man thought Kendra was pretty. Even Kane thought Kendra Troyer was gorgeous, and she was far older than he was. But he also knew it wasn't just her looks. It was the sad light in her eyes that made everyone take a second look at her. He'd even seen Ben do it.

But no way was he going to share any of that. He didn't want Naomi to take it the wrong way — or think Kane didn't think she was just as pretty in her own way.

Instead, he focused on what was important, the fact that both of the women needed to have a good talk as soon as possible.

"Naomi," he said softly. "It's a good thing she shared with him."

"I suppose." She wrinkled her nose. "But I don't get why Nate talked to you."

"Because he wanted to know how he could help. I think he's afraid something bad happened between the two of you."

"It did. She told me something in confidence, and I practically turned away from her." She shook her head. "I focused on me instead of her feelings. Just like I always have."

"I told him you knew you'd made a mistake with her."

"And then what did he say?"

"Nothing. He had to go back to work, and so did I. But then, when he said I could leave early, I decided to find you." He looked around. "I'm sorry you're sitting here by yourself."

"Me, too. I thought I needed time to think. But all I've been doing is thinking, and it's not helping much."

"I'm glad I found you, then."

"Any idea what I should do now?"

"You need to go home." He stood up and held out his hand. "Let's go. I'll walk you."

His statement startled a laugh from her.

301

"Seriously?"

"It's getting dark. No way am I going to let you walk home in the dark by yourself."

"What about your Jeep?"

"I didn't bring it to work today." He reached out for her. "Come on. Take my hand. I've got to get home, too."

She rested her hand in his and let him pull her up. "All right."

Kane helped her walk down the bleachers, though she didn't need any help, then he dropped her hand as soon as they got on the solid ground.

"What's the best way to walk to your house?"

She pointed toward the ball field. "That way. Kendra's place is just on the other side."

"That close? It's almost faster to walk to school than drive, isn't it?"

"It is if you're not carrying around a bunch of books or a cooler."

He smiled at the reminder . . . before realizing how much he'd miss her if she was gone. "Hey, Naomi? Are you still going to leave?"

"I don't know." She walked carefully along the gravel until they came to the manicured path that ran around the perimeter of the field. "When I told Kendra that, I was mad at her. I was sure anything would be better than living with her."

"And now?"

"Now? I realize that was a stupid thing to think."

"Is she really that hard to live with?" Kendra had seemed nice.

Naomi stopped and looked at him in shock. "No. *Nee!* I was just mad at her. She's great."

"Not to be rude, but if she was that great, you wouldn't be thinking of leaving, would you?"

"Not if I wasn't in a snit." Her voice still sounded mystified. "But really, you have no idea . . ."

"About what?"

"About what we have to compare things to. I promise you, even if you tried to imagine a really bad home situation, you wouldn't even come close."

"Oh. So . . ."

They were at the edge of the ball field. On the other side of the chain-link fence was a residential street, illuminated by a street-lamp. Kane could see Naomi's expression, and it was wrecked. She was so upset that she looked beyond tears.

"So, I made a big mistake, Kane. I wasn't sitting on those bleachers wondering where to go next. I was sitting there, wondering how I was ever going to make Kendra understand that my home is with her. I want her to trust me with her heart again."

"All you have to do is tell her that."

She shook her head. "That's not enough."

Kane realized then that Naomi still had a lot to learn about love and trust. "Look, I'm no expert, but I can promise you that love, especially between siblings and family members, isn't about being 'good enough' or never making mistakes. It's just there."

"You really believe that, don't you?"

"Yep." He smiled to himself as they slipped through the narrow opening in the fence and got to her street.

"Here it is," she said.

Looking again at the variety of plants and flowers surrounding the little walkway leading up to the front door, he said, "It's a small *haus,* but really pretty, Naomi."

"I've always thought that, too," she murmured as they approached. "Kendra is a really good housekeeper and gardener."

Stopping on the street, he noticed a faint light shining through the white curtains in the front of the house. "It looks like she's home."

"I'm sure she is. Kendra likes to use a battery-operated light and either work on a sewing project or read in the evenings."

"Maybe she's also waiting for you."

"I guess I need to go in now."

She looked so nervous. If they were closer, he'd give her a reassuring hug. Instead he did the next best thing. "I'll stand here until you get safely inside."

She took a step, then looked back at him. "Would you do me one last favor? After the door closes, would you count to a hundred before you walk away?"

"A hundred?"

"*Jah.* Just in case things don't go well. That gives Kendra a minute or two to tell me off."

He almost laughed, until he realized Naomi was completely serious. "Sure, I can count to a hundred before I leave." Then, he decided to do something even better. "Hey, give me your hand real quick."

As she held out her left hand, he pulled a pen out of his pocket and wrote down his landline number. "This is our kitchen phone. If something goes wrong later or even tomorrow before school, give me a call, and I'll help you decide what to do."

She looked down at her palm. "You're serious, aren't you?"

"Yep." He reached out and folded her hand into a fist. "Now, go on, Naomi."

When she still hesitated, he said, "Sorry, but I really do have to go home."

"Oh, sure. Sorry. But thanks for tonight."

Instead of answering, he made a shooing motion with his hands. Then he stood there as she took a deep breath and finally walked to the house. When she knocked on the door, he stepped a little further into the shadows and held his breath as a couple of seconds passed.

Finally, the door opened. "Naomi!" Kendra said as she pulled her into a hug. "Oh, praise God."

He started counting after the door shut again, but as he saw the faint shadows through the curtains, he knew he was only counting because he had made a promise to Naomi, not because he was worried about her.

By the time he reached ninety, he was whistling softly, feeling pretty good about the whole situation.

Then he hurried home.

When he opened the kitchen door, his mother sighed in relief.

"Kane, we were starting to worry about you," his dad chided.

"I know. I'm sorry I'm home so late. I, well, I had to help out a friend."

His mother, who was pulling his plate out

from the refrigerator, glanced his way. "Oh? Is everything okay?"

"I think so. I'll tell you all about it while I eat."

Ten minutes later, after he'd washed up, he was sitting at the table with his parents and a full plate of spaghetti and meatballs in front of him.

"So, I met this girl. Her name's Naomi, and I like her a lot," he began. He told her story as he ate, realizing as he did that he'd never again take all his blessings for granted.

TWENTY-NINE

"We must have sat there for hours, me and Andy. Talking about nothing. Eventually, I went back inside and put on my now-clean dress, which smelled like his mother's dryer sheets. Then, I helped Andy clean up the kitchen so good, no one would have ever guessed we'd been there."

Friday

She couldn't stop crying. "I'm so sorry," Naomi said into Kendra's neck for about the fifth time. "Will you ever forgive me?"

"There's nothing to forgive."

Naomi knew Kendra would say that no matter what and that she might actually believe it, but she didn't feel like that simple acceptance was enough. "I shouldn't have acted like I deserved to know all of your secrets. I don't know why I listened to Chris."

With a sigh, Kendra pulled away. "Chris

was only trying to help you."

"Sometimes he acts like our parents weren't any different from all his friends' parents," Naomi said. "Like, they just sometimes forgot to buy us milk or something. I don't understand it. Do you?"

"*Nee*. I can't speak for him. I can only guess that he finds that an easier way to cope with the memories," Kendra said slowly.

"So he copes by lying?" she cried. "By lying to us? We know what it was like, Kendra."

"Come on, let's go sit down."

Naomi followed her into the kitchen, sitting down on one of the chairs as Kendra put the kettle back on the stove. Blue trotted over to her, circling her feet. Kendra bent down and patted her dog before walking to the covered cake holder. "I made some blondies. Would you like one, Naomi?"

She got to her feet. "Would you mind if I made a sandwich first? I didn't eat supper." She actually hadn't eaten for hours.

"Help yourself. You know you don't have to ask. Anything that's here is for you."

She grabbed the peanut butter, some freshly made bread, and strawberry jam that Kendra had put up in the spring. The peanut butter and jelly sandwich was anything but simple, thanks to the freshly made ingredients. By the time Naomi sat down again, she felt better. Maybe not completely calmed down but ready to listen and speak without getting overwrought.

Holding a mug of tea between her hands, Kendra sat down across from her. For a few minutes, neither said a word. Kendra sipped her tea and Naomi ate her sandwich. When she was done, Kendra took her plate and put it in the sink. Then she sat back down and finally spoke.

"Naomi, all five of us kids are survivors. But that doesn't mean we are completely healed or don't ever make mistakes. Even survivors can be flawed, don't you think?"

"I never thought of all of us as being survivors."

"Well, I think if we got out the dictionary, we might see that the definition of a survivor fits us like a glove." She leaned back. "I've never actually talked about this with the others, but I think we all coped with our father's abuse and our mother's denial in different ways. The way we grew up wasn't normal. It's not normal to be denied food, shelter, or decent clothing. It's not okay to expect to be hit or yelled at for no reason other than it was easy to abuse us because we had nowhere else to go." Her voice cracking, Kendra said, "It wasn't okay for our parents to expect their oldest child to raise four younger siblings."

"But Chris pretends that it wasn't so bad."

"*Jah.* I think he does that real well."

"But why?"

"I think it's easier for Chris to forget the bad things and concentrate on the man he is now," she said after a pause. "And that man wants to do everything right. He wants to care for his little sister, honor his mother, and forgive his father."

"But what about you? He isn't treating you all that good."

"Well, now, I don't know why," she said, "but he'd rather focus on the things I shouldn't have done in Columbus instead of what I did for him when we were little."

"That's not fair, though."

Kendra waved a hand. "Everyone can agree it wasn't good that I started drinking so much that I blacked out all the time. It wasn't good that I started taking pills and did all sorts of things to support my habit. Having to go to an institution to get clean when I was only eighteen years old isn't something to be proud of."

"He still shouldn't judge you."

Kendra's voice hardened. "No, he shouldn't. But here's where he's wrong,

311

Naomi. He brought it up to you because he thinks I'm trying to be something I'm not. But that's not true. I don't bring it up because I'm not proud of myself, and that's not the person I am any longer."

"I was upset because I never knew. You've been there for me my whole life, but you've kept this big secret. Chris caught me off guard."

"I can understand that. But maybe there's a part of you that can appreciate *why* I never wanted to tell you about something I did back when you were just ten years old."

"That was a long time ago."

"Exactly. I was alone, I was hurting, but I'm not alone or hurting anymore. And I'm okay if you are never okay with my past. You don't even have to understand it, but I would hate it if you took a bad part of my life and decided that those two years were more important than the other twenty-two."

"I don't feel that way."

"I am grateful for that." Kendra stood up and brought over the plate of blondies as well as a couple of napkins. After taking one for herself, she slid the plate Naomi's way. "Now, moving on, I could have sworn I saw someone standing in our front yard when I peeked out the window before I opened the door. Was that my imagination?"

Naomi hadn't been planning to tell Kendra about her walk with Kane, but now she was thinking it would feel funny not to share that experience. "It was Kane."

"Kane, as in the boy who works at Nate's hardware store and has been picking you up in the mornings?"

"Uh-huh. I guess Nate talked to him about our argument."

"What? He shouldn't have done that."

"Watch it, Kendra. If you protest too much, you might have to eat your words about being open and discussing things."

She groaned. "I hear you. So, Nate talked to Kane who talked to you?"

"Kind of. Kane told me he didn't know too much, but he decided to look for me."

"Where did he find you?"

"At the high school. I was sitting on the bleachers by myself. We talked, then he said he didn't want me to walk home alone in the dark."

"That was nice of him."

"He's a nice boy."

Kendra's eyes warmed. "It sounds like it." Just as she looked like she was going to say something else, there was a knock at the door.

Kendra started. "I don't know who that could be. It's late."

313

Naomi stood up. "Let's go together." She ran ahead of Kendra and, ignoring her sister's words of caution, peeked out the front window to see who had arrived. "Uh, Kendra?"

"Who is it?" Not ready for another round of sibling drama, she groaned. "Uh-oh. Please don't tell me it's Chris or Jeremiah."

"It ain't them." Turning to Kendra, Naomi's eyes were wide. "I think all of your friends are here."

"What?" She threw open the door and then gaped at the crowd on her stoop.

"Hey, Kendra. It's *gut* to see that you're home," John B. said as he led at least ten people inside.

She stood to one side as her best friends filed in through the door. Most were members of the Eight, but some were part of their larger circle: Harley Lambright's younger brother, Kyle, and his new wife, Gabby. And Nate. Nate was there, looking like he didn't want to be anywhere else in the world.

As Naomi stood at the door, trying to come up with a reason why they all showed up unannounced so late at night, John B. moved to her side. "Hiya, Nanny."

"Hiya. Uh, what are you all doing here?"

"Let's go sit in your cozy living room,

314

Kendra," Elizabeth Anne said. "We have some news we need to share."

Naomi scanned all of the Eight's expressions. They looked serious and wary, some even sad. Looking back at her sister, she saw Kendra had paled. Yes, whatever had happened was bad. Really bad.

"I'll put on some coffee," Naomi said, more for a reason to escape the tension filling the room than as a desire to be helpful.

"I'll take care of it instead," Katie said. "You go sit down with your sister."

"But —"

"I can help. I'm good at making coffee," Marie said. "Let's make a full pot, Katie. I think we're going to need a lot of it tonight."

Now Naomi was starting to feel ill. She hoped she would be able to keep it together for Kendra.

THIRTY

"And then it was time for me to go. Andy walked me halfway home.

"And as far as I can tell, no one in my family ever figured out that I didn't go to school that day. If the receptionist in the attendance office tried to call, no one ever told me."

Friday Night

Kendra was trying really hard not to bite her nails. These were her best friends in the world, and they'd all shown up after eight at night. This wasn't only unusual, it had never happened before.

Something was wrong — really wrong — and every guess she had was even worse than the last. At first, all she could think was that one of their friends had gotten hurt, but as she looked at all the members

316

of the Eight, she couldn't find anyone missing.

To make things worse, not a one of them seemed ready to divulge the real reason they'd shown up. Instead, Marie and Katie were making coffee in the kitchen, and everyone else was attempting to make small talk with Naomi.

The whole situation was excruciating.

Desperate, she walked to Harley. He was not only standing close to her — and therefore couldn't dodge her concerns — but he wouldn't brush off a direct question. Harley simply wasn't that way.

"You've got to tell me what is going on," she said under her breath.

"Kendra —"

"*Nee,* listen. If whatever you all have come about concerns Naomi, I need to be able to make things easier for her. I can't do that if I'm in the dark."

"I think you should go sit down and relax," he said gently. "Let us worry about your sister for a time."

That didn't make any sense at all. "Harley —" she began but saw he'd already stepped away. She tried a couple of other attempts with Tricia and Logan, but they ignored her question and instead relayed a story about Tricia's latest attempt to drive a buggy.

317

Just when she was ready to interrupt Logan, Marie appeared with a tray of coffee cups. "The coffee is ready," she announced. "Kendra, that is one terrific percolator. It brewed a whole pot in no time at all."

"*Danke,*" she said weakly as she watched her ten friends surround Marie like they were in the middle of a church social in May. After refusing her own cup, she stood to one side while everyone else helped themselves to mugs of coffee.

By the time Marie sat down, Kendra was done waiting. "As much as I enjoy watching you all enjoy my coffee in my little living room, I know you all didn't show up here by accident. Would someone please, please tell me what is going on?"

To her surprise, it was Nate who answered. "Kendra, I'm afraid it's not good news."

"What has happened?"

Nate looked at everyone, then blurted, "I've got a good friend from high school who now works at the hospital over in Millersburg. Brandt knew you and I've been seeing each other."

"Okay . . ."

Looking like every word was getting painfully pulled from him, Nate said, "Brandt called me an hour ago."

"Nate, what happened?"

318

"It's your father."

"What about him?" Naomi asked weakly.

"Kendra, Naomi, I'm very sorry, but your father started having trouble breathing a couple of hours ago. Then it seems his heart stopped."

Kendra swallowed hard. "Stopped?"

"*Jah.* Unfortunately, they couldn't revive him. He . . . he died. Your father died."

And just like that all the air escaped her lungs.

Back in high school when he had torn his rotator cuff after pitching six innings and gotten rushed into surgery, Nate had thought he knew what real pain was.

Now, seeing the devastated look on Kendra's face, he realized he hadn't even come close. Real pain wasn't a physical injury. No, it was seeing someone you loved hurting and not being able to do a single thing to make it better.

Hating the fact that he hadn't found a way to break the news in a gentler manner, and that he now didn't know what to do, he looked around the room. Katie and Tricia were looking at the floor. Marie was holding John's hand and biting her bottom lip. E.A. had wrapped an arm around Naomi and was whispering.

But to his surprise, it was Harley Lambright who knelt in front of Kendra. His expression was as serious as it was set. His eyes full of compassion as he reached out and took hold of both of her hands, he said, "I'm real sorry, Kendra. I know that this is hard news to hear."

Kendra nodded. "I suppose it is."

"What are you feeling?" Harley said the words so quietly that if Nate hadn't been hovering he wouldn't have heard a word.

"Confused," she replied. Raising her chin, she shrugged. "I don't know. Empty?" She looked around the room. "Is that bad?"

"I think you're entitled to feel any way you want," Nate said.

"Really? Do you think the Lord is fine with me not crying right now?"

Harley seemed to think about it hard before replying. "I think He knows you well enough to be all right with you being yourself, Kendra."

"Maybe so." Smiling softly, she squeezed his hands. "*Danke,* Harley."

With a nod, he got back to his feet and returned to Katie's side.

After casting another look in her sister's direction, Kendra stood up. "Thank you all for coming over here," she said. "I am glad you all were the ones to let me and my sister know. That means a lot."

"It feels right for us all to be here," Marie said. After darting a glance in Naomi's direction, she added, "I would never want you to think that you were alone during this time."

"I appreciate that." Still looking shaken but determined, Kendra cleared her throat. "Nate, did Brandt give you any other information?"

Nate knew the only way he could handle telling Kendra was to reply honestly and without any emotion. "Brandt said that for the last two days, everyone knew there was nothing to be done for your father. His liver wasn't working. The poisons in his blood that his liver wasn't filtering were taking over his body. Plus, his heart wasn't working too well, either. He got worse every day."

Kendra nodded. "So it was just a matter of time."

"I suppose so."

"I'm really sorry," Tricia said. "I know hearing such news can be hard."

"I guess." Kendra's eyes widened just before her expression seemed to shatter. "He was such a bad man," she sputtered, tears filling her eyes. "It's no wonder the Lord made him die the way he did, with poisons destroying his body. He was toxic

321

in life, too." As if she'd just realized what she said, she pressed a hand to her mouth and ran out of the room.

While all of them stood there gaping, Naomi started crying harder.

Nate could practically feel everyone's shock. He felt like a bull in a china shop. Surely there would have been a better way to deliver the news. "I'm sorry," he said to everyone. "I thought it would be best to not try to keep anything from Kendra and Naomi, but it was obviously the wrong way to go. I seem to have just made things worse."

"You didn't, Nate," Naomi said as she got to her feet. "It's just . . . well, see, the problem is that where our father and my sister are concerned — their relationship couldn't have been worse."

Releasing a ragged sigh, she turned to E.A. "I'm going to go to my room. Would you please check in on Kendra? I know she's really hurting. I'd try to comfort her, but . . . I don't think I'm who she needs right now."

"Of course," E.A. replied.

All of them sat in silence as they watched Naomi walk down the short hallway and close the door to her bedroom.

"I'm not sure what to do right now," Marie said. "Kendra's the best at comforting everybody."

Katie smiled at her. "You know what? You're right. We've all leaned on her at one time or another. She's always been there for us, making things better."

"I can do that for her now," E.A. said. "And then I'll just camp out here in the living room until she needs me."

"I'll stay here in case they need something, too," Nate volunteered. "I'm not a great cook, but I can heat up a can of soup or something."

"Are you two really that close now?" Will asked.

"I want to be." The moment he said the words he wanted to take them back. What did such a thing even mean?

Marie grinned at him. "Even though this is such a tough time, you made me happy."

"Do you think wanting to be there for someone counts?"

"I think it's half the battle."

Harley stood up. "Katie, we need to get home. You need your rest."

"We'll go ahead, too," Logan said as he and Tricia, and Kyle and Gabby, headed to the door. "In this case, I think less people here is more."

Soon John B. and Will left as well, leaving

just Nate, Marie, E.A., and a stack of coffee cups.

"Want to wash some dishes?" Nate asked, yearning to go check on Kendra but knowing that being alone with her in her bedroom was inappropriate.

"Sure," said Marie. "E.A., what do you think?"

"I'll help, but first I think I'd better check on Kendra. Even if she doesn't want us in her room, I want to make sure she knows we didn't all abandon her."

When the door closed again, Nate walked to the sink and started running the water. "I wish there was something I could do that would help Kendra. Unfortunately, I'm at a loss."

Marie helped him place all the cups in the sink. "I am, too, but I'm glad we're going to stay here tonight. Even if Kendra never comes out of that room, I agree with E.A. I want her to know we didn't leave."

"I want that, too. I think a lot of people have left her over the years."

"That's how life is, though, right? We drift apart, we come back together. Sometimes things are good, and then they aren't. I don't think it matters if things aren't the same. What matters is that we have friends who help us get through the changes."

"Well said." He scrubbed a couple of cups with a soapy sponge, rinsed them, and then handed them to Marie. "I think you've gotten wiser since marrying John."

She smiled. "Maybe I have. Love makes everything better."

"I think I love Kendra," he confided.

"I know you do."

"Really? How can you be so sure?" He'd barely realized it himself.

"Nate, anyone who saw you telling her the bad news would know you loved her," she said as she dried a mug with a dog on it and put it on a shelf. "It was written all over your face when you looked at her. And what we couldn't see was embedded in your voice."

Was that really the case? Part of him hoped so. He didn't want to play games, but he just wasn't sure how Kendra would take a confession of his love. "I don't know if she feels the same way. I continually seem to do the wrong thing where she's concerned."

"Don't be so hard on yourself," Marie said. "You know, I don't think there's one right way to go about having a relationship, Nate."

"You don't think that's oversimplifying things?"

"Maybe, or maybe not. I've recently learned that we don't always need the same things all the time. Sometimes John wants me to sit with him and talk things through, and other times, he would rather I leave him alone so he can go take a long walk. I've had to learn that I need to respect that."

"That's good advice. I need to remember that."

"You will . . . or Kendra will probably let you know," she said with a smile. "Women have a way of making sure their guys know what's right."

THIRTY-ONE

"I never knew about that, either," E.A. said. "That's so strange, because Andy knew you and I were friends."

Friday Night

"I decided not to knock because you need me," E.A. said as she walked into Kendra's room. "So don't even think about asking me to turn back around."

Blue, who'd been sleeping in Kendra's bed the whole time, gave a little bark of alarm. Immediately, E.A. reached down to pet the dog.

Sitting in her beautiful maple rocking chair next to her bed, Kendra muttered, "Do you ever get tired of always being right?"

"Of course I do, but *someone* has to be right all the time. Ain't so?" E.A. chuckled softly before continuing. "I figured if that's the case, that person might as well be me."

327

"Oh, E.A. You are a piece of work."

"I know, but I'm your piece of work." Her voice softened. "Are you okay?"

"I don't know." So far, the only thing she'd been feeling was numb. She hadn't been able to do much of anything besides listen to the quiet murmur of her friends in the living room.

She'd relaxed when she'd heard the eventual sounds of her front door opening and shutting. "I thought everyone had gone," she admitted.

"Most everyone did, but I decided to stay. So did Marie." She smiled faintly. "And so did Nate."

That surprised her. "Nate's still here?"

"Oh, *jah.*" She smiled softly. "I think if Nate wasn't so afraid of you kicking him out, he'd be in here with you right now instead of me."

"I wouldn't have kicked him out. But I don't know what I would've said to him." She curved her arms around her middle, hugging herself tight.

"That's the thing, Kendra. None of us are expecting you to say anything."

E.A.'s comment was so wise and, she reckoned, true. If their positions were reversed and she was the one sitting on the bed offering comfort, she would have done the same thing. Actually, she had said almost the very same words to Naomi before.

But now? Well, at the moment, she wasn't sure what to do. She felt strangely hollow, like all that was inside her was a bunch of emptiness. She sure didn't feel like she was in any position to comfort Naomi.

Looking for the right words, she turned her head to look at E.A. "Do you have much experience with death? I mean, other than Andy?"

"*Nee.*"

"I don't, either. I've had loss and hard times, but I've lost only Andy. This feels different, though."

E.A. sat down on Kendra's bed and kicked her feet out. When Blue snuggled next to her, she rubbed her side absently. "I bet it does. You adored Andy and hated your father."

The words were so shocking, Kendra laughed. "I *canna* believe you just said that."

"Why? It was obvious there was something special between you and Andy."

Yep, E.A. had just sidestepped her father and focused on the boy they both missed so much.

Remembering a day she'd spent with him back in high school but had never breathed a word about to anyone, Kendra said, "There was something special between me and Andy. Some people thought I had a crush on him, but it wasn't that. Andy . . . well, he helped me out one time."

"Really?"

Kendra nodded. "Andy was really kind to me during a time when I sometimes felt really alone. He did me a big favor, and more importantly, he kept that secret."

"I'm impressed." E.A. smiled sadly. "Our Andy really was more than we all knew, wasn't he?"

"I always thought so."

They sat quietly for a bit, Kendra trying to put a name to the way she was feeling, E.A. looking just as reflective. After a while E.A. spoke again. "Your father never apologized for all the things he did to you, did he?"

"*Nee.* I didn't expect it, though."

"Really? Not ever?"

"I don't know if he even remembered everything he did. He had a bad drinking problem. *Mei mamm* used to use that as an excuse, saying he couldn't be held accountable for his temper or for any of it. I never believed that excuse, though."

"Of course not. You were a child, and your parents should have protected you."

E.A.'s voice was so sure, so matter-of-fact, that it almost made her smile. If only life were so cut-and-dried. She swiped at a tear rolling down her cheek. "My mother and my brothers came to see me a couple of days ago. They said my father didn't have much time to live and that I should see him in the hospital."

E.A. shifted. "Did you go?"

"Me? Oh, *nee*. I said I was still angry at him and didn't feel anything for him, but that wasn't the whole truth." Even though E.A. didn't prod, Kendra gathered her courage and admitted the awful truth. "I think there's a part of me that was still afraid of him. Isn't that something? Even after all this time?"

"Of course you were. You didn't know your father could be anything but scary and abusive." E.A. paused, then continued. "Life with my parents was much different, but I think there's always an invisible barrier that's hard to cross. It's hard to defy them."

"I suppose." She shifted. "I guess what I'm struggling with right now is that all I feel is relief. That's it. I'm relieved I won't have to see my father again."

"Kendra, that's okay."

"Naomi isn't going to feel that way. Neither are my other siblings."

"So?" When Kendra stared at her in surprise, E.A. continued, "They aren't children anymore. Not even Naomi. She might be sixteen, but she made the choice to move out of that house and in with your grandparents. Now she just made the choice to leave them and move in with you. She's a girl who knows her mind."

That described Naomi to a T. "I hear you."

"And even if she is upset, if they're all upset, that's okay. You lived your first sixteen years putting their needs first. Because of that, you took the bulk of the abuse and the least amount of food and who knows what else? They can come to terms with the fact that you are just as human as the rest of your family. You aren't Kendra 'Superwoman' Troyer. You're just Kendra."

She was right. All she could be was herself. Imperfect, fallible, maybe a little broken. But she was also a good person, she knew that.

"I didn't know I needed you here, E.A. But it seems I really did."

E.A. reached out and held her hand. "I'm glad about that."

An hour after E.A. went into Kendra's room, both of them came out. E.A. looked thoughtful. And Kendra? Well, she looked much better.

As Kendra walked into the kitchen bare-foot, her dress wrinkled, and her eyes a little swollen, Nate thought he'd never been more transfixed by anyone. She had to be the strongest person he'd ever met.

"*Danke* for staying," she said quietly. "I appreciate it."

"I told him that E.A. and I could handle everything, but he wouldn't take no for an answer," Marie said.

"I only stayed for self-preservation. If I left, all I'd be doing is wondering about you. At least this way I know you are all right."

"I am." She smiled so sweetly, that if they were alone, he would have crossed the room and pulled her into his arms. "Have you seen Naomi?"

Marie shook her head. "I knocked on her door about a half hour ago and asked if she wanted company. She told me to stay out."

"Ouch." She looked worriedly down the hall.

"Oh, no you don't," E.A. said. "Remember what we talked about?"

"Yes, ma'am," Kendra replied. "I *canna* rush over and make everything better. Not anymore."

"Good girl."

"So, it's going on a quarter to eleven,"

Nate said. "I don't know about you three, but I'm hungry. I thought I'd make up some omelets. Anyone want one?"

"You know how to make those?"

"I grew up in a slightly less traditional house. When we were hungry in between meals, my mother told us to go feed ourselves. Me and my brother got pretty good at boiling noodles and making egg dishes."

"In that case, I'd love an omelet," Marie said. "I was just looking through the kitchen to see what I could come up with."

Looking skeptical, E.A. said, "What did you find?"

"Toast," she said sheepishly. "I can make a pretty good piece of toast."

"We'll put you in charge of that, then," E.A. said as she joined Nate behind the counter.

"What are you going to make?" Marie asked.

"I'm going to fry bacon of course." E.A. turned to Kendra. "And before you offer to help, the answer is no, go sit down."

Smiling, Kendra sat.

Nate walked to her and rubbed her back softly. "It's good to see you smile, Kendra." Before she could answer, he kissed her brow.

Though he could tell that E.A. and Marie

were smirking at him, he couldn't care less. He was exactly where he wanted to be.

Thirty-Two

"Well, there's a story there, I think. Maybe four or five days after Andy and I spent the day together, I saw him at the park by the high school. He was walking through with a couple of his buddies, and I was taking Chris to the park to play on the swings. We were walking toward each other, and when we got close, I kind of smiled. But Andy looked like he'd never seen me before in his life. He looked right through me."

Sunday

A full day had passed since they'd gotten the news. However, Naomi felt so raw and confused inside that she figured it might have only been one hour. Her emotions kept flip-flopping. Sometimes she'd feel a deep loss, and minutes later, she would accept his passing. Then, on its heels was a sense of dismay that things with her father had never actually changed. That was the hardest part, she thought. As much as she hadn't really liked her father, she still loved him. And she'd secretly wished he would one day change and be the man she'd always hoped he would be. Now that would never happen.

Soon after Nate had told them about Daed, Kendra's phone had rung. Jeremiah had called to tell them the news. Naomi had overheard Kendra accept the news with little emotion in her tone.

Later, when she and her sister were alone, Kendra had informed her that Mary was due to arrive the next day. She hadn't wanted to stay with Kendra, her mother, or even with Chris. Instead, she'd gotten a hotel room at one of the nicest hotels in the area and had sent word that she'd see them at the funeral.

Which was tomorrow morning.

Yesterday, Kendra had quietly shared that she wasn't going to help with the funeral arrangements or do anything other than attend.

When she'd told Kendra that it didn't seem right to not help at all, her sister had said that Naomi was free to help all she wanted. Then she had given Naomi the option of staying with her, her grandparents, or even moving in with their mother or Chris while the funeral preparations were underway.

Naomi had been shocked. Kendra's actions seemed so callous. When she told her sister that, Kendra had only shrugged and reminded her that she was old enough to do what she wished. She had to make her choices based on what she wanted, not on what Kendra was doing.

And that, she realized, was the price of growing up. She had to take responsibility for her own feelings and actions. No longer would she be able to blame anyone else for this moment, and that made her uncomfortable.

Still not sure what she was going to do, she walked into the kitchen early that morning and found Kendra sipping coffee at her small table, Blue sitting next to her.

On the table was a Bible. Kendra was writing in the margin but stopped when she caught sight of Naomi. Marking her place with a finger, Kendra looked up at her with a smile. "*Gut matin.* Did you sleep last night?"

"Better than the last two nights. What about you?"

"About the same, I guess. For some reason, I was thirsty all night. I kept walking to

338

the kitchen to get 'one more' glass of water." She grimaced. "Then, before I knew it, I was heading to the bathroom just as much."

Naomi smiled. That was Kendra. She never put on airs or tried to be someone she wasn't. "I need a big cup of strong *kaffi.*"

"Sounds *gut.*" Kendra paused, as if she was thinking about saying something else, but she didn't after all.

After Naomi filled her cup and added a good amount of milk, she sat down next to her sister. "I didn't know you read the Bible in the mornings. Or is this only because Daed died?"

Kendra looked surprised at the question. "No, this isn't for Daed. I, um, I started reading the Bible when I was in rehab in Columbus."

"I didn't know that."

"No reason you would. I don't talk about it much."

Suddenly Naomi knew she needed to hear about it. "Does it help you?"

"Reading the Bible? *Jah.*" She paused, then continued. "Some girls in the program had just started partying, then got hooked, I guess. But my counselor knew I had been trying to do whatever I could to forget everything that had happened in our *haus.* Of course, taking pills and drinking didn't

339

actually help me forget. All it did was make it harder to move on."

Looking wary, Kendra paused again. "Naomi, I'm not very comfortable talking about some of this with you."

"If I'm honest, I'm not comfortable hearing about it," she admitted. "But I still think that I need to know more about that time of your life."

"All right, then." Looking pensive, Kendra took a sip of coffee. "When I was in recovery, I discovered it helped to think of other things when all those bad memories surfaced. So, I started reading the Bible. Every time I couldn't sleep, I'd simply open it up to a random page and start reading."

"Just like that?"

Her sister laughed softly. "Kind of. I'm gonna be honest — you know how hard it is for me to read — those words weren't easy for me! It was also especially hard when I would start in the middle of a chapter. I didn't know who anyone was or what was going on."

"Is that why you started writing in the margins?"

Kendra nodded. "The counselor gave me this Bible, you see. At first, I thought it was too special to use. I'd even get worried if any of the pages got wrinkled. But then I realized that was a silly worry. God's word is made to be read and absorbed and thought about. I started writing notes. Sometimes, it was just to help me understand the stories or to underline words I needed to learn the definition of. Later, it was reflection."

Everything Kendra was saying made a lot of sense, and it also gave Naomi a far better understanding of how Kendra had been feeling. "Why do you do it now?"

"Well, I think it's become a habit."

"A good habit."

"Exactly. I need to do this in the morning, to remind myself how long I've been sober and to remind myself that even though something might be hard, I can still do it."

"Like reading is for you."

"*Jah.* Or overcoming addiction . . . or overcoming abuse," she added softly. "That reminder made me stronger. I really think it helped me feel brave enough to make more friends and even open my shop." She shrugged. "Maybe reading the Bible has even helped me do something I never thought I would do, too, such as going to a funeral for one of the people who hurt me when I was small."

Kendra watched as Naomi again eyed the pages she had just written on.

"If you would like a Bible, let me know and I'll get you one to write in. You can give it a try."

Naomi thought she would like to try that, but she was a little worried about studying the Bible, too. She wasn't used to failing, and she really wasn't used to disappointing her sister. "What if it doesn't give me comfort like it does for you?"

Kendra shrugged. "Then it doesn't. It won't make me think less of you, Nanny. I'll still love you no matter what."

Maybe it was Kendra revealing her difficulties or maybe it was the way she'd so easily accepted Naomi's fears, but the time finally felt right to admit what she'd been grappling with for the past two days. "I'm struggling about what to do about the funeral."

"I know you are."

"I'm worried if I don't do the right thing I might regret it."

"I reckon you are."

All of her sister's statements were so nonjudgmental. Not a one of them gave her any direction! "Kendra, you aren't helping! Can't you tell me what to do?"

"Nope. All I can do is let you figure this out on your own. It's too important to simply tell you what to do and hope you'll listen."

"But can't you offer me any advice? Maybe pretend you were in my *shoos*?"

"In your shoes, hmm?" She sighed. "Well, all right." She walked over to the percolator on the counter and poured herself another cup of coffee. "Here's what I would do if I were in your shoes. I would consider my choices first."

"That's easy." Holding out her fingers, Naomi said, "I can go live with Mamm. I can move in with Chris. I can stay here, or I can go back to living with our grandparents."

"So you have four options. Now you have to think of the pros and cons of each. Does that help?"

"Kind of." But not really. She wasn't even sure there were pros or cons for some of her options; she just hated not to consider them.

Kendra laughed softly. "Oh, Naomi. You are older and smarter, but you're still the same as when you were a little girl, always wanting everything to work out."

"That's not true."

"Isn't it, though? You were hopeful about living with our grandparents. You became Mennonite to please them. Then, when they

343

started pressuring you about Mamm and Daed, you wanted to move in with me. When Chris asked you to visit Daed, you did, even though you didn't really want to. Now you are considering temporarily moving back home to make Mamm feel better."

"It's not exactly like that." She was getting annoyed.

"Naomi, I told you the other day that I'm not going to pave the way for you anymore. I can't. If you don't like my opinions or my advice, I'm sorry."

Naomi stood up. "I'm going to go for a walk."

"All right. I have to go to my shop, but when you're done walking, I'll give you three choices: come to the shop to help me, come back home to do laundry and clean, or call up one of your other options and make arrangements to move."

"Fine."

Kendra stood up slowly. "*Danke*, Naomi." She set her coffee cup down and walked to her bedroom.

Now even more frustrated, Naomi walked out the front door and headed toward the high school. It was Sunday, so no one would be around. And she was glad of it. She wanted to walk on the track and think. She didn't know how it had become her safe place, but it had.

As she walked she threw herself a little pity party. She couldn't believe that after Kendra had told her she needed to look within and choose what was right for herself, she had still gone and given her an ultimatum and told her to make up her mind soon.

The sad fact was that Kendra really couldn't relate to her problems. Out of preservation, she'd cut ties with most of the family. But that wasn't Naomi. She'd walked the tightrope, trying to please everyone, but because of that, she was more confused than ever.

She'd just done a second lap when she spotted Kane running toward her. She waved shyly, not sure whether he was running to see her or training for football.

Three minutes later, he was at her side. "I wasn't sure if you were going to stop."

"That's because I wasn't sure if you were here to see me or to work out."

"You." He grinned.

"Why?"

Some of the confidence shining in his eyes slipped. "Well, because I hadn't seen you in a couple of days. And because your sister called our house."

"I didn't know she had your number."

"Maybe she asked Nate for it."

That made sense. "I still don't understand why she called you."

"Kendra said something about you maybe needing a friend right now."

That was her sister, always trying so hard for her. Which was amazing. But part of her wished Kendra would just leave her alone. "Okay."

"What's wrong? Would you rather be alone?"

"*Nee.* She was right. I'm sorry. Right now it feels like even the good things are hard to handle right now."

"I understand."

"Do you? I'm sorry, but you have both of your parents."

"I do, but my brother passed away when I was six."

It was official. She was a terrible, self-centered person. "I'm really sorry. Forgive me for acting so awful."

"There ain't nothing to be sorry about. It's not like I go around introducing myself as Kane, the guy whose big brother died."

She winced. "I suppose not." She was about to apologize again but refrained. It wasn't like two apologies were going to make her remarks better.

"Anyway, what I was trying to tell you is

that when my brother, Andrew, died, I was in a fog for a good month. And even after that, I don't think I felt all right for at least a year, so I understand how hard it can be."

"Like I told you, I had a complicated relationship with my *daed*. I'm just trying to figure out how to feel, much less what to do."

"What do you mean? Isn't the funeral tomorrow?"

"Yes. But it's more than that. I'm wondering if I shouldn't be living with Kendra and maybe be there more for my grandparents or my mother now." She didn't mention Chris because she now knew he wasn't the right person for her to live with.

As they continued walking, Kane gave her a sideways look. "But you just started school here."

"I know."

"And you've been doing well. You've seemed happy."

"I know. But if I moved in with my mother, I could still go to the same school."

"She'd be okay with that?"

That's when she realized she had no idea. She hadn't asked her mother about anything; she'd asked Kendra. Even though some things had changed, a lot was still the same.

Naomi realized Kane wasn't looking for flaws in her logic; he wanted her to realize she'd already made her decision.

She sighed. "I've been making everything so hard. I want to do the right thing, but I think I only thought about how that would look, not how it would actually work out. I haven't lived with my mother in years," she said. "But I suppose I can love her and not want to live with her."

"And what about Kendra?"

"Kendra? She's different. She's who I trust."

Kane nodded. "Well, there's your answer, isn't it?"

"*Jah.* She is who I trust. And I think she is slowly learning to trust me, too."

"When Andrew was alive, I was sure he was everything I always wanted to be. Now that I'm older, I realize that he wasn't perfect or imperfect. He was just Andrew. I'm not saying you need to change your mind or your opinion about what you think Kendra ought to do. But I do think you ought to accept that her decisions might be different from yours."

"I could try, but —"

"All right, maybe put it this way. Is that one difference in opinion worth losing a relationship? If not, then agree to disagree and move on."

What he said made sense. It might take prayer and time, but she could do that. He was right. Her relationship with her sister was worth more than this one moment in their lives. "I'm really glad you came out here, Kane."

"I hope so, because it's really early." He pointed to a fast-food restaurant down the road. "Want to go get breakfast? I got paid yesterday."

Food did sound good, and she always did have a weak spot for those fast-food breakfast sandwiches. "Are you sure you want to spend your money on me?"

"I can't think of a better person. So, what do you say? Are you hungry?"

"I am."

"Then let's go."

She followed him off the track field, feeling better about her future than she had in days. Though she was sure she would have more than a couple of difficult moments in her future, right at that moment, she felt at peace. She had Kane to thank for that.

Well, Kane and Kendra.

No, Kane, Kendra, and God.

THIRTY-THREE

"Of course I was hurt. Here I'd thought we'd become friends, but he'd looked embarrassed that he knew my name."

Will looked stricken. "What did you do?"

"Me? Oh, I didn't do anything. I mean, what could I say anyway?

"But maybe a month after that, I was talking to you, E.A., and Andy, Logan, and Nate were nearby. You all were talking, and I was just standing there feeling awkward. But then, Andy asked if everyone wanted to come over for a bonfire and make s'mores."

"I remember that," Logan said.

Sunday Night
It had been a long day. Kendra had spent it

thinking about her mother, her siblings, ar
her friends. But mostly, she thought about
her time in rehab. After she'd gotten picked
up for a minor drug violation for the second
time, a social worker had interviewed her.
When she'd learned more about Kendra's
history, the woman had pulled some strings
and gotten her placed into a facility for
women. The day she'd entered, she'd gone
four days without a drink or a pill and she'd
felt like she'd been pulled so tight, the
smallest problem would bring her to tears.

She'd been examined, processed, and
eventually placed in a room with eight other
beds, seven of which were occupied. Every
person in the room had silently stared at
her when she'd walked in. She'd felt their
curiosity and their contempt.

She'd never felt so alone or been so scared
in her life. But still, she'd walked to her bed
and sat down.

The hours and days that had followed
were some of the hardest of her life — and
she'd thought that nothing would ever come
close to her childhood. But this time, she
realized the pain she was enduring now had
come from her own making. She'd been the
one harming her body. She'd been the one
who had caused her suffering.

Then one morning, when she'd opened

her eyes and noticed that the sun was shining and her soul felt at peace, she'd known she'd come out on the other side. She was going to beat her addiction. She was going to do something with her life. She was stronger, and she'd rediscovered her faith.

Sitting in her living room by herself, she realized she needed to do the same thing with her anger. Yes, it might have been justified, but if she held on to it much longer, it was only going to fester inside her like all the pills she'd taken years ago.

She needed to go to the funeral.

But just like she couldn't break her addiction on her own, she knew she needed support. She walked to her bedroom and quickly put on a new navy-blue dress and apron. After pinning it closed and putting on black stockings and shoes, she took the time to let down her hair, neatly put it up again, and then finally placed her *kapp* on her head.

After writing a quick note to Naomi about where she was going, she left the house and started walking down the road. Several good friends lived nearby, some even part of the Eight.

They would have been good choices, and she knew they would have helped her in a pinch. But at that moment, she needed someone who was more than a friend. She needed the person she'd fallen in love with.

She needed Nate Miller.

"Hi there, Kendra," Peach Miller said with a bright smile. "Come on in. Now, isn't this a nice surprise. How are you?"

"I'm all right. *Danke.*"

Peach glanced over her shoulder. "Nathan is out with his father, fussing over the chickens."

"He is?" She smiled. "I didn't think he cared too much for his father's fancy birds."

Peach laughed. "He doesn't! Not at all! But he loves his father and is a hard worker." She shrugged. "So he's helping him clean the henhouse and gather eggs. Oh! Would you like to see them? Some of the ladies have quite the personalities."

"*Danke,* but maybe another day? I'll just wait for him right here, if you don't mind."

Mrs. Miller nodded, though she looked worried. "If you'd like me to go out to get him, I can . . . Is something wrong?"

Kendra shook her head. It was in her nature to keep her thoughts to herself, but there was something about Peach's cozy demeanor and comfortable home that made Kendra want to lay down her guard. "I decided this afternoon that I need to go to

353

my father's funeral." She watched Peach's expression. "Do you think I'm making the right decision?"

"Well now. I guess that's not for me to say as much as for you to decide. Ain't so?"

"I wasn't going to go. All this time, I've been angry with both of my parents and didn't want them in my life."

"What changed?"

"I prayed about it, and I started remembering about a difficult time in my life." She blinked. "Sometimes a person has to make a change, you know?" YES, D. DID!

Mrs. Miller nodded. "If you go, then you're going to need people who love you by your side, Kendra."

Kendra smiled. "That's why I'm here to see Nate. I'm going to ask him if he'll go to the funeral with me."

Mrs. Miller smiled. "Kendra, I mean this in the very best sense. I do believe Nathan will be delighted to go with you."

Kendra smiled back at her, just as the back door opened and Nate walked in. "Mamm? Where are you?"

"I'm in here talking to Kendra Troyer! And don't yell, son. It's rude."

Kendra covered her mouth to hide her giggle just as Nate walked in the room. When he smiled back at her, she realized

354

that like that early morning back in Columbus, her life had just been renewed again.

THIRTY-FOUR

"I do, too. Because just after everyone agreed, Andy looked directly at me and said, 'Kendra, you're coming too, right?'

"And that's when I knew he hadn't forgotten anything about that day at all.

"I realized Andy was really good at keeping secrets. He wasn't going to tell anyone about our day and chance getting me into trouble. He wasn't going to tell anyone about my life. I could trust him."

Monday Morning
Kendra now knew for a fact that she had the best friends in the world. Not only had they all gotten together the other night when she'd gotten the news, but they'd also all shown up for her father's funeral.

Even Nate.

Or perhaps most especially Nate. He'd

356

shown up at her house in his parents' buggy a full hour before Kendra, Naomi, and her friend Kane had planned to leave. When she'd asked Nate why he'd come to the house instead of meeting her there, Nate had shared that he didn't want her worrying about either going to the funeral without support or wondering how to get there.

She'd been so grateful, she'd simply thanked him and let Naomi and Kane know. To her surprise, Nanny had asked if she could travel with Kane by herself in his vehicle. Kendra didn't have the heart to say no. Naomi and Kane had gotten really close, and there was something about Kane's quiet presence that seemed to calm her sister.

After sending them on their way, Kendra accepted Nate's help getting into the buggy and sat quietly by his side as he directed the horse to the funeral, which was taking place at her parents' home, per their mother's request.

With Nate firmly by her side, Kendra had been able to enter the building she'd promised herself she would never enter again.

It looked the same. Same faded curtains in the windows. Same worn furniture, now even more worn and more stained. It was spotless, no doubt thanks to Mommi and whomever she'd cajoled to help her clean.

But to Kendra's surprise and relief, the house didn't cause her the flashbacks she'd feared. Instead, she felt slightly like she was entering another person's life. If she'd ever needed a reminder that she had moved on and healed, walking inside the living room was a good one. 18ᵗʰ AVE

Right away, she'd spied Naomi and Kane, who were standing off to one side. Just as she was about to walk over to check on Naomi, the rest of the Eight showed up. After giving her warm hugs, they stayed off to one side while her mother cried and some of their longtime neighbors entered the room.

Minutes later, Jeremiah and Chris appeared in the doorway.

"Hello," Kendra said simply as she walked over to greet them.

"You okay?" Jeremiah asked. She shrugged as Naomi joined their small circle.

Jeremiah hugged Naomi, then gripped Kendra's hand for a long moment. "We'll get through this, *shveshtah,*" he whispered.

"I hope so," she replied, glancing worriedly at Chris. He had clasped Naomi's hand and hers but had otherwise remained silent. Kendra thought he looked lost and out of place in his English suit.

And then, just as Preacher Evan called them all to find their places, Mary walked to her side.

Mary's appearance was a shock. She, too, was dressed English, but she also looked like a model out of a magazine. For some reason, Kendra had imagined that Mary would look much like her. But when Mary murmured, "Oh, Kendra," and hugged her close, Kendra realized that in the ways that counted she was the same.

"Mary," she said gently. "I was hoping to see you."

"I didn't want to come."

"I know." She ran a hand down Mary's short dark hair. "But I'm glad you did. I wanted to see you."

"I wanted to see you, too. And the others." She glanced over at the boys, both of whom were staring like they couldn't believe their eyes.

"I'm here, too, Mary," Naomi said.

She smiled. "Yes you are, Nanny. Looking so grown up, too." Looking beyond her at Kane, who was watching Naomi like a hawk, Mary asked, "Naomi, who is he?"

"Oh. That's my friend Kane. Uh, would you like to meet him?"

"Of course, honey."

Reaching for Kane's hand, Naomi said,

"Kane, this is my other sister, Mary. Mary, this is Kane Law."

When Mary smiled up at him, Kane offered his hand to her. "I'm sorry for your loss."

"I'm glad you're here with Naomi," Mary said simply.

Naomi lowered her voice. "Mary, Mamm is staring at you. Do . . . do you want to go say hello?"

Everything about Mary's posture changed. "Not yet." Naomi's eyes widened, and just as Preacher Evan called everyone for prayer, she whispered, "You're going to have to understand how I feel, Nanny. If not for Kendra, I wouldn't have walked inside that door."

Kendra hadn't been to a lot of Amish funerals — only two, older people in their church district who'd lived to a ripe old age and were respected and loved by everyone. They'd been big affairs held in a barn, with plenty of people to support the family and bring food for after the burial.

Almost two hundred people had attended Andy's service. The shock of losing a man so young had brought everyone out, from his teachers and coaches to friends, neighbors, and other close acquaintances.

In contrast, there were only about fifty

people gathered in her mother's cramped living room, a dozen of whom were the Eight and their spouses. Preacher Evan seemed to be struggling for words. He paused for a length of time after each Scripture verse he quoted, then uttered simple statements about the Lord loving everyone or how prayer helped in times of stress.

Even innocuous statements like that seemed to haunt Mary. Standing beside Kendra, she fisted her hands.

Kendra knew what she was thinking. However, she realized that somehow she was actually doing better than she thought she would be. After finally expressing her hurt to her grandparents and mother, she had let go of her anger at last. She was grateful for that.

She was also grateful for Nate, who had remained by her side. Every so often, he placed his hand on her back. It wasn't exactly proper, but Nate didn't seem to care — and she didn't, either. Just having him there made her feel less alone. He also was doing a good job of reminding her that she didn't have to be strong anymore for her siblings. She might always want to step into the role of provider, but she didn't feel the need to shield them from pain anymore.

After the last prayer, Preacher Evan and Rosanna led the way out the door. Now everyone would follow their buggy to the cemetery. As the older people filed out, Chris and Jeremiah walked to her and Mary's sides.

"Mary, I can't believe it's you," Jeremiah said as he gave her a hug. "You look so different."

"Yeah, I have a feeling I'm going to be hearing that a lot this afternoon."

Chris hugged her next and even pressed a kiss to her brow. "It's good you came."

"I told Kendra there was no way I'd ever let her go to this funeral without me. I may not be a real part of this family anymore, but I'll never be able to repay our big sister for everything she did for us."

Both of their brothers looked taken aback. "Yes, well . . ." Chris murmured before his voice drifted off.

"Well, what?" Mary asked, her voice as sharp as a new needle. "Christopher, are you still bitter that Kendra left us when she did?"

"No. Of course not."

"But?" She raised an eyebrow.

"Mary, now ain't the time to bring up the past," Jeremiah murmured.

The look she sent him was lethal. "Of

course not. We're here to give our respects and pray for our father's soul. Yes, let's go to the cemetery and do just that." She walked out the door in a rush.

"Wait, Mary!" Naomi called. "Kane has to go home and help his mother with something. Can I ride with you?"

She turned in an instant . . . and held out her hand with a smile. "Of course, Nanny," she said gently. "Come on."

Nate, who'd been standing quietly by Kendra's side, spoke to her brothers. "We'll see you at the cemetery."

"Are you a couple now?" Chris asked.

"*Jah,*" Nate replied as he placed Kendra's hand in the crook of his arm and escorted her to his buggy.

When he joined the line of buggies on the way down the quiet street, Kendra said, "If I haven't said it enough, I'm really glad you're here. You're making what could have been an absolutely horrible day bearable." As compliments went, it wasn't a great one, but it was heartfelt. She hoped he would realize that.

He patted her hand resting on his elbow. "I'm glad you're letting me stay by your side."

"My family feels like a soap opera."

"There's a lot of nooks and crannies in all

of your relationships, that's for sure. But I don't know if that's an unusual thing."

Again, he'd known exactly what to say to her. He wasn't sugarcoating her reality but wasn't making her feel awkward about it, either.

"I had hoped Mary would be here, but I didn't really think she would show up. I'm really glad she did."

"It sounds like she came here for you, Kendra. That says a lot about what you did for her when she was little."

"Jah." She smiled slightly. "It does."

"When did she leave to go out on her own?"

"When Naomi was thirteen. Chris was sixteen, and she was seventeen. Jeremiah was nineteen, and I was twenty-one."

"So you'd already been in rehab."

"Jah. I'd been clean and sober for almost three years by then but was not ready to face them."

"Where did she go?"

"I knew at first she went to Mansfield, then to West Virginia. Later, I heard she moved to Pittsburgh. Then we lost touch. I didn't have her address or phone number, and she didn't call. Then, two or three years ago, Chris told me she had moved to Cleveland. He always acted like she was struggling, but it sure doesn't look like it — at least not financially."

"I wonder why he thought she was struggling?"

"I don't know. She might have kept her life from him, or he just decided that was how Mary ended up."

"That doesn't sound right."

Kendra didn't think it did, either, but she wasn't one to judge. "We're all kind of damaged, I guess."

"Kendra, don't take this the wrong way, but I don't think you're as damaged and broken as you say."

"Nate, you don't have to say that."

"No, listen to me. It's obvious all of your siblings respect you. It's obvious that they all know you shielded them from a lot of bad things and that they're grateful for it."

"Oh, Nate. Bad stuff still happened to all of them. Even Naomi, she just doesn't remember it."

"Mary made it sound like she owed you. You need to accept that and take it for what it is — a sign that you did everything you could. And she noticed."

They pulled into the cemetery, and after Nate set the brake, he said, "Stay here a moment until I get my horse settled."

She did as he bid, watching the small

gathering in the distance. Though some were dressed Amish like her, others were wearing English clothes, and some, like Naomi, were obviously Mennonite. Everyone was wearing black and somber expressions. Her mother was in the center of the group, crying, and several ladies were attempting to comfort her.

Standing on the fringes in a tight group were Chris, Jeremiah, Naomi, and Mary. Jeremiah had an arm around Mary's shoulders, and Mary and Naomi were holding hands. All were looking her way.

She still believed she was right — all five of them were a little broken. But as she walked toward them and saw Naomi look up at her with an expression of relief and Chris move over a bit so she could be in the center of their group, Kendra realized that Nate had been right, too.

They might have been a little broken, but they weren't damaged beyond repair.

Maybe they were all okay after all.

Thirty-Five

"Andy really was more than I ever realized," Marie said. "I mean, he was a good friend, and kind, but he was a lot more."

"I think that's true about all of us," Kendra said slowly. "The Lord made us all special. We're flawed, but there's good in each of us. Maybe more than most people see or most people realize. Maybe more than even we realize."

Monday
After the burial, the whole group headed to one of her mother's neighbor's houses. Knowing how difficult the funeral had been for her — and that the next few hours were surely going to be just as difficult — Nate had insisted on staying by Kendra's side. Unlike her siblings, his only concern was Kendra, and he believed she needed some-

one to carefully look out for her.

They joined the procession of buggies clip-clopping slowly down the road. The somber mood seemed to permeate the air around them — even the usual robins and cardinals were as silent as Kendra was beside him.

Her tense manner worried him, but instead of murmuring platitudes, Nate let her have a few moments of silence. There was nothing he could say to comfort her that he hadn't already said several times. Besides, he'd always thought there was too much small talk at funerals, like everyone needed to fill the sadness in the air with mindless chatter.

He wasn't sure if Kendra felt the same way, but he did notice that by the time he parked the buggy in the field next to the house, she seemed to be a little more relaxed. He hoped that was the case.

After he tethered Ten to a hitching post and helped her out, Kendra looked up at him. "Would you mind very much if I spent some time with Mary? I fear that if I don't talk to her now, I might not get another chance. I don't think she'll be staying in town much longer."

"Of course not. I want you to spend time with whomever you want. I'm only here in case you need me."

Her expression crumbled. "You have been so helpful. *Nee,* you've been a godsend," she corrected. *"Danke."*

"There's no reason to thank me. I want to help you, Kendra." He paused, hoping she understood everything he was trying to convey without saying as much. "Now, go see your sister, and I'll go spend some time with all our friends."

She cast him another grateful smile before walking over to her sister. As Nate watched her go, he said a little prayer, asking Jesus to help her during the next few hours. He reckoned she was going to need His guiding hand.

An hour later, Kendra was still sitting with Mary, and Chris, Jeremiah, and Naomi had joined them. The five of them looked like they were chatting easily, and Nate thought Kendra looked more relaxed than she had in days.

While she'd been with her family, Nate had talked with Kendra's mother for a few minutes before joining his friends at one of the long wooden tables that had been set up for the occasion and enjoyed a wonderful meal of baked chicken, mashed potatoes, and vegetables.

Little by little, the crowd had thinned, and they were just standing around and catching up until Kendra was ready to leave. Though no one had said it out loud, Nate knew none of them wanted to leave Kendra alone.

"Here we are, at another funeral," Marie said as she joined them after filling her glass with more lemonade. "All things considered, I like when we gather at weddings a whole lot better."

"Amen to that," E.A. said.

"There's no telling who will be getting married next," Tricia said with a smile.

Logan grinned at Nate. "Who knows? Maybe you and Kendra will be getting hitched before you know it."

Even a week ago, Nate would have laughed off the suggestion. Now, though? He was actually thinking about it. "We'll see. Kendra has been having a pretty chaotic month. She might want to simply relax for a spell."

Marie looked over to where Kendra was sitting with Mary and Jeremiah. "I didn't really know Kendra well until we were in our teens. I remembered she had some brothers, and Nanny, but I don't remember her ever talking about Mary. Were they close?"

"I'm not sure," Nate replied. "Kendra was

glad to see her, though. And Mary? Well, she looked like she was about to cry, she was so happy to see her big sister."

"Maybe this funeral will have a silver lining, too," Katie murmured. "Maybe it will help Kendra and her siblings reconnect in a new way and they can become closer."

"Too?" Nate asked.

Looking a little tentative, Katie said, "Well, we were all together, then drifted apart. It was only when we were standing together after Andy's funeral that we made a vow to reconnect."

Nate knew some of their story, but he'd never talked about it with any of the Eight so openly. "And so you all started seeing one another more? It was just that easy?"

"I kind of think it was just that easy," John said. "I, for one, was glad to have an excuse to focus on my priorities again. And you know what? I wasn't alone."

"Every single one of us missed the way we used to be," Logan added. "We missed knowing we were just a few minutes away."

"I realized that being just a phone call away wasn't enough," Marie said. "Keeping in touch is one thing. Working on a friendship is something else entirely. That can't happen when you only see people a couple of times a year." *yes, it can!*

371

"Well, all of you should be proud," Nate said. "In spite of the obstacles in your lives, you all came back together." He chuckled softly. "Hey, some of you even fell in love and paired off!"

"That we did," Harley said. "But we also realized there was plenty of room for more good friends in our lives." *Not by some!*

Katie pressed her hand onto Harley's arm. "Like Kendra."

"Especially like Kendra," E.A. said. "Though I feel kind of bad she wasn't part of the Eight from the beginning."

"I know you do, but I think she would be the first to tell you that she wasn't ready back then," Nate pointed out. "Everything really does happen at the right time."

Looking at Will, E.A. nodded. "I agree with that."

Glancing at Kendra again, Nate murmured, "In spite of the circumstances, she seems to be doing all right, doesn't she?"

"When you are surrounded by people you love, it's amazing what can take place," Marie said with a smile. "Miracles happen, and Kendra is due for a small miracle of happiness now. It's her time."

Marie's words, though lightly spoken, hit him hard. Nate realized then that he was willing to do whatever it took to make her happy and make sure that from now on, she was surrounded by love. Especially his.

2001

THIRTY-SIX

Kendra nodded. "Maybe at the end of the day, we don't need to worry about pleasing lots of people. We simply need to be pleased with ourselves and the way God made each of us. We need to trust ourselves and trust Him, too."

Two Weeks Later

"Mrs. Warner is the nicest lady in the world," Kendra said to Nate as they walked down the driveway. "I don't know if I'm ever going to be able to be as gracious and welcoming as she is. Every time I've stopped by, she's been nothing but kind."

Nate seemed to consider her words for a moment before replying. "She is a nice lady, but I think she appreciates the company. It's nice of all of you to still stop by."

"I hope we don't stop anytime soon. I enjoy being around her."

"She sure loved the caramel brownies you

brought," Nate said.

Remembering the way Mrs. Warner had looked when she'd eaten her first bite, Kendra grinned. "I think she really did! That made me happy."

"You are such a good cook. Everything you make feels like we're having a little part of your heart."

Kendra smiled up at him. "That is very sweet of you to say."

Nate linked his fingers through hers. "It was sweet of you to include me today."

"I'm glad you wanted to come with me. Not everyone understands why we all stop by so much, especially now that it's been over a year since Andy died."

"To tell you the truth, I thought being at the Warners' house might make me feel sad or that sitting with Mrs. Warner would be really awkward, but it wasn't like that at all." He paused. "Instead, it gave me a chance to talk about Andy with someone who loved him, too. Almost like even though he died, he hasn't really left our lives."

"I feel the same way."

"When did you start going over?"

"I'm not sure when the first visit happened. I think it was either Marie's or Katie's idea to stop by. Or maybe it was John's? I can't really remember. But I do remember we all agreed that it would make Mrs. Warner happy to have some of Andy's friends in the house again."

Nate smiled. "I bet. He was one of the most social people I know. He always was planning something."

"Always." Kendra chuckled. Thinking about the visits, she added, "To be honest, there was a part of me that was sure she'd stop wanting to see us. You know, maybe she thought us sitting in her living room would make it even harder to move on. But I think the opposite is true."

Nate rubbed one of her knuckles with his thumb, showing her without words that he understood. Enjoying that simple connection, she smiled up at him.

She loved holding Nate's hand. She liked feeling the warmth of his skin, liked feeling connected. She even liked that Nate was never shy about holding her hand. It was like he needed her touch as much as she needed his, like he was proud of having her by his side. YES

He never cared who saw them, never cared that some of the older people in their church district frowned upon the simple display of affection in public. He never cared what other people thought. Not even bishops.

That was very Nate.

"Hey, what are you smiling about?"

"Hmm? Oh, something silly. It's nothing."

"*Nee,* I know that smile. It's something. Come on," he cajoled. "Tell me what's going on in that head of yours. I won't laugh."

"All right, but you're going to agree it's nothing important. I . . . well, I was just thinking about how much I love to hold your hand. Laugh if you want, I won't mind."

His teasing expression faded. "I'm not about to laugh at all. You know I like to hold your hand, too. I like it a lot; it keeps you close to me. Is that what you like?"

She nodded. "I like feeling a little part of you by my side. I also kind of like that you never care who sees us holding hands together."

Looking even more serious, he said, "Now that's where you're wrong. It's not that I'm not worried if someone sees us. It's that I want everyone to see your hand in mine. I want everyone to know you're mine."

What did one say to that? "Oh."

"Yeah, oh." Looking even more determined, he drew to a stop. "Actually, Kendra, there's something I've been wanting to talk to you about."

"What's on your mind?"

"It's a little complicated. Can we stop and talk right here?"

They were on an empty street. Trees with thick, brightly colored foliage surrounded them. She supposed they were in as private a spot as one could hope for. Wondering what could be on his mind, she started doing what she always did — she started worrying. "Is everything okay?"

Nate's hazel eyes warmed. "Oh yeah. I mean, I think so. I just wanted to tell you something." He drew a breath. "See, the truth is that sometimes I hold your hand because it's all I have of you."

Wasn't that the sweetest thing? "Nate. It's not all you have. You have my heart, too."

"I love having your heart. I love holding your hands. But it's not all I want."

She figured her eyes were as big as saucers. "What do you want?"

"You. Kendra, I want to marry you one day. I don't want you just to have my heart. I want you to have my name, too."

"You're proposing? Now?"

He nodded. "I love you, Kendra Troyer. Will you marry me?"

Kendra blinked. Nate Miller was asking her to marry him right there, on an empty street in the middle of a Wednesday on the way home from the Warners' house.

He knew who she was. He knew her past, knew her imperfections, but he loved her anyway.

She really believed that.

And so, after so many days of doubts and worries and recriminations, Kendra realized that she trusted Nate, too.

Was there anything she'd ever wanted more?

"*Jah,* Nate," she said quietly. "I will marry you."

Grinning, he took hold of both her hands and stepped closer. "You scared me for a minute, there. I thought you were going to say no."

"*Nee,* I needed a minute only so I could remember this moment. I'm starting to learn that there are some things a person doesn't want to ever forget."

"You won't forget. I'll make sure you'll always remember this day and never regret it," he said as he wrapped his arms around her and held her close.

Kendra rested her head on his shoulder, breathed in his scent, and realized Nate was not wrong. She was going to remember this moment always.

Always.

Standing in front of all of their friends, in

front of all the people whom she held most dear, Kendra finished her story.

"Everyone, I loved Andy Warner. I loved him for what he did for me that day. I loved him for being my friend. But most of all, I loved him for reminding me that I was going to be all right. That one day in the future — in spite of everything that had happened — I was going to be just fine."

She smiled. "And you know what? Andy Warner was right. I turned out just fine."

Looking up at the sky, she pressed a hand to her heart and said a prayer.

And trusted that He would let Andy know she was glad to have known him. No, that she was glad to have been his friend.

ACKNOWLEDGMENTS

I worked on this series for almost two years and I couldn't put all my notes, notebooks, and research papers away without first taking a moment to thank the many people who helped bring these books to life. First, I owe a debt of gratitude to my agent, Nicole Resciniti. From the time I first emailed her about my idea for the Eight, she helped champion this project and my move to Simon & Schuster. Nicole is my cheerleader, confidant, sounding board, and voice of reason. I hope every writer has someone like Nic in their corner.

There are so many people at Gallery and Pocket to thank. They've made a new-to-them author feel welcome and have *all* gone out of their way to not only help me feel included but also to help make these books the best they can be. I especially want to thank my editors Sara Quaranta, Molly Gregory, and Marla Daniels for their guidance through all four novels and three novellas. I really am a writer who needs an editor, and I'm grateful for their feedback. The same goes for all the folks who copy-edited and proofread the manuscripts. Editing all those Amish phrases, words, and actions isn't always easy, and I'm in awe of their patience with me.

I'd also like to thank Lynne and Laurie, aka Team L & L. Lynne is my invaluable first reader, and Laurie not only manages my street teams but also does about a hundred other things for me throughout the year.

No note would ever be complete without mentioning my husband, Tom. He cleans the house when I can't, brings me soup when I won't leave my desk, and never points out that all the "people" I'm worried about are actually made-up characters from my books. He's the best.

Finally, I owe a huge thank-you to my readers. You're the reason I still love to write. I write books that I hope you'll want to read. I'm so grateful for your letters, Facebook chats, tweets, and smiles. Truly, I am blessed.

READER QUESTIONS

1. What did you think about Kendra's hurt and anger at Nate's careless remark in the opening scene? Have you ever been the recipient of a thoughtless comment? Or have you ever been like Nate and said something you regretted?

2. What did you think about Kendra's relationship with the Eight? How do friends' relationships change over time? Are you friends with someone now whom you weren't especially close to years ago?

3. Kendra is one of my favorite characters I've ever imagined. I loved how much she sacrificed for her siblings. How do you think those sacrifices affected her siblings? How did they affect her? Do you think her life would have been different had she been more selfish?

4. I enjoyed writing about Naomi's struggles. I purposely wanted her to have some growing pains and to make some mistakes. How do you think her mistakes and struggles will help her as she grows older?

5. What did you think about Naomi's and Kane's relationship? What do you think will happen to Naomi and Kane in the future?

6. How do you feel the Lord is your "Trustworthy One"?

7. How could you apply Psalm 37:3, "Trust in the Lord and do good," to your life?

8. How could you relate to the Amish proverb, "Instead of pointing a finger, why not hold a hand?"

ABOUT THE AUTHOR

A practicing Lutheran, **Shelley Shepard Gray** is the *New York Times* and *USA TODAY* bestselling author of more than eighty novels, translated into multiple languages. In her years of researching the Amish community, she depends on her Amish friends for gossip, advice, and cinnamon rolls. She lives in Colorado with her family and writes full time.

The employees of Thorndike Press hope you have enjoyed this Large Print book. All our Thorndike, Wheeler, and Kennebec Large Print titles are designed for easy reading, and all our books are made to last. Other Thorndike Press Large Print books are available at your library, through selected bookstores, or directly from us.

For information about titles, please call:
    (800) 223-1244

or visit our website at:
    gale.com/thorndike

To share your comments, please write:
    Publisher
    Thorndike Press
    10 Water St., Suite 310
    Waterville, ME 04901